UNDER THE MAPLE TREE

A Beach Brew Novel

Manda Mazanec

ISBN: 979-8-9867630-0-2

Cover design: Amanda Walker

Editor: Beth at VB Edits

Proofreader: Sarah Burr at Reed Editorial Services

Mom, this book isn't for you. Not yet.

This is for Ang, Sue, and Sabrina. For getting me through the thick of it.

Disclaimer: Mental health and addiction are discussed in this book.

CHAPTER ONE

Sasha

"G et out!" Sasha screamed, her voice sharp as she threw a ceramic mug at Greg's head, missing by mere centimeters, only for it to explode against the wall and shatter into a million pieces.

"What the fuck, Sasha?" Greg yelled through gritted teeth as he jerked away.

"Get out! Get the fuck out!" Sasha grabbed another mug from the countertop and raised it in the air. Her heart thundered while long, exasperated breaths escaped her lips as she waited. Waited to see what he'd do next.

"Okay. Damn. I'm leaving." He grunted, raising his hands in truce before reaching for the door handle, his dark eyes not trusting her.

Turning the handle, Greg pushed the door open. "You'll be sorry about this. Don't think I didn't warn you." His attention darted from her to Blake.

Sasha held her breath as she narrowed her eyes at him, praying he'd just leave.

A second later, he disappeared, and then she exhaled, her arm falling to her side. Her chest heaved unsteadily as she placed the mug on the counter, though her fingers still gripped the handle. If he came back, she wouldn't hesitate. And she wouldn't miss.

"Sasha." Blake's voice was soft and full of concern.

"I want you to leave too," she said quickly, looking down at her trembling hands.

"Sasha, can we talk about this? I want to—"

"Help? You want to help? Haven't you done enough? Please. Just get out." Sasha lowered her voice as it wavered. She couldn't look into his dark green eyes. If she did, she'd lose it. She hated him for ripping apart her life. For shattering everything she'd ever known. He'd destroyed it the moment he walked into the coffee shop last week. He was pure sin. And yet she craved him. More than anything. She wanted him to wrap his muscular arms around her. To lean in to her. To touch her lips the way he had yesterday.

Blake walked toward the front counter slowly, as if each step might break the wood beneath his feet, and stopped only when he was mere inches from Sasha. His large frame stood still. He watched and waited, but she wasn't about to cave in like he'd probably hoped she would. She could hear his breath as he inhaled, and it took everything in her not to look up.

"Sasha." His words were nothing more than a whisper, a plea.

"Blake, I need you to leave," Sasha bit back, holding in tears that promised to escape. She wouldn't let him see her fall apart again.

Sasha heard his feet move, his shadow following as he turned toward the same door Greg had just exited. When the rattle of the door handle echoed in her ears, Sasha sucked in a deep breath, her heart racing.

"I'm sorry, Sasha." His voice broke.

And then…he was gone.

Throwing her hands to her face, Sasha crumpled to the floor, letting the tears fall down her cheeks. The cries came out muted as she tried to catch her breath. "Why? Why me? Why is this happening?" she sobbed, hating her red hair. Hating that Blake had moved here. That he'd found her. Hating that she'd never known she was lost in the first place. Hating that she'd let Greg back into her life. She was a stupid girl. Stupid, stupid, stupid.

CHAPTER TWO

One Week Earlier

Sasha

"I still can't believe you're married. And you're moving too." Sasha's voice melted as she gave Claire the best pouty lip she could muster.

"Oh, stop with the face," Claire laughed, waving her off. "You know I'll be back. And besides, you'll always be my muse."

Sasha stood behind the counter of her coffee shop, Beach Brew. Well, it wasn't hers just yet, but it would be soon enough. The owner was living in the Bahamas, and Sasha had been managing it for him over the last few years with the intention of buying it once he was ready to sell. Last night, the call had come through.

"Sasha, you think you're ready?" Mitch's deep voice had flooded the receiver.

"Are you serious?" she sang with excitement. "I can be ready by next month. I'll need to secure a loan, but yes. Hell yes."

And just like that, Sasha had been on cloud nine, eager for what the future had in store for her.

But now, Claire stood in front of Sasha, telling her that she was moving. It felt like a fire iron to the heart. Claire had started off as a customer a few years ago. As a writer, she had come in every morning, like clockwork, to work on her novels. But as the days ticked by, she'd become more of a friend, like an older sister or a mother figure. Though Sasha was happy about Claire's recent marriage, she didn't want to say goodbye.

The two of them looked up in unison as the bell on the door rang behind them. A stereotypical firefighter walked in. The kind who belonged inside a calendar spread. Tall, wavy brown hair, tan, and buff. He was so ripped his muscles stretched through his tight navy-blue T-shirt. And his eyes. Shit. He was staring at her. Slightly embarrassed, Sasha looked away, heat rising in her face, which was odd, because Sasha wasn't shy.

Claire must have noticed too, because she nudged her from the other side of the counter. "Close your mouth," she whispered in a tone so soft Sasha was surprised she even heard it.

"Not my type," Sasha mouthed back, scrunching her nose. It wasn't a total lie. She didn't normally go for the buff guys, but those tattoos, those tattoos were a dead giveaway that he was all her type. A sleeve on one arm and a half sleeve creeping close to his elbow on the other was enough for Claire to raise her eyebrows.

"Liar," she laughed. "I'll call you when we get settled in Asheville." She handed her a set of keys. "Thanks for the coffee. Love ya."

Keeping her promise to watch over Claire's house while she was away, Sasha placed the keys in her pocket. "Love you too," she mumbled.

As Claire turned to walk away, the hot firefighter opened the door for her, then headed to the counter.

"Morning. What can I get started for you?" Sasha asked, trying to sound professional while still avoiding eye contact. He was definitely easy on the eyes, but she'd been gawking, and she knew that men like him got stared at all the time. She didn't want to feed into his ego.

"I'll just take a large black coffee, thanks." His voice was deep and inviting, and when she did finally manage to look up, his eyes screamed sex. Maybe she was imagining that last part because it had been so long since she'd actually had sex. But damn if that wasn't the first thing she'd thought about when he'd slipped through those doors.

The last date she'd been on had been a total bust. A guy she had matched with on one of those dating apps, Jake, all of five feet and maybe five inches, had greeted her at a local dive bar with long blond hair that probably hadn't seen a bottle of shampoo in the last decade. She didn't have anything against short guys, but getting botulism wasn't exactly on her bucket list. Okay, maybe botulism was being a bit dramatic, but she was pretty positive she saw lice staring back at her when she excused herself to use the restroom. And Jake's profile placed him at six foot two with short brown hair. He'd lied. When Sasha escaped the bar, she knew she had been catfished.

"Dark roast okay?" she asked. A smile formed as she tried to steal another glance at his eyes.

"Sounds perfect."

She turned around and grabbed the handle to the coffeepot but froze when he spoke again.

"Paige?"

Her back was to him, but the sudden mention of someone else's name gave her shivers and yet felt strangely familiar.

"Paige?" he asked again, his voice barely audible.

Sasha shook her head. Maybe someone had walked in, or perhaps Mr. Firefighter was talking on the phone. She glanced around. Neither guess had been correct. Shifting her attention back to him, Sasha watched as his lips parted and his face drained of color.

Furrowing her eyebrows, Sasha tilted her head before asking, "Me?" She pointed at herself.

When he stared at her, unresponsive, with those dark emerald eyes, she continued. "Oh, sorry. No. My name's Sasha." She turned back to the coffee and poured what was left into his cup. When she placed the warm cup on the counter, Sasha's stomach twisted. He was still staring at her, and not in the seductive fashion she'd first hoped for. Not in the same way she'd gawked at him when he'd walked into the café.

He shook his head. "No…it can't be. You're…you're Paige."

Fuck. She groaned. Mr. Firefighter, a.k.a. Sex Eyes, must be mistaking her for someone else, probably a one-night stand. Tilting her head and giving him her full attention, she repeated herself, "I'm sorry, my name's Sasha." She almost added that he could call her anything he wanted tonight but figured that would only encourage his strange behavior, and she wasn't about to go down that rabbit hole, no matter how gorgeous he was.

She turned around to avoid any additional eye contact, hoping he'd leave and fighting her intuition that his full lips were calling to her. Grabbing the dish towel, Sasha busied herself by wiping the counters, hoping another customer would come in to save her from the uneasy awkwardness. But no one came.

Instead, he just stood there, unaware of the silence that sat between them.

"Wait, I'm sorry. Can I start over?" he asked after several seconds, confusion in his voice.

She exhaled before turning back to face him. He was still appraising her, studying her face.

"You look familiar. Someone I haven't seen since I was a kid."

The poor guy looked like he'd just lost his best friend. Sasha almost felt bad for him.

"So I look like a kid?" she laughed, trying to ease the tension. It was better than being mistaken for an ex or a one-night stand. And his eyes were kind of dreamy, so why not make small talk?

"No. No, not at all. That's not what I meant. It's just…" His voice trailed off.

"It's okay. Honestly, I get it all the time with my red hair. Something about redheads and freckles. I guess we all look alike." She breathed a sigh of relief. He wasn't crazy, just mistaken. She could work with that.

"Do you live nearby? I haven't seen you around," she asked, hopeful they could move past this Paige person.

Sex Eyes ran his fingers through his thick brown hair with a bewildered look still stretched across his face. "I moved here a few weeks ago. Is it that obvious?"

"We have our regulars and then we have the tourists. You aren't dressed for the beach, so you must be new," Sasha said, motioning toward his uniform.

"Yeah, I just started at the fire department." He smirked as he placed his hand on the warm cup. "I'm from the Cocoa Beach area. Moved here for the job, and I've been meaning to come by to check out the coffee."

Her heart fluttered as she bit her lower lip. She liked new people. They didn't know her. Sasha didn't have to explain anything about her past. It had been the reason she'd moved to St. Pete herself.

"Our coffee's the best." She smiled her best smile, brushing loose strands of red hair away from her face, tucking them behind her ear. "That one's on the house," she added, pointing toward his cup.

She scribbled her number on the back of a business card and slid it across the counter. "Just make sure you come back before your next shift. Here's my number. If you text me ahead of time, I'll make sure to have a warm cup ready for you."

The second the words left her tongue, she watched as Sex Eyes' face went white. Damn. Was that too forward? It's not like she made a habit out of seducing her customers, but this guy was definitely worth flirting with. Maybe it was because she'd just been on an awful date the other night or because of her envious feelings about Claire finding the love of her life, but either way, Sasha didn't think she was overstepping. She did this with all the customers she thought would become regulars. She hadn't thought the mention of a text would send him back to weird.

"I. Umm, I need to go. Thank you for the coffee." He shifted his focus away from her, not bothering to take her number.

Before Sasha was able to respond, before she could say a word, he was at the door, turning the handle. But before he pushed it open, he turned to look at her once more, his eyes narrowing as if he were trying to figure something out. "It was nice to meet you. Sasha." He paused before saying her name, like it was difficult to roll off his tongue. Then he was gone.

What just happened? What was that all about?

Feeling her chest restrict, Sasha breathed in a slow, deep breath before exhaling. Go figure. It was always the hot ones who acted strange.

For the rest of the morning, Sasha tended to the café, greeting customers and making coffee, trying to think about anything other than Sex Eyes. Around noon, her dad texted to ask if she wanted to join him and her sister for dinner. "Of course," she responded, adding a smiley emoji at the end.

This is what they did every week. He'd text her about dinner, and she'd reply with a fun emoji. It was his way of keeping tabs on her, something he'd started once Sasha had gotten her own place. She didn't blame him, especially after the hell she'd put him through. She would want to keep tabs on herself too. And if Sasha were being honest with herself, she was damn lucky her dad still texted her at all.

Later that afternoon, after she'd cleaned up and closed shop, Sasha hopped on the road and drove toward her dad's house, passing beachgoers and tourists until she made it into town. It was early, so the sun was still a few hours from setting, masking the sky with shades of vibrant red, orange, and yellow.

In less than fifteen minutes, Sasha pulled up to the small two-story brown bungalow, a home she'd never lived in. Her dad and sister had moved there from her childhood home in Tampa when she was twenty, when she needed them closer to help her. But she didn't want to think about that now.

Instead, Sasha felt a sudden wave of relief when she saw both of their cars in the driveway. She closed her eyes for a few moments before getting out of her own car. It had been a month since she'd last seen her sister, Margo. They'd gotten into a nasty fight over Margo's choice of friends. Her sister had screamed at her about how hypocritical it was for Sasha to judge her. How she, of all people, had no room to talk. And she was right. Sasha had made plenty of bad decisions growing up. Most importantly, her choice in friends.

But Margo hadn't allowed Sasha to apologize. Instead, Margo stormed out of the house, and Sasha hadn't seen her since.

Today would be different. She'd sit down with her sister and make things right. Margo was a good kid: smart and driven. She should trust that her sister would make smart choices.

Knocking on the door as she pushed it open, Sasha called out to her dad and Margo, but neither of them answered. "Hello? Where are you guys?" she yelled across the hallway. Again, no response. Setting her bag on the bench near the door, Sasha walked toward the kitchen. From there, she heard their muffled voices.

When she peeled back the curtains to the back door, Margo came into view. Her long strawberry-blond hair blew with the slight wind. She waved her arms erratically, angry about something Sasha could only assume involved teenage hormones. Her dad stood next to the grill, his arms folded in front of his chest, his mouth in a scowl.

Shit! Sasha had *not* anticipated Margo being in a bad mood already. No way could she have a conversation with her if she was already pissed off.

How did her dad do it? Putting up with teenage-girl hormones was not for the faint of heart. She, herself, had been terrible. And now, at twenty-four, she'd witnessed hundreds of girls getting caught up in ridiculous drama at the café. It was the one stage of her life she was happy to be past.

Just then, her dad looked past Margo and spotted her through the glass. He raised his eyebrows, and his scowl disappeared as his lips curled upward. His arms relaxed, and he waved. Margo followed his gaze and locked eyes with Sasha. Then she stomped her foot like a toddler before she grabbed the handle and yanked the door open.

"Hi, Margo," Sasha said, but Margo ignored her and bumped her shoulder as she stormed through the kitchen.

"Nice to see you too," Sasha mumbled after Margo was out of earshot.

"Hey, honey. How've you been?" her dad said as he stepped inside and kissed the top of her head.

"I'm good. What was that all about?" Sasha asked, both intrigued and scared at the same time.

Her dad brought his hands to his face and rubbed his eyes like he was tired. Tired of pretending to be happy. Tired of pretending everything was okay. Sasha had seen the same look when her mom died. That bright spark he once held in his eyes had dimmed the night they'd cremated her body. Then she'd watched what little light he still had fizzle away when she was seventeen, when she'd overdosed for the first time.

"What is it?" Sasha asked, grabbing his hands, expecting the worst.

"She's a teenager. What do you think?" he grumbled, suddenly looking much older and worn down by years of grief. Grief she knew she'd contributed to. Gray peppered his brown hair. Deep lines etched his forehead.

Sasha pressed her lips together, and she looked into her dad's sad eyes, praying and hoping he wouldn't say what she was thinking.

CHAPTER THREE

Blake

Blake pulled up to the firehouse less than fifteen minutes after he left Beach Brew, but he hadn't budged from his truck. He was early, and he needed the extra few minutes to think. The longer he sat, the quicker his heart raced, his anger rising. He slammed his fist onto the middle console.

Fuck.

Sasha. That wasn't her name. He knew it wasn't. He'd seen that scar emblazoned across her forehead. When she'd brushed her fiery red hair behind her ear, he'd seen it, the crease that zigzagged from her temple to the top of her ear, the same one Paige had. The reminder of the injury he'd witnessed when she was only four years old. When he'd slammed his bike into hers, and she'd fallen onto a chunk of glass.

Fuck.

A tight knot climbed up his chest, and his eyes burned. He should be happy. Ecstatic. This was something he'd dreamed of. But instead…he felt dark and empty, like his gut had been ripped out. It had been so long. Years. Almost twenty, to be exact. They'd all but lost hope of finding Paige in the last half decade. Given up on the dream that she would ever return home. And yet, there she was, at a damn beach café only a handful of hours away from where she'd gone missing.

Taking a deep breath, Blake scrolled through his contact list until he found Porter's name. He stared at it for a few seconds before pressing the blue Call button and then closed his eyes as the phone rang.

"Hey, man. What's up? How's St. Pete?" Porter's husky voice echoed through the phone after the second ring. "Haven't heard from you since you left."

"Yeah, I'm not really settled in yet. I'm about to head into work now, but I wanted to call to see how you've been. How's the family?" Blake winced at the word family, his thoughts shifting to Paige.

"Mom and Dad are okay. Worried sick now that Penny is twenty-one. You know how they are though. Always expecting the worst. Other than that, things are good. I'm holding down the fire station over here, so no need to worry about that," he laughed. "But I'm actually about to walk into a class right now. Trying to finish up annual training, so I can't talk much longer." Porter was an EMT and worked at the same fire station Blake had worked at in Cocoa Beach before he transferred here.

After promising to invite Porter and his family over in the coming weeks, Blake wished his friend well. He wanted to mention Paige but couldn't put Porter through the heartache with such little information. Porter wouldn't believe him anyway, not after all these years. He'd say it was a coincidence—that Blake "thought" he'd seen her. In Porter's eyes, his twin sister was dead. It was the only thing he could believe to move forward with his life.

But Blake knew it was her. She'd been right there, right in front of him.

With a quick search, Blake pulled up the photo he had stored in his phone, and the freckle-faced five-year-old appeared on his screen. He sighed. It wasn't hard to see the similarities this girl had to the girl at the café. But now that he wasn't there any longer, thoughts of misidentification swirled in his head. It was possible he'd imagined the scar. He wanted to believe it was there because, as she said herself, people often thought others with red hair and freckles looked alike.

Unconvinced, he typed Paige Knight into the search bar on the website for Missing and Exploited Children, focusing on the age-enhanced photo. A low growl fell from his lips as he clenched his jaw. *Shit*. If there had been any doubt, any second thoughts, they were gone now. The barista at Beach Brew was none other than his childhood neighbor, the little girl who'd tagged along with him and the other boys in town. The fiery, redheaded tomboy who loved to play hide and seek. She'd been so good at it that no one had ever been able to find her.

Until now.

Blake slowly stepped out of his truck and into the sweltering humid air. He tucked his phone into his pocket, struggling to understand. *How did Paige get here? Did she even know who she was?* She'd hesitated at the name, hadn't she? He didn't know where to start, who to tell, but he had to learn more, find out more about her before he told Porter.

Entering the firehouse, Blake wrestled with his bags, careful not to spill his coffee.

"Blake, we're ordering pizza for dinner tonight. You want in?" Jay leaned his chair back and called from around the corner. "The guys said they'd do sandwiches for lunch. Marcus brought in a bunch of ham and turkey and a shit ton of sub rolls." Jay was always thinking of food. From their very first conversation when he'd arrived three weeks ago, Blake knew he'd never go hungry. It was as if Jay woke up every morning with food on his mind, making sure he had every meal planned and prepped for the entire week.

"Sure, sounds good." Blake set his cup on the table and dropped his bags to the floor.

Jay eyed him suspiciously before disappearing behind the corner, only to reemerge seconds later. "You know we have coffee here, right?" he said, walking toward him, tipping his white Styrofoam cup in Blake's direction.

"Yeah, I know. I've been wanting to try the place by my condo. It's pretty good," Blake said.

"Good? It's coffee. Don't you start being one of those guys." He nodded at the cup on the table.

"Those guys?" Blake lifted an eyebrow.

"I'm assuming you met Sasha, the redhead?"

Blake sucked in a sharp breath, and his body grew tense, the muscles in his jaw tightening.

"Oh shit. It's already started," Jay laughed, his stomach bouncing. "Sasha is never gonna let you near her. She's all fun and games, but that's just her spirit, part of her ploy to get you coming back for more. Every newbie thinks he's special, and once they set eyes on that firecracker, the bets start coming. But I'll be honest with you, I wouldn't go near that place. Take it from me, firsthand experience. She's trouble." Jay's expression was serious, though he laughed as the words fell from his mouth.

Before Blake could ask what he meant, Marcus walked in, his chest puffed out. Marcus was easily the tallest man there, and at six foot six, he could have been an NBA star. When the chief asked why Marcus had turned down the opportunity for a full ride to UCLA to play basketball, he simply replied: "My heart wasn't in it." Instead, he became a paramedic and worked his way into the firehouse.

"Are you talking about Sasha?" Marcus asked, his voice deep and gravelly. "Did she give you her number?"

Jay chuckled, and Marcus fist bumped him.

"Twenty bucks he keeps trying to get in her pants for the next two weeks," Marcus said.

"With that look, I'll double it and say he's in it for the next month before he comes to his senses," Jay replied.

"I'm not interested in the girl. Just the coffee," Blake lied to them. It wasn't that he was interested in Sasha so much as he wanted to understand how she'd *become* Sasha. A part of Blake wanted to question Jay more. What had he meant by "trouble"? He seemed privy to information Blake wasn't aware of, and he wanted answers. He wanted anything that would shed light on who Sasha was. But that didn't seem possible now. Not with the way they were clowning around.

Tossing his bag into his locker, Blake finished his coffee and met the other guys in the training room. After a few classes and a late lunch, the department received calls one after another. By sunset, most of the guys were exhausted. While most of them herded to the kitchen for pizza, Blake headed toward the weathered sofa and sank his tired body into it. He pulled out his phone and stared at the black screen, debating whether to pull up Paige's photo again. Hesitating, he decided against it. Instead, he opened Google and typed Paige Knight into the search engine.

And there she was. A five-year-old girl with that fire-red hair, smiling at the camera with the same freckled face he'd just seen. And then his heart broke. He closed his eyes for a moment, remembering the last time he'd seen her. It was her birthday, and she'd wanted to play hide and seek. A few of the other kids joined in, and they all huddled under the maple tree, taking turns hiding and seeking. "It's your turn. Start counting," she'd said to him.

Blake must have fallen asleep staring at the picture because the next thing he knew, the alarm was waking him up.

"All hands on deck!" Jay yelled out. "Fire on Ravenwood Drive. Suit up."

In a matter of minutes, Blake, Jay, Marcus, and a handful of other men were speeding through the streets of St. Petersburg, one fire engine behind another. And in no time, they were pulling up to a small brown bungalow. Blake was the first to jump out as Jay barked orders. From a quick assessment, it looked like the fire was coming from the backyard. An older man with gray hair stood on a ladder, leaning over the fence and sprayed what little water he could toward the back of the house. A short woman propped her body against the ladder, steadying it from tipping on the uneven earth. When the firemen pulled up, she let go and ran over. "Dan's back there. He isn't waking up! You need to do something."

"Anyone else in the home that we should know about?" Jay asked as he pointed toward the house.

"Maybe his daughters. Their cars are in the driveway. He was grilling. I haven't seen them though." Her voice shook and her arms trembled.

With that, Blake, Marcus, and two other men ran toward the house, sealing their masks and securing their helmets. The front door was a solid piece of glass, allowing Blake to get a good view of the layout, including straight to the back door where the fire was blazing the hottest. But the truth of the matter was that the fire had already spread throughout the whole lower level.

"Fuck! Marcus, you and Ty are better off jumping that fence to get to the man. Break any lower-level windows you see. Mike, you and I need to get to the girls." Opening the door, Blake rushed in, followed by Mike, who closed the door behind them. Flames clawed up the walls and smoke engulfed the air. Taking the railing in his hand to check for durability, Blake led the way upstairs, yelling for the girls. "Firefighter. Call out!"

The heat was growing intense when he heard a voice from a room in the corner.

"In here!"

The door was closed, and while it was on the opposite side of the house from where the fire looked to have started, he noticed the quick shift of flames gravitating toward that room, which meant a window was open.

"We're coming in. Stand away from the door."

With a gloved hand, Blake twisted the handle and pushed the door open. He assessed the room and quickly noticed a girl with a baseball cap looking out the window. "Are you both in here?"

"No, my sister jumped. They got her. Is my dad okay?" Her words came out fast, but before she could say more, Blake scooped her up and placed her over his shoulder. "Get eyes on the sister," he called out to Mike. And then Blake dashed out of the room and down the stairs, covering the girl's head from any possibility of danger. "Is there anyone else in the house?" Blake asked.

Her head was against his back, but he could hear the muffled voice acknowledging there wasn't.

At the bottom of the staircase, Blake looked at Jay, who was opposite the glass door. Jay swung it open, and Blake rushed out.

After he carried the girl out of the house, he brought her to the ambulance and laid her on the nearest stretcher. She moaned and brought her hands to her face, but before Blake could do anything, two paramedics were standing over her. Turning around, he tore his helmet and mask from his head and breathed in the fresh air that surrounded him. A few firefighters from neighboring stations started their hoses and blasted the flames, depriving the fire of oxygen.

"The sister will be fine. She said your girl helped her climb down the back, and then she had to jump the rest of the way. The dad though…" Marcus shook his head. "Looks like he took a blast to the head. He's conscious now but can't remember what happened. And he has some burns."

"Looks like the propane tank to the grill exploded. The neighbors were outside and heard a pop. They called 911 when the fire started," Jay said, heading their way. "Good work in there." He patted Blake on the back.

"I'm fine. I just want to see my dad and sister," the girl behind him said in the same sharp voice he'd heard upstairs.

Instinctively, Blake turned around. When he caught sight of the same red hair he'd seen earlier, his heart paused. How had he not noticed? Trying to catch his breath, he put his hand to his mouth. He watched as Sasha pushed loose strands of hair away from her face. Her white baseball cap fell to the ground. Then, in the next moment, she was turning toward him, and her eyes went wide with recognition.

CHAPTER FOUR

Sasha

It felt like a dream. Everything happened so fast. One minute Sasha was imagining Margo being entangled with drugs, sex, and pregnancy. But then, in the next moment, she was hugging her. There were no sex tapes or babies. Her sister was smarter than her. She was growing up.

"She wants to leave. She got accepted into Harvard," her dad had said before she sprinted up the stairs to congratulate her sister.

"Harvard? I can't believe it. Who would have thought? My sister, going to Harvard. What made you want to go there in the first place? I mean, I didn't even know you were applying to schools yet. And you know Dad. He isn't mad. He's just going to miss you. Losing his baby girl is going to be hard on him."

"I'm not leaving tomorrow. It's still a year away. And I need something different. This place reminds me too much of Mom." A pout formed on Margo's lips.

Sasha understood that all too well. She had lived in Tampa for most of her life. And when her mom had taken her own life, Tampa no longer felt like home. Instead, it was a hub of terrible memories that invaded her mind. But where Sasha turned to drugs to numb her pain, Margo became a bookworm, surrounding herself with make-believe stories to get through each day.

"I know. But Dad will be okay. He just needs time." Sasha hugged her again.

That's when it happened. A loud pop interrupted their conversation. They didn't notice anything at first, even after looking out the window. It wasn't until minutes later that they'd smelled the smoke.

"What the hell?" Sasha said, poking her head out the window for a second time. She assumed her dad was burning the burgers, but she still couldn't see him. Instead, she saw bright orange flames ascending the far side of the house.

"Oh my God!" Margo gasped.

"Stay here," Sasha said to her sister, but when she reached for the handle to the bedroom door, it was hot on her skin. "Shit!" she yelped, pulling back her hand. "We need to get out of here. Do you see Dad anywhere?"

When Margo shook her head, Sasha leaned out and devised a plan. She didn't know much about fires, but she remembered a firefighter in elementary school telling the entire auditorium that they spread quickly. "We need to move fast. I'll help you out the window. Try to grab that ledge and then inch your way down as far as you can before you jump. It's not too far. I'll be out as soon as you're safe."

Without hesitating, Margo gripped the edge of the window and climbed out feet first. As Sasha watched her sister slide her way down, a voice called out from behind her. And then, in a whirlwind, she was hanging upside down over someone's shoulder.

"Is there anyone else in here?" a deep and muffled voice asked as she was carried down the stairs.

"No." She coughed, inhaling a cloud of smoke. She wanted to tell this man that she could walk, that she could take care of herself, but before she knew it, Sasha was falling onto a stretcher.

When she opened her eyes, a young blond woman hovered over her. "Hi, sweetie, does anything hurt?"

"My sister. Is she okay? Is my dad okay?" Sasha coughed again, trying to sit up.

"I need to check your vitals first," the blond said, pressing a firm hand to Sasha's chest.

And that's when she noticed him. From the corner of her eye, Sasha spotted Sex Eyes, the fireman that had called her by someone else's name. He was right there, staring back at her with that same damn intensity he'd held at Beach Brew. Sasha opened her mouth to say something, but nothing came out. Time seemed to slow down as the paramedic walked around her, checking her blood pressure, her pulse, and her heart.

"Blake?" A voice rang out, breaking the silence and slow motion that swayed between them, even in the chaos that unfolded.

Without turning away, Blake yelled back, keeping his attention on Sasha the entire time. "Yeah?"

"They're taking the dad and the sister to the hospital now. The girl can follow behind. They want them all checked out."

"My dad? Is he okay? What about Margo? Where is she?" Sasha asked, panic suddenly setting in. She tried to sit up again, but the paramedic held her down.

"You need to lie down. You'll see them at the hospital. We'll get an update on the ride over there for you," the blond said. And then she turned to look at Blake. "You're new. You did a great job out there. You were quick with her. My name's Mal. I'm at the station across town." She flipped her bleached hair and swayed her hips. "Maybe I'll see you around sometime."

"What the fuck? Flirt with him on your own time. Can't you just get me to the hospital so I can be with my family?" Sasha spat out, trying to ignore the jealousy that rose in her chest. But Sex Eyes hadn't even looked at the girl, didn't even acknowledge her presence. Instead, he kept his focus on Sasha.

"Your family?" His voice was low and harsh.

Then, suddenly, his irises went dark and he looked away.

"Come on honey, let's get you moving," Mal gritted out. She strapped Sasha to the stretcher, cinching her in a little too tightly.

Sasha frowned, confused with Sex Eyes' change in demeanor and question. She tried to catch his gaze as Mal and another paramedic pushed her into the ambulance, but all she saw was his back as he headed toward a fire truck.

What the hell? What was that guy's problem? Could today get any worse?

Oh, things could always get worse. Way worse.

At the hospital, Sasha was cleared to go home within the first hour. The shortest hospital visit she'd ever had. No joke. And it felt strange being discharged so fast. The last time she'd been at this hospital was four years ago. When she overdosed on Percocet. It was the last time she'd touched a drug of any kind, even prescription painkillers.

The withdrawal had been brutal. She'd woken up disoriented. Bile had risen from her throat as the smell of her own sweat seeped through her hospital gown. And the tremors were terrible. She'd thought she'd die on more than one occasion.

But then, as the physical symptoms had begun to subside, the cravings had kicked her ass. That's why her dad and sister moved down there. To get her through the worst of it. To help her stay clean. She had stayed at the hospital for three days before being admitted to a drug rehabilitation program.

"Room 304, sweetie," a tall nurse said, pointing down the corridor when Sasha went in search of her dad.

When she found his room, she knocked on his door before entering, though she didn't wait for a response.

"Dad! Are you okay?" Sasha exhaled. She ran in and gave him a hug.

He sat on his hospital bed beneath white cotton sheets. His arm was resting on a small portable table, and both his head and arm were wrapped in heavy white bandages.

"I'm fine, I'm fine. Don't worry about me. Where's Margo?" His voice trembled as he cleared his throat.

"She's still down in the ER. She twisted her ankle pretty bad, so they're fitting her for a boot. I heard they're keeping you overnight for observation. The nurse said you have a concussion and second-degree burns. You got really lucky. This could have been worse if your neighbors hadn't called for help."

"I don't even remember what happened. No one has told me much of anything. Just that you and Margo were okay and that the house caught fire. Is it bad?"

Sitting on the edge of her dad's bed, Sasha replayed the events for him, leaving out the details of Sex Eyes. But then, as if the mere thought of him triggered something, the world carried the tall, tanned God into her dad's room. She parted her lips, ready to thank him, but he didn't allow any time for her to force the words out.

"Mr. Patterson?" he asked, walking straight to her dad's bedside. "My name's Blake Ryan. I'm one of the firefighters that was at your house today. I retrieved this woman from one of your upper-level bedrooms this evening." Blake stood tall and lean and very serious. And it seemed as if he were avoiding all eye contact with Sasha, but she couldn't be sure or understand why. She'd never seen anyone act so strange.

"You're the one who saved my daughter? Thank you so much. I don't know what I would have done without you. Sasha was just filling me in on all the—" her dad gushed, but before he could continue, Blake extended his arm and placed his hand out to stop him.

"Mr. Patterson, I don't want you to thank me. Actually, I'm not here about the fire."

Sasha couldn't stop staring at Blake, but he wouldn't even look in her direction.

"I'm here as a courtesy to let you know that a detective will be in shortly to ask you some questions."

"A detective?" Sasha asked, her voice sharp. "Over a propane tank?"

"It's okay, dear. If that's what they need to do, they can ask me anything." Her dad patted her on the arm.

"Like I said, I'm not here about the fire," Blake continued. His attention shifted to the floor.

Sasha waited as the seconds dragged out. Her eyebrows furrowed in confusion the longer the time stretched.

"Mr. Patterson, can you ask…" He pointed toward her.

"Sasha. My name's Sasha."

"Can you ask…Sasha…to leave while I speak with you?"

Silence filled the room. Had she heard him right? She looked at her dad, who looked just as puzzled as she felt. Then she turned to Blake, but he still wouldn't meet her gaze. Her pulse quickened and her chest tightened. "What the fuck is going on? I'm not going anywhere until someone tells me what's happening. Dad, tell him I'm not leaving."

CHAPTER FIVE

Blake

Every time he heard them utter the words family, dad, and daughter, Blake winced. Family? Her real family was less than two hundred miles away. Her real family had been worried sick about her for nearly two decades. Her real family didn't include this man sitting in front of him on a hospital bed.

"No. I'm not leaving," Sasha said, holding firm at the man's side.

Blake couldn't bring himself to look at her. Didn't know whether to call her Sasha or Paige. He had no idea what she knew. What the man had told her all these years. Had he brainwashed her? Held her captive until she was willing to comply?

Blake knew he should wait for the detectives. But he needed something. Anything. And he'd be kidding himself if he thought the detectives would let him sit in on an open investigation. He had to do this now. His own way.

"Sweetie, I'm sure it will be okay. Why don't you go check in with your sister? Hopefully she'll be ready to leave soon. Can she stay with you tonight?"

She stood up and exhaled loudly, clearly upset about being left in the dark. But Blake couldn't say anything in front of her. He didn't want to hurt her, cause her any pain.

"All right," she acquiesced and kissed the top of his head. "I'll be down in the ER. I'll come back and check on you once she's discharged."

Taking a side step so Sasha could get around him, Blake tightened his lips and looked up just in time to catch her gaze. He anticipated daggers, eyes that would slice right through him. After today, he would have deserved it. He was about to flip her life upside down. But instead, her eyebrows arched, and a crease formed in the center of her forehead, baring soft, tender eyes that were filled with worry. And in that moment, he did everything in his power not to go to her and hold her. He'd thought about this moment a million times. What it would be like to finally find her. But none of his dreams had ever played out quite like this.

When Sasha left the room, closing the door behind her, Blake pulled out his phone and held it up to Mr. Patterson's face. "This girl. Does she look familiar?"

"Of course. That's Sasha. What is this about?" he asked, shifting his weight on the bed.

"This girl. The one in the picture. Her name isn't Sasha," Blake growled. His heart was heavy. A part of him felt relieved that this man had confirmed the girl's identity, that the picture was the girl who'd walked out of the room. But the other part of him was furious. He wanted to rip this guy apart for kidnapping her. For taking her from her family. For brainwashing her into thinking she was someone other than Paige.

"Of course it is. That's my daughter. And how in the world would you have gotten your hands on a picture of her?"

Was this guy kidding? The nerve of him to call her his daughter. "This girl is not your daughter. Her name is Paige. Paige Knight. She was kidnapped when she was five years old," Blake bit back, trying not to yell. He didn't want to make a scene and be escorted out just yet. He knew it would be inevitable, but he needed more time. He needed more information.

"Listen, you've got the wrong girl. Let me look at that picture again," he said, reaching for his glasses and placing them on the bridge of his nose.

"I'll show you again. This time I want you to look very closely." Blake held the phone out, expanding the picture to show her face. Her bright hazel eyes. Her freckles. Her fire-red hair pulled up in a high ponytail. The scar that zigzagged across her face. "This scar. This one right here," he said, pointing, "is the same scar that girl has that walked out of this room."

"I don't understand. Sasha got that scar from falling off her bike when she was four," Mr. Patterson said.

Blake's face went dark. "How the fuck do you know that? Who are you? Why did you take her? Her family has been looking for her for almost twenty fucking years, and you've had her all this time." His voice was thunderous, and he seethed with each sentence.

"Hey, I'm not sure who you are, but I'm going to have to ask you to leave," a police officer said as he entered the room, two more trailing behind him.

"No. I can't. I need answers. That's Paige Knight. He kidnapped Paige Knight." His face was hot, and his eyes burned. Not from tears. Fuck the tears. He didn't have time to cry over this again. He had cried too much as a kid. Now they burned with rage.

"I don't know what's going on. Can someone tell me who Paige Knight is?" the man pleaded.

With that, Blake launched himself at the man, but an officer stepped in his path, grabbing him by the arm. "Let me handle this, but stay close. If this is the same girl, we'll need her family to confirm her identity."

It took every fragment of willpower he had to walk out of that hospital room. And when he did, he was surprised to see that there were at least four more officers waiting in the hallway, all looking at him. But none of them budged from their positions.

Taking a few steps away from the crowd, he leaned against the wall and pulled out his phone. *Damn it.* It was time. He knew he had to make the call. He couldn't put it off any longer. Taking in a deep breath, Blake dialed Porter's number for the second time that day.

CHAPTER SIX

Sasha

S asha and Margo took the elevator to the third floor and walked out into a sea of cops.

"Whoa, what's going on?" Margo asked, limping along Sasha's side.

"Oh my God!" Sasha said, noticing the men going in and out of their dad's room. She quickened her pace, leaving Margo to hobble along by herself.

"Is this about the fire? I can't believe this is all over a stupid grill," Sasha said harshly to no one in particular, but none of the officers responded. They all looked at her like they didn't know what to say.

She turned toward her dad's room, but one of the officers placed a hand on her arm, stopping her in her tracks. "I'm sorry, you can't go in there right now."

"Is Dad okay?" Margo asked, worry in her voice.

"Let me in his room. I have a right to see my dad," Sasha demanded.

"I can't do that," the officer said, blocking Sasha from the door.

"Is he under arrest?" she scoffed. She couldn't comprehend a world in which her dad would be arrested, especially over a malfunction with a grill.

When the officer didn't respond, Sasha's jaw dropped, surprise catching her off guard. She scanned the crowd, and that's when she saw him. The firefighter. Sex Eyes…whatever his name was. He was rounding the corner, placing his phone inside his pants pocket.

"You! You did this. Tell me what's going on," Sasha demanded when he looked up to meet her gaze.

But he didn't respond either. He just stopped in his tracks. It was as if the entire hospital had a secret. As if they all knew and couldn't tell her. She looked from face to face until she saw Margo, with her big brown eyes, tears welling up and spilling down her cheeks.

"Someone tell me what the fuck is going on," Sasha pleaded, unable to move.

Finally, Blake inched forward. It felt like hours had passed before he maneuvered his way through the cops. She kept her eyes on his, but she couldn't make out what he was thinking. She couldn't decipher his motivation.

"I need you to sit," he said, motioning to the chair against the wall.

"I don't need to—"

"Sit." His voice was strong, yet soft.

She didn't want to be told what to do. She didn't want to listen. But hearing the demand in his voice made her entire body tremble.

"Is there anyone you can call to pick up your sister?"

Sasha looked at Margo and then back at Blake. "She can call her boyfriend. He can drive her back to my condo. We don't have any other family."

Blake nodded and then walked back toward the group of officers. Two of them nodded and then walked toward Margo. Together, they escorted her to the elevator.

When Blake came back, he sat in the chair next to her. They were so close. She wanted to ask him again. To beg him just to say it. What could be so wrong that he couldn't just tell her? Her mind raced with thoughts of her dad dying. Of him being arrested for wrongfully starting a fire. Her stomach twisted into a knot and her heart beat erratically.

"Please," she whispered. "Please just tell me what's happening."

"There is no easy way to say this. I have to show you." He reached into his pocket and pulled out his phone. After a few clicks, he held it to her, placing it in her hands.

She didn't know what she was looking at. Somehow, her eyes had become blurry. There were two pictures. Both of them were of her. One was a toddler-age Sasha. The other was of a girl who looked like her but was clearly computer generated. She shook her head. Tears slipped from her face and dropped onto the screen.

"No. No. No." She shook her head, not understanding and unable to register any other words.

"Your name is Paige Knight. You were abducted when you were five years old. Your family has been looking for you for close to twenty years," Blake whispered, his hand now resting on her arm.

She knew he was still talking, words still spilling from his mouth. But she couldn't hear him any longer. The room spun and her head became fuzzy. This was a horrible mistake. She had a loving family. Her mom had loved her with everything she had. It was what kept her mom alive for so long. That's what she told herself. And her dad. He was the sweetest, most gentle soul on the planet, always giving, always helping. And her sister. They were the truest of frenemies. Their love-hate relationship growing up was as typical as in any household. This was all a huge mistake. Too cruel to be a joke. It was downright wrong.

Sasha stood and then wiped away her tears with the back of her hand. "You have the wrong girl. That's my dad. My mom died when I was seventeen. No one ever took me. You're wasting your time," she pleaded for him to understand.

Blake took the phone back, his breaths just as ragged as hers, but he didn't argue. Instead, he pinched the screen and zoomed in on the picture of the little girl, the one who looked like five-year-old Sasha but was clearly someone else.

"Do you see it now?" he asked, his green eyes growing darker, his voice soft.

Sasha's focus landed on the phone for a second time, and then she gasped. Her hand intuitively drew to her face, to her hairline. To the scar that the little girl wore. The same one that looked back at her in the mirror every morning when she woke up and every night before she went to bed. Her eyes darted back to Blake. "You're wrong. There's an explanation…there has to be."

"Blake?" a gravelly voice yelled from down the hall.

Blake's eyes went wide as he lifted his head in the direction of the voice, causing Sasha to turn her head only a second later.

A tall, redheaded, freckled man came running down the hall at full speed. And then his arms were on her, wrapping themselves around her shoulders. Pulling her into an airtight embrace. Only, an embrace would be welcomed, and this wasn't. Her pulse accelerated and her stomach twisted. The idea of a stranger's hands on her was bad enough, but under these circumstances…

"It's you! I can't believe it's you! Holy shit! Paige!" the guy said, squeezing her tighter. And then he took a step back, her shoulders still in his grasp. Looking at her from arm's length, he smiled as if he were taking her all in. But it didn't take long for his lips to turn directions when he caught sight of what must have been a dreadful, confused look that covered her face. The look that told him she had no idea who he was.

The pain in her abdomen was so raw she pushed the man away from her and yelled, "I'm not Paige! I don't know who you are, but you've got this all wrong." She couldn't take it any longer. She shrugged out of his hold. Taking a step back, she placed more distance between them.

The man rocked on his heels at the sudden withdrawal, his eyes large and confused.

"I don't know who you are, and I don't know who this Paige girl is. My name is Sasha. After you talk to my dad, you'll see."

And then the man's eyes darted to Blake, the arch of his brows sinking. "What the fuck is she talking about? I thought…"

"Porter. I told you not to come yet. You're supposed to wait until—"

"Are you fucking kidding me? You found my sister, and I was already in Tampa, but you expected me to sit on my ass and wait?" he growled as he shifted his attention back to Sasha. "If you're not Paige, then who are you? Because you sure as hell look like me, wouldn't you say?"

And that's when it struck her. She'd watched him running down the hall and when she'd pushed him away, but she hadn't really seen him until that moment. His hair was the same fiery red as hers. The same color that made it unnecessary for her to dye it because it was so vibrant and full of life. Most redheads showcased a softer auburn or strawberry-blond hue, like Margo. And his nose, the narrow ridge that landed perfectly on his oval face, was almost identical to hers.

Just then, the door to her dad's room opened and a man in uniform looked up from his notepad. He stopped in his tracks the moment he saw Sasha and the man claiming to be her brother.

CHAPTER SEVEN

Blake

"I don't care what you say. This shit is messed up," Porter said as he folded the blanket he'd slept with last night.

"You realize that girl has lived the last two decades not knowing she had a brother, right? You can't expect her to remember things from so long ago," Blake responded, throwing a black T-shirt over his head. "Detective Spencer said she might not ever remember, and you have to be okay with that."

Blake had made the decision to call Porter last night, but he hadn't thought his friend would come running the second they'd ended their call. Cocoa Beach was two and a half hours away, but Porter hadn't been at home. Somewhere in their conversation, Porter had failed to mention his classes were in Tampa, so he'd shown up at the hospital less than an hour after Blake had called him.

"I'll never be okay with that. Fuck, it's like, what if someone took Carter? I sure as hell would hope he'd remember me and Tina if something happened." Porter's son Carter was almost five. Almost the same age Paige had been when she was abducted. And the thought of the same thing happening to him worried them all.

Porter ran his hand through his hair and paced the kitchen floor before continuing. "How am I supposed to tell my mom and dad? I can't keep something like this from them. Tina won't be able to either. You know how she is."

Blake did know. Too well. A secret to Porter's wife, Tina, was like a shiny diamond necklace wanting to be touched and worn and shown off. When Tina was given news, she could typically hold her tongue, because it was just that—news. But the second she was told not to tell someone, it was as if her tongue was on fire, and there was no water to stop the flames from spreading. It was a bad analogy coming from a firefighter, but it was true. She never did it with ill intent, never with malice. That's just who she was.

"My mom will call her at some point this weekend to see how we're doing. And Tina is going to slip. I'd rather tell her myself, but how the hell do I tell her that her daughter doesn't remember her? Doesn't remember any of us?" Defeat was plastered all over Porter's face.

Blake couldn't imagine what Porter was feeling. To lose a sister at such a young age. To go through life never knowing what happened, thinking the worst. And then, just when he'd finally given up hope, she reappears, only to not remember.

"Just give it some time. Try to look at it from her viewpoint. She just needs time." He patted Porter on the back, trying to comfort him.

"I know. And I appreciate you helping. I can't promise I won't be back tonight with the whole gang though," he chuckled, but the humor couldn't hide the sorrow that dripped from his voice. The whole gang included Porter's mom and dad, his sister, his wife, and his son. Blake knew it was a real possibility that they'd all show up. Where one went, they all went. If news of this spread, Blake was sure they'd all be in his living room before the day was over.

"You are all more than welcome. You know that," Blake reassured Porter.

An hour later, Blake pulled up to Beach Brew. He wasn't exactly sure what he was doing there or what he was hoping for. Porter had taken off. He'd gone home, probably disheartened at the reunion he'd received. "If you hear anything before I do, call me," he'd begged.

"I'm not family. No one will call me. They'll call your mom."

They both knew this would be tricky. Sasha was an adult. She wouldn't just be returned home now that she'd been found. She had her own life here in St. Pete. A job. A sister and a dad she seemed to love. And since Sasha was adamant about her identity, she'd refused all but a DNA test, which would take a few days to produce results.

Blake half believed Sasha would be at work. Being rescued from a house fire was one reason to stay home, but finding out you had another family out there, after all these years, well, that was a whole other ball game. Sasha, however, struck him as someone who needed to work to distract herself. Like being preoccupied would help take her mind off anything and everything.

He clung to that hope when he finally mustered enough courage to push open the café's door. He'd made it two steps inside before his feet stopped. The cool air that pushed out from the air conditioner encircled him as the scents of freshly brewed coffee and warm cinnamon rolls filled the air. But that's not what stopped him. It was the sight of Sasha, leaning over, helping an elderly woman with the sleeve to a hot coffee. Her red hair was pulled into a messy knot on the top of her head. Loose strands fell around her sullen face. Shit. What was he supposed to call her? Paige? Sasha? Neither felt right.

She looked up after the woman thanked her, her expression soft and sweet, though there was no spark in her eyes. Instead, her cheeks were flushed and swollen. Her shoulders drooped, and her movement was slow and exaggerated as she wiped down the counter. And yet, she was still beautiful.

"Hi." It was the only thing he could think to say.

What the actual fuck? Destroy this girl's life and just say hi?

He wanted to punch himself in the face for sounding so stupid.

"Hi," she said back, giving him a half smile, her eyes tired and red-rimmed.

"I wasn't sure if you'd be here today. I mean, you shouldn't be here, not after everything," Blake continued, trying to hold back from touching her hand.

"Yeah, well, when you're about to be the owner, you have to show up and unlock the doors, right?" Sasha turned around and poured a cup of coffee. When she finished, she placed it on the counter, pushing it toward him.

"You own this place?" Blake asked, his eyebrows lifting in surprise. "That's impressive. Twenty-four years old and you have your own business."

"Twenty…" Sasha started but then stopped and shook her head.

Blake knew what he'd said a second too late. Her age. "I'm sorry. I just…"

"Listen, I don't hold grudges. You did what you had to do because you felt it was necessary for those people. The detective talked to me after you left. He showed me pictures. Explained how that little girl was taken from her birthday party. But that's not me. And I don't feel the need to explain anything other than that." She poured a bag of coffee beans into a grinder. "But what about my dad? They said once he's released from the hospital, they have to arrest him, pending my DNA results. My scar is enough to label him a suspect. They have an officer watching his room. Like he's going to run or something."

A tear trickled down her face at her last sentence. Blake wanted to reach out. To wipe her face with his thumb. To console her. To pull her into an embrace. But he was nothing more than a mere stranger to her. She had no idea of the pain all of this was causing him or the memories it dredged up.

"I don't know what happened to you. I don't know why you don't remember anything, except that you were so little. But it's your reality, and I believe your reality." He paused and took a deep breath. "But I also have my own reality. And I do remember." Blake opened his wallet and pulled out a few singles. He placed them on the counter. Underneath the bills, he laid an old, worn picture with crinkled edges. Then he left, knowing she might not even look at it.

CHAPTER EIGHT

Sasha

Relief washed over Sasha after she heard the bell chime. Sex Eyes was gone. She didn't have to turn around to know that. The silence was proof enough. His absence created a void she hadn't anticipated, and now she was alone.

It was crazy how drastically things could change in twenty-four hours. Yesterday Sasha had been on cloud nine. She planned to apply for a loan today, to move forward with acquiring Beach Brew. Today, her dad was in the hospital, his house had been destroyed by a dumb accident, and it was likely he'd be arrested upon his discharge. She knew she should talk to a lawyer, but she didn't have enough strength. Not this morning.

Instead, Sasha pulled out her phone and typed a quick text to her sister.

Sasha: *Hey, you awake?*
Margo: *Yeah. About to shower.*

Sasha: *Do you need anything today? I'll be home early. We can get dinner.*

Margo didn't respond right away. The little blue dots appeared and disappeared a few times, causing Sasha's heart to skip a few beats, worry and dread washing over her. They'd talked and argued well into the morning after Sasha had gotten home from the hospital. Margo had been left in the dark, completely unaware of why all the police officers had surrounded their dad's room. Sasha was left with the daunting task of explaining the terrible mistake to her sister.

"What's going to happen to him? Are they taking him to jail? Will we need a lawyer?" Margo had asked, tears flooding her eyes when Sasha had finally gotten home.

"I don't know. But I did a DNA test to prove to them that this was all a misunderstanding. They want you to do one too."

"Me? Why me?" Margo asked, her voice pitching, surprise catching her off guard.

"They said if Dad abducted me, he may have taken you too. But we know that's not the case. I was there when you were born. Grandma and I were in the waiting room. And look at us, Margo. We look alike. We both…"

"We don't look anything alike," Margo responded, cutting Sasha short. "Aside from our hair, we look nothing alike. And even that…even that is questionable."

Sasha's eyes narrowed and her mouth dropped at her sister's words.

"You've always had such bright red hair, and it's soft and shiny and straight. Mine is coarse, and curly, more strawberry blond, like Mom's. Your face is oval and mine is super round. And then our eyes? You're the only one with hazel eyes. We all have dark brown." There was a pause before she continued. "Oh my God. Sasha. What if they're right? What if they did take you? Think about it. Mom always suffered from depression. What if that's the reason why?" Margo clasped her hand over her mouth.

"No. Don't say that," Sasha snapped. She stood solid and continued, her voice still raised. "Mom was depressed, but not because they kidnapped me. Mom was sick." The blood rushed to her temples at her sister's words. Her mom was her world. Her mom was the one who'd taught her everything she knew.

As teachers, her mom and dad had agreed to homeschool Sasha from the beginning, allowing curiosity to dictate what she learned. They'd said a public school would only hold her back. So her mom took a permanent leave of absence, which allowed Sasha to learn at her own pace, to grow, and blossom on her own, allowing them time to visit museums while others sat at wooden desks at a school that was bound by government rules. Margo, too, had been homeschooled, but only until she turned ten. That's when their mom had lost her battle with depression, leaving their dad with no other choice but to put her into the public school system.

But Margo had gone to bed unconvinced. She had been so young when their mom died. And while Margo handled it better than she had, Sasha wanted to shelter Margo from any more pain.

After what felt like an eternity, Sasha's phone buzzed again.

Margo: *Drew is going to pick me up and take me to do the DNA test. Then I'm hanging out with him today.*

Sasha let out a deep sigh. She wanted to connect with her sister. But man, that was proving to be more difficult than she'd imagined. Putting the phone back in her pocket, Sasha scooped up the money Blake had left on the counter. Underneath, a picture with edges that curled caught her attention. Sasha brought the photo close to her face and swallowed thickly as her eyes settled on the three kids who stared back at her. A little girl and boy with bright red hair stood side by side next to matching bicycles, wearing identical smiles. Another boy, taller, with dark brown hair, stood behind them with a bigger bike. Sasha ran a finger over the front, dragging it from face to face, and then flipped the photo over, feeling the paper underneath. *I'll be home today if you want to talk. If you want to know more.* It was signed by Blake and had his address and phone number beneath his message. She was about to toss the paper out when she peeled it from the back of the picture and noticed the words on the picture itself. *Paige and Porter Knight, four years old. Blake, six years old.*

Confusion crossed her face. She'd assumed Blake had mistaken Sasha for this Paige girl, recognized her somehow, but hadn't thought he was related. Not linked to the case. And yet, this picture told another story. Blake knew Paige. But his last name had been left off, leaving more questions than answers.

She didn't want to indulge in something that was causing her dad and sister so much heartache, but over the next several hours, it was all Sasha could think about. It consumed her. She wanted to ask her dad. She wanted to find out what he'd told the police. But her dad was off-limits, at least until her DNA results came back. And that could take a few more days, if not longer.

By early evening, Sasha was driving herself mad. When her stomach growled, she knew it was time to get out of there. She had to eat something. Pizza. Yes, she would order a pizza and bring it home. If her sister didn't want to eat with her, she'd be fine on her own. Sasha grabbed her keys and purse and was just about to lock up when she hesitated. The pizza place was right around the corner from Blake's address, she was sure of it. If he'd written his address correctly, he lived just a few blocks from the café. *Fuck it*, she thought to herself and pivoted on the balls of her feet. She retraced her steps and reached for the paper Blake had left behind.

Ten minutes later, Sasha found herself in an unfamiliar hallway, knocking on a door she'd never seen before. Nerves ran through her veins. When the knock went unanswered, she brought her fist back up to the solid brown door, but before she could rap her knuckles against it again, it jerked open.

Blake stood to the side, shirtless, his hand still on the bronze handle. Wearing nothing more than a pair of black running shorts, his chest glistening with sweat.

"I…" Sasha whispered, her lips parting slowly. "I shouldn't have come. This was a mistake." Heat rose in her cheeks. Quickly, she turned, wanting to escape. But before she could make it two steps, a gentle hand clutched at her elbow.

"Please. Please don't leave," Blake pleaded, his voice rugged and firm. "I don't know what to call you."

"Sasha. I told you my name is Sasha," she said, unable to bring herself to turn around. Not wanting to look into the eyes that drew her breath away. But she didn't move forward either. She wanted to stay. Needed to stay. Truth be told, she didn't really want to be alone tonight. And more importantly, she wanted to find out more about this Paige girl. She wanted to show this man she wasn't the girl he thought she was.

"Sasha. Sasha," he repeated himself, letting a deep exhale leave his lips when he was finished. "Please. Come inside."

She turned around to face him, biting her lip in indecision. If she left, she wouldn't be any closer to understanding any of this. But if she stayed, she might hear things she wasn't ready to hear. Her sister's theory about her mom and how they didn't look alike replayed in her mind. She steadied herself before nodding. And then her feet were moving as Blake pulled her inside.

"I just moved here, so I don't have much."

Sasha glanced around. The apartment looked fully furnished but lonely. White walls. No pictures. Nothing to suggest what kind of person Blake was.

"I don't have much food. I just got back from a run and I'm starving. You hungry?" he asked, throwing a white T-shirt over his head, the sweat instantly bleeding through where it stretched across the defined muscles of his chest.

"Starving," was the only word Sasha could conjure, and she wasn't only thinking of food.

Blake looked at her a second too long, causing Sasha to wince and bite her lip again, not knowing if Blake could see right through her. That she'd spent a second too long looking at him too.

He smiled. And then his expression lit up. Grabbing her hand, he pulled her back into the hallway.

"I hope you like pizza."

CHAPTER NINE

Blake

Sitting across from Sasha at a small table outside, Blake pulled a slice of pepperoni pizza from the cardboard container and bit into it. "It's pretty good," he said, watching as Sasha toyed with the piece that sat on her paper plate, uneaten. "It tastes better when it's in your mouth."

She looked up at him, unamused, and then turned her attention to the sky. Dark clouds rolled in, blocking out the setting sun. "I know. They've got the best pizza around." She turned toward him. "Actually, that's why I came by. I was going to order a pizza to take home, but then I remembered your address and realized you lived around the corner." She looked back at the sky for a brief second. "Looks like it might rain." Clutching the pizza between her fingers, Sasha brought the slice to her mouth and took a bite. She closed her eyes and let a low hum escape her lips.

Blake watched as she chewed, smiling gently. "You saw the picture."

Sasha nodded.

"Okay, I know you weren't coming to invite me to dinner, which I wouldn't have minded, by the way. But I'm sure you have questions. Go ahead and ask me whatever you want," Blake said and then took another bite.

Her eyes flashed open at his words. Licking the red sauce from her lower lip, she found her voice. "Tell me about that girl. And how you're connected to her. I'm assuming that guy at the hospital the other day is her brother. But who are you?"

Blake tilted his head and took her in. He watched as worry creased her forehead. He had to tread lightly. If he said the wrong thing, insinuated that she was Paige, she'd run. She had to make sense of the past before she could connect herself to it. He knew that. The last thing he wanted to do was to overwhelm her. This was his only shot. After wiping his hands on a napkin, he cleared his throat and began.

"That guy yesterday, his name is Porter. He's Paige's twin brother. I'm his neighbor. Well, I used to be. He still lives in Cocoa Beach, just a few blocks from where we grew up."

"Cocoa Beach? That's only a few hours from here." She furrowed her eyebrows.

"Yeah, not far at all. Have you ever been there?" he asked, curious about whether she'd ever been back to the town she had been abducted from, going unrecognized.

"No, but my boss, the current owner of Beach Brew, has a house over there," Sasha said.

"It's a coastal town, so not all that different from here. Porter's an EMT. He works at the same fire station I just came from."

Just then, a gentle breeze danced between them, leaving strands of red hair covering Sasha's eyes. Blake sucked in a deep breath; she was so beautiful. The way she didn't care about how messy her hair had become as it blew in the wind. The way her dark freckles contrasted with her pale skin, and how they dotted her nose and scattered across her face, highlighting her high cheekbones. It was a different version from yesterday, when she'd worn makeup that covered up the freckles and had earrings that dangled to her shoulders. She was gorgeous then, but nothing compared to the raw beauty she displayed now.

Sasha drew her hand up to her face, tucking the strands that had come loose behind her ear, and that's when his eyes went wide and he inhaled sharply. That scar. It was right there. He wanted to reach out, to touch it. To tell her he was sorry. But the wind came back, causing her hair to fall loose again. He knew he had to wait. He couldn't mention the scar again. Not yet.

And then, as if by pure force, her eyes shifted to his, their gazes meeting through her tousled hair. Her hand lifted to her face. Her fingers trailed the lines from her forehead to her ear.

"This. Tell me about this," she said, her voice low and unsteady.

He shook his head. "I can't. Not now." His breath hitched.

Confusion swirled in her eyes before she put her hand back in her lap.

"Then tell me what happened when that girl was taken."

That girl. She kept referring to herself as that girl. He understood why, but it didn't make it any easier on him. He had to walk this at a snail's pace or he'd lose her, and losing her again wasn't an option.

"It was their birthday party. Porter and Paige had just turned five. Their parents threw a big party. We were all playing hide and seek." He paused and wet his lips before continuing. "One minute she was there. The next, she was gone."

Sasha straightened in her chair. "Okay, let's pretend what you are saying is accurate. This girl has been missing for what? Twenty years? Is it odd that I look like her? Yes. And I agree, it's even more strange that I have this scar that looks like hers. But I grew up in Tampa. I was at the hospital when my sister was born. My grandma too. So, if someone took me, that means my entire family would have been in on it. Don't you find that a little hard to explain? And people who get kidnapped, aren't they usually locked up? Not allowed out of the house?" The minute the words left her mouth, she slapped a hand over her face.

"What? What is it?" Blake asked, his words coming out sharper than he intended.

She shook her head, her eyes wide in alarm.

"You remembered something, didn't you?" He reached out and grabbed her free hand, the heat searing through his own.

"It's nothing."

"I call bullshit on that. Just remember, I'm not the enemy here. You came to see me this time." His voice was rough, and for a second, he thought maybe it was too rough, too quick and demanding. But her eyes let him know it was fine. Damn, it was impossible not to look at her eyes.

"It's probably nothing at all, seriously. I wasn't locked up. Never. Not once. My parents didn't even ground me. But…" She paused and looked away.

He brushed the back of her hand with his thumb, giving her time to process her thoughts.

"I was homeschooled my entire life. My sister too. My dad only registered Margo for public school when she entered fifth grade, when my mom died."

Blake clenched his jaw when Sasha mentioned her dad and mom. It made him want to punch something. That this girl was talking about other people as her family infuriated him, but this wasn't about him, it was about her.

"It could be nothing at all," he acknowledged, moving his hand from hers, suddenly aware of his actions. "Have you been back to the house yet? To see the damage? Most people are shocked to see so much stuff get ruined, but it's really not as bad as it looked yesterday." Blake changed the subject. He was too afraid to push her. She'd just offered up a tiny bit of information, and he wanted to respect that. He also wanted it to simmer there. Maybe she'd remember something later. This had to be done on her time.

"No, I hadn't even thought about it with everything going on. Maybe I'll go by tomorrow."

Just then, Blake's phone buzzed. The noise startled them both. When Porter's name flashed across the screen, Blake silenced the call, but it was too late. Sasha had already seen his name, and her demeanor changed immediately.

"I should get going. I need to get back for Margo. She'll be home soon." Her lips tightened and her shoulders squared as she pushed from her seat.

He'd seen that look before. At the hospital. And he knew if he pressed on, if he asked her anything else, she would backtrack. But he wanted to see her again, so if that meant she had to leave now, he was more than willing to say goodbye.

"If you need anything, if you just want to talk, you can text anytime. Or drop by again."

He added the last part without hesitation. Meaning dripped from his lips. But she didn't say anything in return. She just kept her lips pursed in a tight smile as she stood up.

"I mean it. I'd like to see you again," he added before she could turn to walk away.

She bit her lower lip as if contemplating what to say next. Her eyes locked in on his. "This is all just so weird. I'm sorry. I really do need to go."

Blake nodded in agreement. And then she was gone. Again.

Once Blake made it back upstairs to his condo, his phone vibrated again. "Hey, Porter. What's up?" he asked, finally answering the call.

"I've been trying to get in touch with you. My mom knows. She wants to meet her."

"Shit, Porter. I thought you were going to wait to see what happens with the DNA results," Blake snapped.

"Like I said, Tina can't keep a secret. My mom came by. She didn't believe Tina at first, so she drove over and interrogated me. Once I mentioned the scar, she panicked. She called the police station over there to see what's going on and started crying."

"And?" Blake asked.

"They told her they couldn't answer any of her questions until they had a positive identification."

Blake knew where this was leading. Porter wanted him to pull some strings, and not with the police. He wanted Blake to ask Sasha if they could meet. But if Porter's mom met Sasha now, it would only make things harder for Sasha, and he wasn't sure that was the right choice just yet.

"She's not ready," Blake responded. He grabbed the back of his neck, knowing full well how Porter would react. Hell, he would react the same way if it were his sister.

"You have no fucking idea what this is like for us, Blake! My sister is this close, and she has no memory of us. And we have to wait, what? A week? Longer? Just to get her DNA results when we already know who she is. This is fucked up. And that man who took her gets to sit in a fucking hospital bed. They should be investigating. Searching his house. Something." Porter's voice was frenzied as he lashed out. "My mom will go insane if she doesn't get eyes on her."

"Porter. I know how hard this is…you're right. But you saw her yesterday. It's been two decades. She has to start somewhere. She needs to remember something, or your mom will be even more devastated when Sasha pushes her away. Today, when we were talking about her in the third person, she…"

"*What*? You saw her today? When? Why didn't you start with that?" Porter yelled through the speaker.

CHAPTER TEN

Sasha

The next morning, Sasha woke long before the sun was up. She'd always been an early riser, but this was taking it to new heights. She had tossed and turned throughout the night, unable to stop the grave visions of her parents from invading her thoughts. Each time her eyelids fell, the nightmares would return. And each time, someone was dragging her, pulling her into a car, taking her away. In the last one, she was an adult, and she sat with her dad on his hospital bed, only to be dragged out by the boy who looked like her. She'd screamed, begging for him to let her go, but he wouldn't.

"Sasha. Sasha." Margo was there, shaking her by the shoulders. "You're having a nightmare."

When Margo's words finally cut through her nightmare, Sasha sat up and wiped the sweat beading down her forehead.

"I couldn't sleep either," her sister murmured. She shoved her feet under the covers when Sasha pulled them back for her. It had been ages since they'd slept together in the same bed, probably since before their mom had died. And while it was nice to have her sister here, so close after years of struggling to maintain a healthy relationship, it made it that much harder to fall asleep.

Sasha waited until Margo's breathing deepened before she snuck out of bed. Walking through her small condo, she glanced at her phone to check the time. Barely four in the morning. Yikes. She should jump back in bed and pull the covers over her face and pray for sleep. But she shook her head. She was too awake for that. And she did not want any more of those nonsense nightmares returning.

After pouring water into her Keurig and waiting for a fresh cup of coffee to brew, Sasha opened the door to her balcony and dropped down into a wicker chair, tucking her feet under herself. Without the sun, the air was crisp. She adjusted her weight in the chair and pulled a gray fleece throw over her lap. Then she swiped the screen of her phone. It was too early to call or text anyone, so Sasha resorted to browsing social media. She scrolled through post after boring post, past pictures of old friends graduating from college and starting families, past updates about weddings and new job announcements.

It wasn't that she didn't care. Okay, that was a lie; she didn't care. Social media wasn't really her thing. She knew how devastating it could be to one's self-worth, so she didn't go on it very often. Typically, her involvement was limited to browsing when she was bored or tired, a way to pass the time. This morning, however, her mind was elsewhere.

One picture did cheer her up though. It was of her friend Claire and her husband. The two of them hand in hand at the airport, on their way to Asheville, no doubt. Claire wasn't much for posting anything other than things associated with her writing, especially pictures of herself, so the sight of her face made Sasha smile. Oh, how she was going to miss Claire. But even as she studied the image, her thoughts traveled back to Blake.

She recalled his broad shoulders. His wavy brown hair. The way the word "Paige" had fallen from his lips. It had sounded familiar, but she hadn't known why. She wasn't Paige. But his voice. Something about the way he spoke. He'd sounded so convinced. She replayed their conversation about Paige over and over in her head until she couldn't take it any longer.

She stood, stretching and rolling her neck until a flash went off in her mind. She wasn't sure what Blake's last name was, but she might be able to find it. Porter's last name was Knight. She'd start there. Typing his name into the search bar on Instagram, she crossed two fingers and prayed she would find something. Anything. She clicked Enter. A dozen pictures popped up, but it was easy to spot the one she was looking for. Clicking his icon, Sasha scanned each image. Porter looked like he was married and had a kid. A son. And he apparently loved his job as an EMT.

Scrolling to the bottom of his page, Sasha spotted a few baby pictures toward the end, though they didn't seem to be Porter's son. These baby pictures were of older quality and aged. She clicked on one, enlarging it for a better view. It seemed to be Porter as a toddler with his twin sister, Paige. The two of them sat on a brown couch with old-school flower wallpaper as a backdrop, hugging one another and smiling at the camera. Underneath, there were a few hashtags. *#Neverforgotten. #HappyBirthday. #Oneday.*

Sasha's heart sank, a heaviness falling over her at the thought of Porter losing a sister. And then she let out a sigh, as if that would help. Her eyes trailed over to the hundreds of likes it received from the friends and family who'd undoubtedly felt just as bad for Porter. It was dated from last July. July. Her heart skipped a beat. That's how she'd prove them wrong. Her birthday was in March. She couldn't be Paige if they had different birthdays. Sasha felt the urge, then, to find something else, anything else that might prove them wrong. She clicked through the list of likes, scanning each name, not really knowing what she was looking for. She hadn't made it far when she stopped on another name. Blake.

When she clicked on his name, his profile popped open. Damn, it was private. She couldn't see anything aside from his profile picture, but the image was enough for her heartbeat to accelerate. The light next to his name flashed green, which meant he was online, which meant he was awake.

Sasha checked the time again. Only fifteen minutes had passed since she'd sat down, and the sun was no closer to making an appearance. *Oh well, here goes nothing,* she thought. Then, without a moment to second-guess herself, she scrolled down and clicked on the name she saved for him in her contact list. Sex Eyes. She listened as the phone rang through the speaker.

"Hello?" The voice was rough but alert.

"Blake? Oh my God. I can't believe I'm calling you this early," Sasha said in a whisper, as if she were hiding, not wanting people to hear.

"Pai—Sasha?" Blake asked, stumbling over her name.

"I'm sorry. I know it's early. I really shouldn't have called."

"Are you okay?" he asked, panic dripping from his words.

"Oh, yeah. I'm fine. I just..." Sasha paused. She didn't even know why she had called, why she'd clicked on his name. But now here she was, on the phone, and she had no idea what to say.

A loud exhale drifted through the phone. "I'm glad you're okay. And I'm glad you called."

"You are?" she asked in disbelief.

"Of course. Now I have your number."

A slight blush rose in her cheeks. There was something in his voice, his ability to calm her while also making it known she was wanted. Or at least, that's what it felt like when he spoke.

"I couldn't sleep. I've been thinking about heading to my dad's house, like you suggested. To see what's damaged and what's salvageable. But also, to see what I can find from when I was little."

"Now? It's awfully dark out there, and I don't think they've turned the power back on yet," he laughed. There was a bit of flirting in his voice. An ease and familiarity that pulsed through the phone.

"Not now, silly," she laughed back. "Do you work today?"

"Nope. I don't go in till tomorrow. Why? You want to take me to breakfast? I love breakfast," he hummed.

"I wasn't planning breakfast. I was thinking about my birthday," Sasha began, suddenly feeling giddy.

"Your birthday? Your birthday is still a few weeks away." Blake laughed at first, but his tone changed by the end of his sentence. "Sorry. I…"

"No, it's okay. That's what I was going to say. My birthday is in March. If I find my birth certificate, I can show you I'm not this Paige person."

There was a long pause before Sasha continued.

"Okay, so I know the birth date doesn't prove anything. But it will have my name, and I think if I went back there, I could find more things. Things that *will* prove I'm not Paige. Do you want to come with me? This way, you can see for yourself that this is a mistake." The words slipped out so fast she didn't have time to catch them. She hadn't planned to ask him, but now it was too late to take them back. Although, she didn't want to take them back. She wanted to see him again.

"What time do you want me to pick you up?" His words danced in her ears.

A few hours later, Sasha found herself sitting upstairs on her dad's bedroom floor with Blake on the one side of her and their bagels on the other, their backs to her dad's bed. Charred black walls and ash surrounded them, but she didn't care. Sasha wanted—scratch that; she needed—to find her birth certificate.

After she'd asked her friend Rebecca to open up Beach Brew and take her shift, Sasha took a quick shower and waited for Blake to come get her. While it wasn't unusual for Rebecca to cover a shift, it'd be her first time opening, which made Sasha nervous. But Rebecca had been asking for more responsibilities, and she knew it would only be a matter of time anyway. "I'll call if I have any problems, but I got this, Sasha!" Rebecca had squealed excitedly.

"Other than your birth certificate, what are we looking for?" Blake spread a stack of manilla envelopes across the floor.

"I'm not sure, but I feel like there's going to be other stuff in here that'll help you understand who I am. Look at this—my dad kept everything. I just wish things were labeled," she said, waving a few documents in his direction. Her dad was sentimental, not organized.

The sun, now fully awake, streamed through the curtains, shining across Blake's chest and arms, making it impossible for Sasha to focus or think straight. His tattoos were an assortment of chaos, bulging as he flexed. He reached across her body and grabbed his bagel. The sensation of his arm brushing against her legs brought butterflies to her stomach. She held her breath and watched, dazed, as his arm retreated, unable to take her eyes off his hand.

"Do you want some help?" he asked, opening his palm once he finished chewing.

She blew out a deep breath and ignored the swan dives in her stomach. "Yeah, you can go through these." She laid a few envelopes in his hand. "The birth certificate won't be hard to identify. I just don't know which one he kept it in. And I'm not sure what else might be useful."

Opening the first envelope, Sasha leafed through the contents. Old bank statements and credit card bills. Scrunching her nose, she shoved them back in and moved on to the next envelope. Her dad's military papers from when he was in the Marine Corps spilled onto the floor, including some old photos of him in his dress blues.

"Your dad was in the Marines?" Blake nudged her bare knee as he lifted a picture close to his face.

The contact made her flush, but she tried to hide it as she snatched the picture from his hands. "Yes. Before I was born," she said defensively.

Blake tilted his head and looked at her. "I was just going to say that's awesome. I just got out last year. Served eight years."

"You're a marine?"

"Does that surprise you?" he asked, his voice deep and gravelly.

"No. I mean, I guess I didn't expect that from you. I should have known though," she stammered, still feeling the heat from his legs against hers.

"Should have known?" His eyebrows lifted.

"I don't know. I mean, you have the look. Clean cut, muscular, lots of tattoos." Her voice dropped an octave. She lifted her shoulders, and then she reached out to touch the tattoos that covered the length of his arm. Somehow, she had allowed her fingers to trail up his arm, and when her eyes met the edge of his sleeve near his elbow, she instinctively inched it up, the tension rising between them. She let her fingers investigate the designs, one intricate pattern woven into another, blending between the branches of a tree.

By the time she had his sleeve all the way up, she had managed to change positions. Kneeling next to him, lost in thought, she released a ragged breath. Her heart was pounding, though she hadn't been sure when that began. Then she lifted her head, slowly drawing her attention to Blake's emerald-green eyes. He was staring back at her, his gaze dark and dripping with desire. She pressed her lips together before drawing them apart to lick them. The energy between them suddenly filled the room. She wasn't sure what she was doing, but she knew exactly what she wanted.

CHAPTER ELEVEN

Blake

The sensation of Sasha's fingertips on Blake's arm sent goosebumps down his spine. He'd had people admire his ink before, but no one had ever traced over them, inspecting them the way she had. Each one was carefully placed to form a collage. And for a brief second, when she trailed across the bicycle near the base of the tree on his upper arm, he held his breath, unsure of whether she'd say something. But she didn't, even though her fingers slowed as she traced the wheel, as if she recognized it. But why would she say anything? The tattoos didn't mean anything to her the way they'd meant something to him. Not yet at least.

When her fingers reached the top of his arm, heat rose in his chest. There was something about her. Maybe it was the way he suddenly felt alive when she touched his skin. Or the unmistakable look of desire when she raised her head, her hazel eyes flashing. The silence between them was almost suffocating. The air charged with temptation. Blake had already been staring, watching her every move, but when she parted her lips to wet them, a carnal desire pulsed through his body. Without second-guessing himself, Blake reached for Sasha's waist and pulled her in, lifting her by the hips and dragging her onto his lap. Then he crushed his lips to hers. A low moan echoed through her mouth as she kissed him back, biting at his lower lip and running her fingers through his hair.

This girl. This damn girl. She was all fire, alluring and captivating, setting his world ablaze. But this wasn't just any girl. This was Paige. And the idea of Paige and Sasha being the same person complicated things. The thought swirled in his mind, making him dizzy as he ran his hands up her back, but he couldn't stop. She wouldn't let him stop. Everything was rushed and frenzied, like neither of them had touched another person in ages. Their breaths quickened. In one swift movement, Blake pulled from her perfect mouth, tilted her head, and dropped his mouth to her neck, brushing her long red hair over her opposite shoulder. She hummed in pleasure as he cradled her head in his hands.

When Blake reached the crook of her neck, her body shuddered. And in that moment, Blake forgot everything. No one else existed. It was just the two of them.

Then she closed her eyes and fell into his lips. This time the kiss was softer, sweeter, slower. Sasha's chest swelled, and in a whispered plea, she exhaled. "Blake."

The sound of his name set off an inferno. His body pulsed, desperate to respond. To whisper her name back. But he didn't know what to call her. She was Paige to him. She'd always be Paige. And yet, she was also Sasha. If he called her anything but that, she'd withdraw. And he wouldn't blame her. It was a slippery slope. So instead, he crushed his lips to hers again, a low growl forming in his throat.

Just as she gripped at his shirt, a voice snapped them to attention.

"Hello? Is there anybody here?"

With wide eyes, Sasha pulled away, one hand firmly on his jaw, the other with a fistful of his shirt.

Chest heaving and out of breath, Blake stared into Sasha's eyes, watching them gleam in the light. But when she didn't say anything, didn't move, he cleared his throat. Then, wetting his own lips, Blake yelled over her shoulder. "Yeah. We're upstairs." Then he planted a simple peck on Sasha's lips. "You're sitting on me. If he comes up here, he'll see you on my lap, which might make him uncomfortable." He smiled and arched an eyebrow.

"Oh. Oh my God. I'm sorry," Sasha said, as if she hadn't known what she was doing. As if the heat hadn't risen between the two of them. As if neither of them had been hungry for more just a second earlier.

Just as the words fell from her mouth, her fingers released his jaw, and then she pushed to her feet as if nothing had happened. "There! There's my birth certificate." Reaching across his body, Sasha grabbed the paper. And as she rocked back on her heels, Blake grasped her wrist, forcing her to look at him.

"Don't be sorry. Never be sorry." And then he planted another kiss on her lips.

They both got to their feet just as Detective Spencer stepped into the room. "What are you two doing here?" He scrunched his nose.

Sasha flattened her shirt as she caught her breath. "Looking for proof." She leaned down and grabbed a piece of paper from the floor before placing it in front of his eyes.

"Looks like a birth certificate." He nodded. "But did you look at the names on it?"

"What do you mean? It has my name right here," Sasha said, flipping the document over to scan it again.

"It's missing something. Isn't it?" he asked, scratching the back of his neck.

"I don't understand," she responded, her eyes still on the paper.

Blake stepped in closer. It had her name on it, all right. Sasha Patterson. Mom, Sharon Cohen. Dad, blank.

"Your dad, the man in the hospital…he isn't your biological father. That much we know. He gave us some information this morning, but we wanted to confirm it before coming to talk to you. You might want to sit down."

Blake reached for her hand and led her to the bed. Sitting beside her, he squeezed her tight, reassuring her that he was there.

"Your dad told us he met your mom when you were five years old. Your name used to be Sasha Cohen. But after he and your mom got married, they petitioned the court to have your last name changed. That's why you go by Patterson," Detective Spencer said, shifting his weight from one foot to the other. "He said that in order to get his name on your birth certificate, he would have had to formally adopt you, but they'd never gotten around to it."

"No. If I was five, I'd remember that," Sasha snapped back, but Blake held her firmly in place, interlacing his fingers with hers.

"That's what you'd think. But children that go through trauma forget. They have holes they can't fill. Void out bad experiences to accept the positives in their lives."

"But nothing bad happened. I mean, you're still treating this like they stole me from another family. The worst thing is that my dad lied to me about their marriage. You can clearly see my mom's name on the birth certificate. So what if my dad's name isn't on it? He's still my dad." Sasha's voice shook and her chest pitched with each breath.

Blake couldn't stand to watch her in pain. But he had a feeling this wasn't the worst of it. He didn't know Detective Spencer well, but he'd worked with other detectives long enough to know they didn't ask a person to sit down for a little bit of news. Afraid of what was coming, a part of him wanted to protect Sasha from the truth, to keep everything hidden. He hated that she'd have to learn about the ugly truths of her childhood.

Detective Spencer cleared his throat and blew out a ragged breath, looking in Blake's direction. Knowing this wouldn't be easy, Blake laid his free hand on top of hers. The hand that was already gripping at his fingers.

"There's more. According to the Social Security Administration, Sasha Cohen died when she was four years old. She died before she became Sasha Patterson."

CHAPTER TWELVE

Sasha

Sasha wasn't sure she'd heard him right. It sounded like Detective Spencer had just announced that she'd died twenty years ago. She was unable to move, unable to process the information. The only thing she could feel was the tightening of fingers. Blake sat beside her, clutching her hand. A muted laugh escaped her mouth, but she couldn't force herself to speak. To look at Blake. To meet his eyes. She knew he was feeling sorry for her. And she didn't want sympathy. She wanted answers.

"Your DNA results haven't come back yet. It might be a few more days. But your dad was willing to work with us right away. The day Paige was abducted, your dad hadn't even met your mom yet. At least that's what he told us. He was stationed at Pensacola at the time. We were finally able to confirm the second part this morning."

"No. That's not true." More confusion spread across her face. "He said he got out before I was born. The documents are over there." Sasha released her hold from Blake. She shuffled through the papers until she found his discharge papers. August 2002. She shook her head. "No. He wouldn't have lied to me this whole time. He wouldn't have made this up."

Tears burned the backs of her eyes as they began to spill over. She'd seen Paige's missing person report. She was abducted in July of 2002. A month before her dad had been discharged. If her dad had lied about this, what else was he hiding?

"But my parents got married in September 2002. If my dad didn't know my mom because he was in the Marines, how…why did they get married so fast?" Sasha asked frantically, disbelief edged in her words. She dropped to her knees, dumping the contents of each envelope onto the carpet. Her hands pushing and shoving as she looked for their marriage license.

"Sasha, there's something else you need to know," the detective said patiently. "When we sorted through your dad's story, a common factor seemed to stand out. And I'm really sorry I have to bring this up…because of your history."

Sasha's breaths came fast, a sharp contradiction to how she sat with her eyes glued to the detective, waiting for his next words. What did he know about her history?

"We know about your mom's suicide. Your dad said she battled with depression for as long as he'd known her. Said they'd been dating for a month before she had a breakdown and he had to call 911. He said you wouldn't leave his side the entire time."

Visions of her mom clawed their way into her memory. Of her mom lying on a stretcher, silent and unmoving, as two men hurried her out of the apartment.

"Everything will be okay," her dad had said as he tried to console her. That was the first memory she'd had of her mom being hospitalized, but she wasn't sure which time that had been or how old she was.

"And according to your mom's social security number, the last place she worked was in Cocoa Beach. At the same school Paige attended. The same school Paige's mom also works at. Your dad is still being considered a person of interest until we sort out the rest. But you need to be prepared when those DNA results come back. Everything is pointing toward a positive identification."

The detective swallowed harshly. "And I'm really sorry for having to say this now, after what I just told you, but you two are going to have to leave. This is about to be an investigation site. Our analysts will have to sort through all those papers." He pointed at her hands.

Sasha sat frozen, unable to speak. Tears dripped from her eyelashes. Her birth certificate and her dad's discharge papers slipped through her fingers and floated to the floor. Everything around her turned hazy. What was she supposed to tell Margo? When would she get to see her dad? How was she supposed to pretend like nothing was happening?

In the next moment, Sasha was in Blake's truck. Silence sat between them as they drove through the busy streets of St. Pete, but time passed in a blur. When they pulled up to Sasha's condo, Blake shut off his engine. She didn't move. She couldn't force her fingers to unbuckle. Staring out the window, she felt helpless. Lifeless. Like the world was crumbling. Crashing into pieces.

In the past, she'd go straight to her drug of choice. Pills. Any pill would do. Any pill would take the edge off until she'd gotten hold of what she really wanted. But she'd been clean for four years. Four years since she'd touched a pill. And now, now the craving was back. Remembering the days and weeks that followed her last use should have been enough. It should have forced her brain to think logically. But it didn't. And that scared her. It terrified her like it had in those early days of sobriety, when she wasn't sure if she'd be able to say no.

Just then, Blake was opening her door. Lost in her thoughts, Sasha startled when he leaned over to unbuckle her. She lifted her eyes to meet his gaze.

"You okay to get up?" he asked, adoration pouring from his voice.

She nodded and swung her legs around the edge of her seat, lifting herself out. She wasn't sure how they'd gotten from the parking lot to her condo. A gray haze fogged her brain. But Blake must have opened her door, because her vision returned as he pulled the key from the deadbolt.

Stepping inside, Blake allowed Sasha to stand there in the small entrance that connected to the kitchen. To breathe. But she couldn't breathe. She felt ill. Lightheaded. Like she was about to throw up from all the thoughts crisscrossing in her mind. Of a little girl with fire-red hair being taken. Of a family that grieved her disappearance. Finding her mom's lifeless body. And now her dad's lies.

She felt Blake's hand on the small of her back, but before he could say anything, before he could move, Sasha bolted to the bathroom, not bothering to close the door, and fell to her knees in front of the toilet. Shaking and sobbing, she heaved repeatedly until she had nothing left in her stomach. When she looked up, she saw Blake through blurry eyes. She hadn't seen him come in. Hadn't heard him. But there he was, gently gliding his hands through her hair, pulling it into a ponytail. Sitting on the edge of the tub, Blake met her gaze, a weary smile pressed to his face. But he didn't speak. And neither did she.

Time ticked by as Sasha sat on her knees. Numb and unfeeling. As if she were sitting at the bottom of a well and a thousand bricks were about to be dropped down. She laid her head in Blake's lap as he ran his hands up and down her back.

Finally, when she felt Blake shift his weight, she pulled back, letting him push to his feet. She lifted her head, watching as he reached his hand into the shower. Then, in one fluid motion, Blake was pulling her to her feet. Taking her by the waist, he lifted her into the shower.

The water ran down her face as Blake pulled her close, rotating her so she was completely engulfed in the steady stream. The rhythm of the water beat against her back as it soaked through her cotton T-shirt. Warm. Calming. Reassuring. When Blake tightened his hold, her tears broke free again. They raced down her cheeks, and then her chest heaved with muffled cries as she buried her face in his chest. Blake didn't move. He wordlessly continued holding her while she broke down. Anger and frustration. Betrayal and confusion. Every damn emotion bled from her soul.

She couldn't be dead. That didn't make sense. She was Sasha. She had to be Sasha. Her parents would never have kidnapped a kid. There had to be a reasonable explanation for this.

A short while later, Blake loosened his grip around Sasha's waist as he reached for the handle to shut the water off.

"Not yet," Sasha whispered, blinking back the tears.

Nodding, Blake dropped his hand, letting it fall to her waist. Then he leaned in and kissed the top of her head. They stayed like that until the water cooled and goosebumps ran down her arms. Until all her tears disappeared, and she was nothing more than a hollow shell.

"Now?" Blake asked, running his hands up and down her arms.

Sasha nodded in confirmation, and Blake reached up and turned the handle until the water stopped. Then he slid the shower curtain open and reached for a towel and wrapped her in it before peeling his soaked T-shirt off over his head. She watched him, remembering how his lips felt on hers. She wanted to feel that again; she didn't want to feel anything but him. Letting the towel fall to her feet, she reached out and set her lips on his.

But Blake pulled back. "Not like this," he said, shaking his head. He reached for the towel and wrapped her back up. Then he scooped her up and carried her to her bedroom. "You should change. I'll be waiting on the other side of the door."

"You won't leave?" Her voice cracked.

"Not if you don't want me to."

She shook her head.

Once he slipped away, Sasha caught her reflection in the mirror. Swollen eyes and hair a hot mess. After a second, she turned away. The last time she looked like this, she'd been detoxing. And she didn't want to think of that. She didn't want to think of pills or how they could make her feel.

She pulled the wet clothes off and replaced them with a dry T-shirt and a pair of cotton shorts. When she finished dressing, she swung open her bedroom door, surprised to see Blake waiting just on the other side.

Her surprised look must have caught his attention, because he reached for her hand. "I told you I wouldn't leave."

"Yeah. But I..." she trailed off, not finding the words she was looking for.

"It's okay. I'm here." He pulled her wrist to his mouth and pressed his lips to it before releasing it to tighten the towel around his waist.

"You're wet. You don't have any clothes," she said, her voice small.

"I'll be okay. I'm more worried about you."

"Why?" she asked, confused as to why he was being so nice.

"I…I can't imagine what you're going through. I mean. I don't even know what to call you. You're Sasha to so many people. But if I say that, I feel like I'm betraying others. And I know you don't want me to call you Paige."

He ran a hand down his face before finishing his thought.

"So if I'm struggling with just your name, I can't imagine what's going on in that head of yours. And I don't want you to be alone." Blake breathed a sigh that sounded like relief. Like he'd finally gotten something heavy off his chest. Sasha was grateful for that. His honesty.

"I am Sasha. I've been Sasha for as long as I remember. I feel like this is all a nightmare and I'll wake up and it'll all be over." Her voice cracked, and she lowered her head. "But I know it's not. And I'm scared." The last words were nothing but a whisper.

"Scared?" Blake asked, lifting her chin.

"My dad. Margo. They're my family. They're all I have. I almost destroyed them a few years ago. And now? Now this is going to destroy them all over again."

CHAPTER THIRTEEN

Blake

Blake had watched in agony as Sasha broke down at the detective's words. At the mention of Sasha's birth name. Sasha's death. Her mother's suicide. When the detective asked them to leave, Blake carried her to his truck as the tears poured uncontrollably down her cheeks. He held her hair back as she made herself sick. He pressed his body against hers as she sobbed in the shower.

And he listened as she told him that she was scared.

Blake squeezed her tighter. He hadn't expected that. He hadn't anticipated things being so complex. She had a family that she loved. A history that tied them together in a way he couldn't conceive. Blake had imagined a lot of things, but he had never predicted a day that Paige wouldn't want to be saved. And yet here they were. His childish dreams of a happy return seemed foolish now. He already felt like he'd crossed a line somewhere.

When he had first set eyes on her at Beach Brew the other day, all he'd seen was Paige. The little girl who'd gone missing. The girl who caused all his nightmares. The one whose disappearance he blamed on himself. The reason he went to therapy. But now? Now he saw Sasha. Somewhere between pizza last night and bagels this morning, he'd become completely captivated by this woman. And all he wanted was to protect her. To keep her safe, no matter how that looked.

"This isn't your fault," Blake said, feeling the dull ache in the pit of his stomach. "You didn't cause any of this."

"You don't understand," she said, looking away.

Lifting her small frame, Blake carried her back to her bed and sat her down. "No. *You* don't understand. You have done nothing wrong. Whoever is at fault for this, it isn't you. And you can't think about them when you have yourself to think about right now."

She shook her head. "No. They won't understand. My sister won't be okay with this. They've already been through so much."

Blake paused and took a deep breath. "Your mom?" he asked, not wanting to say the words aloud. The suicide.

"No." Her words were loud and bold. "Me."

Blake looked at her but kept his questions to himself.

Sasha brought her hands to her face and rubbed her temples. Then she dragged them down her cheeks. "I had a problem with pills. Before my mom died, I started experimenting with them. It started off with my mom's pills. And then others. Eventually my mom ran out and refused to tell my dad because she didn't want him knowing I was abusing them."

Blake reached for her hand and slipped his fingers between hers.

Looking away, Sasha chewed on her lower lip before continuing. "She cycled. Every few months, my mom would get depressed, even with the proper medication. So without it, the withdrawal hit her hard, and then the depression came fast. And then one day…one day, I found my mom's body. I was already high, so I didn't even call 911."

Sasha blew out a breath before she continued.

"I passed out next to her. I don't know how long we were like that or who found us. The next thing I remember was the stretcher and the paramedics taking her the same way they had when I was little. But this time, she didn't come home. So I took more pills and ran away from home. I only came back when I needed money. I put my dad and Margo through hell for four years. Four years of spiraling out of control because I contributed to my mom's death."

"No, you—" Blake began.

But Sasha held up the hand not entwined with his.

"No. I did. I was selfish and spoiled and I didn't tell my dad that she'd run out of medication. I knew. She had been in treatment for years. She'd had years of therapy. I knew her medication was important. I knew what it was like when she came off her meds or when she needed them to be adjusted. We'd learned early on that she had to stay on them to live a normal life." She paused before continuing. "I'm telling you. This is going to destroy my dad and Margo again. Because…because all I can think about are those pills again. The craving. It's real." Her body folded as she exhaled.

"Let me help you," he whispered, slipping his fingers around her jaw and forcing her to look at him. Her hazel eyes were still swollen and puffy. "Let me be here for you. Let's just get through today."

She nodded.

Leaning in, Blake laid a gentle kiss to her forehead and helped her lie down. He wasn't sure what he was doing, other than trying to make her feel better, but he followed her lead as she snuggled up close to him and closed her eyes. He felt the warmth of her skin as her arm slid across his bicep, her fingertips soft against his arm. They were almost nose to nose, and Blake watched as her long lashes twitched with each rise and fall of her chest. Curled up next to one another, in the middle of the day, they fell asleep.

Sometime later, Blake woke to the sound of his phone buzzing. Lifting his head, he pulled his arm out from under Sasha's sleeping body, careful not to wake her. He meant to steal a quick glance at her before rolling over, but he paused at the sight of her scar. The faded line that edged her temple. Blake frowned as he traced it with his eyes. He was about to reach out, to touch her face, when his phone buzzed again. Startled, Blake shot up. It buzzed a third time before he found it beneath the covers.

He released an exaggerated exhale when Porter's name flashed across the screen. Pushing to his feet, he slipped from the room.

"Hello?" Blake said in a hushed tone.

"Hey. Have you talked to her yet? Has she started remembering things?" Porter's voice poured through the speaker.

"Hey. Yeah. I mean no," Blake said, trying to keep his voice low. "It's kind of complicated." Shit. How was he supposed to tell Porter what happened in the last twenty-four hours? Pizza was one thing last night, but this morning? How was he supposed to tell him about their kiss? And how he'd wanted to keep kissing her? To wrap his arms around her waist and never let go?

"What do you mean, it's complicated? You've either talked to her or you haven't," Porter responded, irritation edging his words.

"Yes, we've talked. But the detective came by today when we were at her dad's house. She's pretty upset. She's kind of fragile right now."

"Her dad? Fuck. That's not her dad. Did you know they called my mom last night? Asked her if she ever worked with a woman named Sharon Cohen. My mom freaked out. She said you had her for first grade. Do you remember her?"

A vision of a face entered his mind. A woman with sandy brown hair with a hint of strawberry blond soaked in.

"Wait. You were with her today? What did you guys talk about?" Porter continued, not allowing time for Blake to respond.

"Porter, I'm trying, but you're desperately looking for something she can't give you. Not yet. She just found out her whole life was a lie. You need to give her some time."

"Time? Fucking twenty years is plenty of time. My mom is a basket case. She wants to see her." His voice was demanding, a plea woven through his words. "She swore she'd drive herself to St. Pete."

"Porter. I…" His words trailed off as he caught sight of Sasha staring at him as she leaned against the frame of her bedroom door. Her face pale. Her eyes still swollen and full of sorrow.

"Porter. I'll talk to her. I work tomorrow. Tell your mom she should wait for the DNA results. She just needs some time. I have to go."

Before Porter could respond, Blake ended the call and walked over to Sasha. "How long have you been standing there?"

"Long enough to hear you think I'm a delicate flower that'll break if you say the wrong words," she responded. A small crease formed around the edge of her lips as she lifted her hands to his jaw.

"I didn't..."

Shaking her head, she interrupted his words. "My life wasn't a lie. It happened. Maybe not the way you or Porter think it should have, but I wasn't mistreated or unloved. I still don't know what to believe. But if I break, it's not your job to hold me together."

Damn, her words shot right through him, contradicting what her hands were doing. Slow and soft, her fingers trailed across his five o'clock shadow, begging him to take her. But her words reminded him that they barely knew one another.

He leaned down, bringing his mouth to her ear. "What if, when I hold you together, you're actually holding me together?" he whispered. The words left his mouth before he could stop himself, which caused Sasha to pull back.

Her eyebrows lifted, and her hands ran to the top of his face. She stood on her tiptoes to reach him. She didn't have to say another word after that because within seconds, his lips were crushing against her mouth.

Grabbing her waist, he lifted her until she had her legs wrapped around him. She ran her hands through his hair, the heat rising between them as Sasha's back hit the wall. Blake held her thighs as he explored her mouth, their chests heaving as one, their breaths quick and short. Wanting to continue what they'd started that morning, Blake dragged his mouth to her neck, causing her back to arch.

Just as a soft moan escaped her lips, the front door rattled. Sasha snapped her head forward.

Blake instinctively released his grip, allowing her to slip from his fingers until she was on solid ground.

"Hey!" a voice called out once the door swung open.

"Margo. Hey," Sasha said, flattening her T-shirt and smoothing her hair. "This is Blake. He is…" She stopped short when she turned back to look at him. At his bare chest.

A smile crept through his lips. "I'm a friend. I kind of…I saved your sister from the fire the other day." He reached out to shake Margo's hand, but she didn't reciprocate.

"Friend?" she scoffed, disbelief clouding her eyes as she scanned his chest, her lips paper tight. "Aren't you the guy from the hospital? The one who said my dad kidnapped her?" Her words were cold and calculated. Like she'd had time to stew over the idea of her life being forever altered by his presence.

"I was at the hospital. Yes." His voice softened as he withdrew his hand. Damn. He'd deserved that.

"I was just coming back to get my work clothes. I'll be out of here in five minutes." She grabbed some clothes that were balled up on the couch and shoved them into a bag. Then she turned and walked to the bathroom.

When the door slammed shut, Blake raised his hands, defeat written all over his face. "Sorry, that was definitely my fault."

Sasha's face flushed, which was the sexiest thing he'd ever seen. She didn't strike him as the type to embarrass easily, but damn, did it look good on her. Turning away, he reached for his T-shirt that had been drying on one of the kitchen chairs and pulled it over his head.

"You aren't leaving, are you?" Sasha asked, her brows furrowing.

"I don't want to, but we should go get some food. We haven't eaten all day. It's late and I'm starving. Plus, getting you up and out of here will be good for you," he added. "And I need to change; this shirt is still wet."

CHAPTER FOURTEEN

Sasha

"**I** don't care what you say, your sister *does not* like me." Blake laughed as they walked into his condo. "But I'd dislike myself, too, if I were in her shoes. Actually, why don't *you* hate me?" he asked in a serious tone as he tore the damp T-shirt from his head.

And there he was again, his broad chest nothing but lean muscle. And his arms. Sasha liked his arms the best. The way his tattoos curved and stretched so perfectly around his biceps. "I think I did hate you in the beginning," she replied as he turned to walk toward his bedroom.

"In the beginning? Like when I first walked into your café? Or was it later, like when I was rescuing you from certain death?"

"More like when you demanded I leave my dad's room at the hospital." Sasha walked around his small living room, admiring the empty bookshelf made of dark mahogany. She ran her finger across the stack of books that sat at the edge, waiting to be shelved. She scanned them, curious about what he liked to read. She assumed they would all be about firefighting or how to pump iron, but she was surprised to see an assortment of thrillers and mysteries. A smile tugged at her lips. Blake was a reader.

Suddenly, the setting sun peeked through the slanted blinds and reflected off a large metal frame that sat in the corner of the room, catching Sasha's attention. Turning her head to see it more clearly, she noted the large group of uniformed men and women behind the glass. She found Blake easily, but the person next to him surprised her. It was like looking in a mirror.

"Porter," Blake said, standing behind her.

Startled, she turned quickly. He was so close to her that she could smell his cologne—something woodsy, like sandalwood and cedar. Dressed in a pair of navy-blue shorts and a white T-shirt, Blake made wearing something so simple look so hot. Nodding, she took a step back. She needed room to breathe, or she might end up back in his arms. Which, at the end of the day, might not be so bad.

"I know." She shrugged. "It's just, well, he looks like me."

"He looks nothing like you." Blake's eyes darkened.

Sasha bit her lip. She felt herself warm and knew her cheeks were flushing.

"You can't do that," he said matter-of-factly.

"Do what?" Sasha asked, half unaware and half pleading for him to kiss her.

"You can't bite your lip and then not expect me to do this."

In a flash, Blake closed the little distance between them and took her head, crushing his lips to hers. When he peeled himself away, his chest rose sharply. Or maybe it was her own, she couldn't tell. But she liked it. In the midst of feeling like utter crap, he was making her feel whole.

"We need to leave. Now. Or we'll never get any food," he said, his hand trailing purposefully around her waist to reach for her hand.

With her stomach doing flips and her heart on a racetrack, she followed Blake to the door. When the two of them made it outside, the sun was just starting to fall, the horizon a canvas of reds, oranges, and yellows. The air was warm, with a gentle breeze. Walking with her fingers interlaced with Blake's, Sasha smiled, unsure of how they'd gotten so comfortable with one another in such a short amount of time. How they could go from wanting to devour one another one moment, to being content and calm the next. She wasn't sure when the last time she'd felt like this was. Having a strong attraction toward someone was one thing, but when it came to relationships, she typically wasn't interested in spending time with someone for more than a day or two. This made her feel like a teenager all over again.

"How about tacos?" Blake asked, stealing a glance at her.

"Tacos sound great." Her smile widened as he gripped her hand tighter.

They'd only walked a few blocks when they stopped at a small Mexican restaurant neither of them had been to. She opted for shrimp tacos while Blake ordered chicken.

"So, back to our earlier conversation," Sasha started once the waitress took their menus.

"Earlier conversation? About your sister not liking me?" He grinned.

Shaking her head, she pressed her lips together before continuing. "Your call earlier. With Porter." She watched as he gathered his thoughts and studied his face as the silence engulfed them.

"Porter said your mom—his mom—wants to meet you. She's going stir-crazy waiting," he said slowly, but was quick to add, "but I told him you needed time. I know this is a lot. No one expects you to just be okay with this."

"But he does. The way he yelled at me at the hospital. I know he's upset."

"I think he's upset because, well, we all dreamed up our own versions of you coming home. I mean, Paige coming home. We all had our own expectations. Like it would be this great thing where everyone would be excited. No one really thought about the age and years that would play a role in all of this."

"You keep saying 'we,'" Sasha replied. "What did *you* envision?"

Blake leaned back and scratched the back of his neck. "I don't know if we have enough time for me to tell you what I hoped for. Each year my visions changed. A lot was shaped by how Paige vanished. How close I was to Porter and his family. What they told me, to help me sleep at night."

"What do you mean?"

"I guess at first, I imagined you being returned home. Safe. Like you'd wandered off and someone would find you. But as days turned into weeks, I started having nightmares. I imagined bad people lurking behind every corner. I became obsessed with watching the news. My parents didn't care. They thought watching the news was good for me. But then my visions grew dark."

Blake lowered his gaze to the table and inhaled a deep breath before blowing it out.

"I imagined the worst. That if anyone ever found you, there would be cadaver dogs involved. I must have said something like that in front of Ned and Olive, because the next thing I knew, I was in therapy. I wasn't allowed to watch the news anymore. Sometime after that, my visions changed again, but mostly in dream form. You'd be happy to come home. There'd be a party. Lots of tears, but more laughter."

"You still think I'm Paige?" she asked, her eyes locked on to his. "You keep saying 'you' in reference to her."

"I don't think. I know," he said, unflinching. "I just don't know how to call you Sasha, because you're Paige. But I also care about you and don't want to call you something you aren't comfortable with. I can't imagine someone calling me by another name when all I know is Blake."

Appreciating his honesty, Sasha held his gaze. "Let's say hypothetically I believe you, which I don't. What kind of people are Porter and his mom?"

Blake's eyes brightened, and a curve formed around his lips. "Porter and his mom are great. So are his sister and his dad. They basically raised me. My parents worked a lot. Still do. My dad works for the government and travels all the time. My mom runs IT for several companies, so she's also busy, especially in the off hours, when most people get off work. So, I spent a lot of time with Porter."

Over the next hour, as they ate their tacos, Blake talked about Paige's family as if Paige weren't there, respecting Sasha for who she was. It felt as if she were on a date, learning about Blake through another person's family.

By the time they'd finished eating, Sasha had learned that Porter and his dad, Ned, had both served in the Marine Corps, just as Blake had. Just as her dad had. Ned was also a firefighter. Sasha could tell he played a significant role in Blake's life by the way he talked about him. He spoke as if Ned had been the one to raise him rather than his own father.

"What about Porter's mom and his sister?" Sasha asked, not taking her eyes off Blake.

"Olive teaches kindergarten. She's been teaching for years. Penny is twenty-one now. She's had it pretty rough, being the baby of the family and all. She had a lot of watchful eyes on her growing up. No one ever let her out of their sight."

"Did she go to school?"

"Of course. I think it helped that Olive worked at our school. She was never too far away, and all the teachers kept an eye on her."

"I didn't mean school like that." She cringed. "I meant college. I know most people weren't homeschooled like Margo and me, although it's not as uncommon as you think."

"I'm sorry. I didn't mean it like that. Wow. I kind of put my foot in my mouth with that one. Yes. She went to college. I mean, she has one more year, I think. She's a business major." His face scrunched up as he spit out the last of the words. It was kind of adorable.

"Honestly, you'd love them. They're great people. And Porter really isn't a prick. You caught him on a bad day. He'd just learned they might have found his sister, whom he'd long believed was dead."

"Dead?"

He nodded, frowning.

"So this is all hypothetical again, but when you were on the phone earlier, you mentioned I needed some time. That they should wait for the DNA results. Do they want to see me? To see if I'm Paige?"

He nodded again, allowing her to continue.

"Blake. I…I keep going over everything in my head. But it doesn't make sense. I love my parents. And my dad…he'd do anything he could for me. He's the reason I'm sober. He moved to St. Pete to help me. He literally packed up and moved to get me through the worst of it. I can't imagine a world in which he just took me from someone else. He's the guy who gets disgusted when people don't separate their garbage, when people don't recycle. He doesn't have a bad bone in his body."

"And your mom?" Blake asked.

She sighed. "I just don't know. Why would the detective say I was dead? What does that even mean?" She rubbed at her eyes, closing them to release the stress that had built up behind them. "I want to get to the bottom of this. I do. But I don't know if I can trust myself. If I can trust anybody, to be honest."

"Do you trust me?"

Surprise caught in her throat as Blake's words hit her ears. She did trust him. And she hadn't even known when or how that happened.

"Is it weird that I do? At this point, I might trust you more than I trust myself."

Blake reached for her hand across the table. "Then trust me when I tell you Porter's family are good people. They've been desperately holding on to hope for two very long decades. I know you need time. But tonight, after I drop you off, let yourself fall apart and then consider meeting them. Maybe you'll remember something."

A moment came and went before Sasha was able to respond, but when she did, her words were laced with emotion. "What happens if I disappoint them?"

CHAPTER FIFTEEN

Blake

By the time Blake dropped Sasha off at home, it was well past midnight. They tried being quiet, but Margo was still awake.

"Have you heard from Dad yet?" she asked once they stepped through the door.

"No. And I don't think we will for a few days. Not until our DNA results come back," Sasha responded softly, dropping her keys on the counter.

Margo's focus shifted from Sasha to Blake before darting back to her sister, ignoring his presence completely. "How will we know if he's still at the hospital? They won't arrest him without those results, will they?" Her voice was forced as she choked out the words.

Sasha shrugged. "I'll call the detective working the case tomorrow. I have his card in my purse."

When Sasha turned to look at Blake, a smile tugged at her lips.

Damn. That smile. He dragged his hand through his hair, knowing full well he needed to go before he got in over his head. He knew Margo wasn't on board with having him around.

"I need to get going. I know you work early, and I have an early start too."

He'd left with nothing more than a goodbye. But once he'd gotten ready for bed, a flood of texts poured through his phone.

Sasha: *Hey. You still awake?*

Sasha: *Hope I'm not waking you up.*

Sasha: *Just wanted to thank you. For all your help today.*

Sasha: *Not sure if I'd have been able to get through it by myself.*

Blake: *Yes. Still awake. And you're welcome. I wouldn't have it any other way.*

Sasha: *Coffee tomorrow? You can stop by before work if you want.*

Blake: *Absolutely.*

Sasha: *Okay. Go to bed.*

Blake: *You too.*

But they didn't go to bed. Instead, Blake stayed up well into the morning reading and responding to Sasha's messages about Porter and Paige's family and about the possibility of meeting them when she was ready.

When Blake did finally fall asleep, nightmares plagued him. Images of kids he once knew swam behind his eyelids: eating birthday cake and singing "Happy Birthday," playing tag and hide and go seek. Then a tornado of red and blue lights flashed before him, turning the tears of adults into rivers and streams. A police officer crouched down to meet him at eye level. "Where did you last see Paige?" The question replayed like a broken record, and he was left unable to respond.

He'd woken in a cold sweat, darkness surrounding him. When he rolled over to look at the time, he panicked. His alarm had been going off, and he'd slept right through it because he'd left his phone on silent. With fifteen minutes before he had to be at work, Blake brushed his teeth and threw everything he needed for the day into his work bag. Then he grabbed his keys and darted out the door, sending a quick text to Sasha.

Blake: *Woke up late. Don't have time to come grab coffee. Meet you after work tonight instead?*

Sasha: *I have Rebecca coming by to help. I can drop off a coffee for you at the station. But yes. Tonight too.*

When Blake stepped into the firehouse, he was met with hooting and hollering as the guys all came crashing through the front office.

"Damn, Blake! You've been here what, two weeks?" Marcus bellowed as he wrapped his arm around his neck. "It had to have been the fire. Right?" A husky laugh escaped his throat.

Surprise caught him off guard. "Fire?"

"Oh, Blake. You saved me. You're my hero!" he continued, his eyes fluttering like he was having a seizure, voice pitched mockingly as he laid his hand over his heart.

Blake shifted forward, dropping his bag to the floor, confusion still swirling in his mind.

"Oh, come on. Sasha. For crying out loud. One day. One fucking day. A fire breaks out at her house, and she's eating out of the palm of your hand. That's some bullshit right there," Jay complained as he pulled money from his wallet.

Blake's attention leapt from Marcus to Jay, his brows pinching in the middle as tension built in his shoulders. "What do you mean?"

Jay waved a coffee in his face. "Someone came by to see you this morning. Said this might help after last night?" His eyebrows lifted in exaggerated movements. "Like I said though, you need to be careful with that one."

He heard the implication in Jay's voice. He'd said something similar before. But he chose to ignore it for now.

"You dirty dog!" Marcus winked, releasing his hold. "I ain't paying shit though. The deal was he'd keep trying. Nothing about him actually getting laid." He shoved Jay's hand away and started for the door. "I want details later."

Details? A sudden smile tugged at his lips as he suppressed a laugh. Had Sasha done that on purpose, implication written all over her simple sentence? He imagined her walking in, coffee in hand, insinuating they'd slept together without saying or denying anything. It wouldn't surprise him. He had seen bits and pieces of her feistiness. Her ability to call out the paramedic who'd been flirting with him while she was stuck lying on a stretcher, waiting to go to the hospital. It was one of the things he liked about her. Her "I don't give a fuck" attitude. And her ability to switch gears during appropriate times, somehow mastering the right emotions as needed. He was drawn to that, wanted more of that, craved that.

Thankful for the much-needed caffeine, Blake downed his coffee before heading to his locker. The rest of the day went by relatively fast. When he wasn't training or filling out reports, he was checking his equipment and cleaning up. He'd even managed to get in a quick workout with some of the guys. The only calls that came in had been minor. A woman had locked herself out of her apartment and a suspected gas leak which had proved to be a false alarm.

By the time dinner rolled around, Blake had managed to avoid all conversations regarding Sasha. That he didn't know what was going on between the two of them was reason enough to keep silent. But he didn't know what the other guys knew in terms of Sasha being Paige. If this were Cocoa Beach, news would have spread like wildfire. It would have been the topic of every conversation. But no one had so much as whispered her name since the morning. That was, not until everyone piled into the kitchen, ready to inhale the lasagna Jay's wife had baked for everyone.

"Jay. Blake. You two were at the fire over on Ravenwood Drive the other day, right? The one where the grill kicked back?" the chief asked as he bent to grab a plate.

Jay's eyes shifted to Blake before responding. "Yeah. That was us. Why? Everything okay, Chief?"

"Just heard that's an investigation site for a missing girl. Someone who's been missing for twenty years. Did either of you notice anything unusual?" he asked, brushing his white hair from his forehead as he poured extra sauce over his noodles.

Blake held back a choke at the chief's words. Shit. Here it was. With a mouth full of food, he turned toward Jay, watching as confusion washed over his face. Jay's brows arched and his mouth twitched as he brought his hand to the back of his neck. "Missing girl? Like someone's *missing* or someone was *found*?"

"Found. One of the girls is suspected to have been abducted when she was five."

Jay's mouth dropped, and then his entire body rotated to get a better look at Blake.

Blake met his stare for a moment but let his eyelids shut as he thought, waiting to find the right words.

"Sasha Patterson. Her real name is Paige Knight. She's from Cocoa Beach." Blake wet his lips before continuing. "She's been missing for almost twenty years," he breathed, and the room fell silent. All eyes landed on him as if he'd just exposed a secret.

"Sasha? The barista from Beach Brew?" the chief asked, doubt caught in his throat as he shot Blake a disbelieving look. "Was that her house?"

"No. It was her dad's house. That's where we put out the fire."

"Is this true?" He turned to look at Jay, who hadn't moved since the revelation, his lips pressed firmly together.

"I, umm…" he stuttered. There was no doubt that he was still surprised at Blake's words.

"It's true. I reported it." Blake stood, dropping his fork to his plate. In that moment, he knew he should have included the chief in his report. He should have gone to him before he talked to the police. As a fireman, anything unusual should have been reported. But he hadn't called the police as a fireman. He'd called as Blake. As a person who'd recognized Paige. As a person who'd known her from once upon a time.

"My office. Now," the chief barked, slamming his plate to the table. "You too, Jay."

"What the fuck?" Jay said once the chief disappeared around the corner. "What's this all about? Sasha? There's gotta be a mistake."

But all Blake could do was suck in a breath and shake his head.

Standing at attention in the chief's office, Blake was suddenly thrown back to when he served in the Marine Corps, waiting to be reprimanded for not following protocol. He should have explained, even if it wasn't right away. He'd had all day to say something. But he hadn't, and now he was dragging Jay into this.

"Sit down. Both of you," the chief said, leaning against his desk. "Start at the beginning. But you might want to tell me everything, because the media already has a hold of the story. Once your name is mentioned, camera crews will do anything to get footage of you. They'll want a statement. And I don't like cameras."

Blake sat calmly, his breaths steady and his eyes focused on the chief. Years of therapy had taught him this. How to remain calm in uncomfortable situations; how to remain centered. Taking in one last deep inhale and exhale, he began. "When I first saw Sasha, before the fire, I knew she was Paige Knight. There was no doubt in my mind that it was her. I was seven when she was taken. She was my neighbor. And I'm at fault for her disappearance."

CHAPTER SIXTEEN
Twenty years earlier

Blake

"Everyone outside! Cake time!" Olive called from the kitchen as kids ran around her feet, rushing out the door to find the perfect seat at the table. Every kid wanted to sit next to the twins. But Blake's mother held on to his shoulder, reminding him that it was a family party, to let all the cousins have a seat before he joined them.

"Oh, Nancy, it's fine. Let Blake go sit down. He's just as much a part of the family as any of the others. Go ahead. I know you need to get going. Blake will be fine." Olive smiled, taking him with one hand while leading him outside as she carried the cake in her other. His mother waved goodbye and then she drove off to work.

In the sweltering heat of the summer, more than a dozen kids sat impatiently along four folding tables with alternating pink and blue plastic tablecloths. Each one was accented with a combination of pink and blue balloons, paper plates, and napkins.

Setting the cake in front of Paige, Olive squeezed a chair in next to Porter and motioned Blake to sit. "Here you go, honey. Sit here," she said before turning to address the crowd. "All right! Are we ready to sing 'Happy Birthday'?"

Blake cheered with the rest of the kids and sang along. At five years old, Paige and Porter were only two years younger than him, and they were his best friends, always attached at the hip. If one was riding a bike, they were all riding their bikes, tricycles included. If one was putting a puzzle together, the other two were shoving a corner piece into a spot it didn't belong.

Their moms called them three peas in a pod, and Blake loved it. He didn't have any brothers or sisters of his own, and his parents worked a lot, so Blake spent a lot of time with them, running from yard to yard, digging for worms, and playing with anything they could get their hands on.

Once everyone finished eating, the kids scrambled in all directions. Some went back to the pool while others ran to play freeze tag, but Blake stayed behind to help Olive clean up. "Oh, sweet boy. Don't worry about that. Go play." She patted his head and ruffled his hair. "I got this. You go have fun."

No sooner had she added the last sentence than Mrs. Cohen, his first-grade teacher, walked up, blocking him between her and the table. "Olive, thank you again for inviting me. This was nice, but I do need to get going."

"Oh, Sharon, it's still early. Stay awhile longer. I have a glass of sangria with your name on it. Let me just put this away and we'll chat. I want to hear all about this new place you're moving to," Olive cooed, her voice warm and convincing.

Mrs. Cohen let out a deep sigh, letting her shoulders sag. "Your twins are adorable. Okay, one drink. And then I really need to go." She lowered her gaze to Blake. "Good luck in second grade next year. I'll miss you the most." Inching away from the table, Mrs. Cohen smiled at him.

"Thanks. Bye, Mrs. Cohen," he said before squeezing by.

"Porter! Paige! Let's play hide and seek!" Blake yelled as he ran to find the twins in the front yard by the big maple tree. It was their favorite game. Only, it was never any fun when it was just the three of them. Not when the twins still yelled out where they were hiding. But now? There were tons of kids. This would be epic. "I'll count. Everyone hide," he said.

They played for hours, taking turns running and hiding, seeking and being found. By the time the sun disappeared behind the tree line, most of the kids were exhausted and people were beginning to leave.

"One more round," Paige begged.

Blake waited under the maple as he heard the last of the kids scamper away. "Ready or not, here I come," he shouted.

Porter was the first to be found, giggling beneath a pool towel near the pool. Tony, the big kid from down the street, was discovered in the storage box. Floaties and pool noodles covered his body, but not his face. Then Andrea and Eric, the twins' cousins, were found inside the house. One inside the kitchen pantry and the other beneath Porter's bed. Blake pulled back curtains and lifted blankets to find Paige, but each time he peeked into a possible hiding place, he came up empty-handed. He couldn't find her. "I give up!" he shouted after a third trip around the house. But Paige never appeared.

He walked out of the house with his shoulders down and a pout across his face.

Olive was there. "You okay, Blake?"

"I can't find Paige. She won't come out of her hiding place."

"*Oh*, she has a good spot, huh?" she laughed.

Blake twisted his lips and folded his arms.

Brushing her red hair from her shoulders, Olive nudged him with her hand. "Come on, let's go find my girl."

They walked around the yard, calling her name, searching between the bushes, and checking the trees. They asked those still at the party if they'd seen her. Before long, everyone was calling her name. Even Porter, who'd fallen asleep on the bedroom floor, was now awake and looking.

"Ned. She's gone. She isn't here. Oh my God. What do we do?" Olive pleaded to her husband when everyone came back empty-handed.

"She's gotta be around here somewhere," he said, his voice full of worry.

And then time seemed to stall. Leaning under the maple tree, he couldn't remember when the cops had shown up, when the flashing of red and blue lights first splashed across the lawn. He just stood there, waiting for Paige to come back.

"She's probably around here somewhere. In the meantime, let me jot down what she was wearing and who the last person to see her was," an officer told Paige's parents.

"Blake. He was playing hide and seek with her. Blake, honey, can you help us?" Olive's hands shook as she bent down to look at him.

"Hi, Blake. My name is Officer Spellman. I want to help find Paige. I'm sure she's hiding really well. Do you remember any of her hiding places? Where she likes to go?" the officer asked, crouching in front of him.

But Blake couldn't respond. He didn't know how to. How could he when his last words to Paige had been "find the hardest place to hide. Where no one will find you." Tears welled in his eyes before the officer stood back up.

"We'll need to ask your guests some questions. Make us a list of people who were here earlier. We'll need to get in contact with all of them as a last resort."

Blake wasn't sure when everyone had left, when Olive had tried to get him to come inside. All he remembered was standing under that tree. Waiting. Waiting for Paige to come back.

"Your mom is on her way home. You can't stay out here by yourself. Come inside," Ned said, his voice soft and full of worry.

When Blake didn't budge, Ned scooped him up and tossed him over his shoulder. And that's when it happened. Blake couldn't contain it any longer. The second his feet left the ground, he began screaming. Yelling. Pleading to be put back down. He had to wait for Paige. He had to stay. This was his fault. He'd told her to hide. To not come out. If it got too late, if it got too dark, she'd come out. She had to. But Ned tightened his grip, bracing Blake's back as he hung over his shoulder, whispering words of comfort, even though everyone in the house was inconsolable.

CHAPTER SEVENTEEN
Present

Sasha

Waking up that morning was difficult. Sasha had spent all night talking to Margo, reassuring her that their dad would be okay. She hadn't mentioned anything that the detective had told her the day prior, nothing about Sasha Cohen being dead. Nothing about her birth certificate or their dad's military paperwork.

Instead, they sat on the couch and reminisced. They ate popcorn and shared an oversized down blanket Sasha pulled from an old oak chest her mom used to keep in her bedroom. The combination of the wood scent and vanilla brought back a flood of memories.

"Do you remember Mom keeping all of our sheets in here? I swear, sometimes I asked Mom to do laundry just so she'd make my bed with one of those sheets," Sasha said, bringing the comforter close to her nose.

Margo smiled, but her eyes hung low. "I don't remember that. But I do remember when Dad brought her home from the hospital one time. You'd taken me to the store to buy her a new blanket before they got back, and she cried. She wouldn't even take it. She just cried. She said it was the most beautiful blanket she'd ever seen, but she couldn't even hold it." Margo dipped her head and pulled the comforter up to her chest, nestling into the cushions behind her. Irritation stuck in her voice.

Sasha frowned. She remembered that too. Poor Margo was only nine years old when their mom had come back from in-patient a year before their world shattered. Their mom shouldn't have come home; she hadn't been ready. Their dad had begged and pleaded with the insurance company to keep her longer, to admit her for another week, but they'd denied him. They claimed she was safe to come home. She was being compliant, and they said her new meds would help. But their dad had known better.

"She needs to adjust to her meds. She isn't ready yet. You don't understand," he'd cried into the phone as Sasha listened, trying to keep Margo entertained while she played with her dolls in the living room. But Margo had always been perceptive. Always aware. And Sasha knew what their dad had been thinking. That Margo's heart wouldn't be able to handle their mom coming home when she was still so depressed. Margo was the healer, the one who'd always wanted to fix everyone. To put them back together. But their mom couldn't be put back together. She couldn't even fake a smile.

None of that stopped little Margo from trying though. All she had known was that their mom was sick and that the last time she'd seen her, she was screaming over a ripped blanket she'd taken out of the dryer. So Margo begged Sasha to take her to the store. She spent every last dollar of her chore money on a new blanket for their mom. When Margo handed it to her, she smiled. "Look, Mommy, I bought you a new one."

At first, their mom just stared at it, unmoved. Then the tears came, followed by uncontrollable sobs.

"Don't you like it, Mommy?" Margo asked.

"Margo, Mom loves it. Let's give her some space." Sasha grabbed Margo by the shoulder and tried to lead her out of the room, but Margo pushed back.

"If you don't like it, I can buy you another one."

With that, their mom fell to the floor and wailed. She threw the blanket and clawed at her face.

Their dad rushed in and slid to the floor. "Sharon. Sharon, it's me." He reached for her hands and held them down. "Shh. It's okay, honey. It's okay. Just breathe. I'm here."

Margo ran to her bedroom and locked herself inside, and their mom went back to the hospital.

Sasha placed her hand on Margo's knee. "You know Mom loved us, right?" she asked. "You know she was sick."

Margo exchanged a knowing look with her but took a few seconds before responding. "I know. It doesn't make it any easier though."

Over the next several hours, Sasha reminded Margo of the good times, the happy memories, but found it increasingly difficult to convince Margo of their mom's love for her. Instead, Margo revised each memory with her own version, their dad being the loving and supportive parent. And while Sasha could never deny that, it made her heart hurt to see how differently they perceived the experiences they'd had with their mom.

Sometime hours later, Sasha awoke to Margo's feet in her face. The two of them had fallen asleep with the lights on. Sasha pushed her weight off the couch, careful not to wake her sister. Reaching for her phone as she shut off the lights, she checked the time. Just past eleven. She sent a quick text to Blake, asking if he was still awake.

Her heart skipped a beat and the corners of her lips curled when she saw the indication that he'd read her message pop up. Without waiting for him to respond, she shot off a few more messages. And before she knew it, it was well into the early hours of the morning, and she reluctantly set her phone aside and forced herself to get some sleep.

By the time her alarm went off a few hours later, Sasha was ready to get her day started. Always the early bird, it didn't take long for Sasha to stretch and shower before heading to work.

"Hey, Rebecca. Thanks for coming in early again," she said as Rebecca slid through the back door.

"No problem. I actually love opening. The people who come in early are so different from those in the afternoon. Like, they actually go to work rather than loiter around." Rebecca gestured toward the other end of the café, where people tended to sit and chat as they enjoyed their day. It wasn't just the drinks that brought them in. It was the experience. A chance to get out of the sun and into the cool air.

Sasha just rolled her eyes as she turned on the coffee grinder. She loved Rebecca, but that was the one clear difference between them. Rebecca was all business while Sasha was a people person.

Wanting, desiring, needing to have human connection. And Beach Brew allowed that. With its prime location across the street from the beach, Sasha had gotten to meet an assortment of unique people. With the right amount of charm, and maybe even flirting, she'd been able to create loyal customers out of plenty of the locals.

Just as Sasha unlocked the doors, her phone buzzed. It was Blake. Unable to grab coffee because he was running late. Darn. She had hoped to see him that morning. When he left last night, she couldn't not look at his eyes, the sharp green swirls that darkened when their gazes met. And his lips. Just the memory of the way he tasted had her body temperature rising.

"What are you daydreaming about over there?" Rebecca giggled, pulling her dark brown hair into a messy knot on top of her head before she grabbed the broom.

Looking up from the counter, Sasha caught Rebecca's stare. "Oh. I was just cleaning the counters."

"Not buying it. Spill," Rebecca demanded. "You were staring off into space. That is *so* not Sasha. You're usually unlocking the doors by now. Does this have anything to do with that firefighter? You never did finish telling me about your dad's house."

Sasha slid the rag down the counter, pretending not to hear her, tossing her hair over her shoulder as she moved.

"Oh come on! Now I know there's more!" Rebecca sashayed to the counter, dropping the broom to the wall. Leaning on one elbow, she tapped her nails against the counter. "I'm waiting."

A smile crept across Sasha's lips. "Okay. But it's not a big deal," she said, trying to downplay her feelings. She filled Rebecca in on all the details. About the fire. About Blake. But not about the possible abduction or how she'd had to do a DNA test. That, she wasn't ready for.

"Sasha! Do you hear yourself? You're swooning!"

She knew she had it bad for Blake. She definitely felt it as the words tumbled from her lips. Blake had somehow captured her heart. She'd realized it when he brought her home. After the detective had told her that Sasha Cohen was dead. After he took her into the shower and held her close. Those arms. Those muscular arms holding her tight. And yet, this wasn't like her at all. She hadn't fallen for a guy since high school. But that was different. That was a lifetime ago. And no boy had ever made Sasha feel so safe in such a short period of time.

"Take your man some coffee. Just because he can't come to see you doesn't mean you can't go see him!" Rebecca said, nudging her. "Make those other men drool too while you're at it."

At the fire station, all eyes were on her as she strutted inside, the room stilling at her presence. "Can I help you?" a tall man with a dark complexion asked, stopping in front of her. A curious grin crossed his face. A knowing look.

"You're Marcus, right?" She grinned when she recognized him from her café.

"Yeah. Everything okay?" He scanned her face.

"Yes, I'm okay." She was thankful she'd gotten his name right. "Is Blake around?" she asked, voice pitched with excitement over seeing the man she couldn't stop thinking about.

"No. He isn't in yet. Running a bit behind. Can I do anything for you?"

"Oh, no. I just brought him this coffee. Can you let him know I stopped by? Tell him this will help after last night."

When a few heads turned her way, she winked at them, knowing full well what her words insinuated. And then she laughed and walked away.

Within an hour, Sasha's phone went off, vibrating, alert after alert. All from Blake.

Blake: *Thanks for the coffee.*

Blake: *You didn't have to do that, but I appreciate it. Really needed the caffeine today.*

Blake: *Did you really say it would help after last night? You do realize what they think you meant, right?*

Blake: *Can't wait to see you tonight.*

Sasha: *I'll meet you at your place. I'll bring the food.*

No sooner had Sasha clicked send than her phone rang. An unknown number appeared on her screen. "Hello?" she asked, curiously.

"Sasha Patterson?" the voice barked.

"Yes. Who is this?" she questioned. Annoyance over the caller's demanding tone ripped through her.

"It's Detective Spencer. I'm the one handling your dad's case. I just wanted to update you on what's happening. Your dad had a heart attack late last night. A surgeon performed bypass surgery this morning, and he seems to be doing—"

"A heart attack? Is he okay? Can I see him? Why didn't anyone call me last night?" Sasha's words were rushed. Tears stung the backs of her eyes as she imagined her dad being alone.

"The doctor said the surgery went well. Your dad is resting now. They didn't call earlier because they had to contact me first—"

"You?" Sasha spat out. "Why would they need to call you? I'm his emergency contact. They should have called me."

"I'm sorry. Right now, they can't. Not with the open investigation. I'm letting you know as a courtesy. I'd want to know too. I can't imagine what you're going through right now."

Sasha gritted her teeth. "You have no idea. Can I at least see him?" A heavy breath blew through the phone, followed by what felt like an eternity of silence. "At least let Margo. Please," she whispered, but she knew the response before he even said the words.

"I'm sorry. It's still an ongoing investigation."

She didn't press him. She'd heard the defeat in his voice. The same way she'd felt defeated. "But he's okay?"

"Yes. He's recovering. Doing well. He'll have to stay here at least a week now," he said, his voice shifting. "There is one more thing I wanted to talk to you about. The DNA results. If they come back with a match to Paige, it'll be enough to arrest your dad. He may need a lawyer."

CHAPTER EIGHTEEN

Blake

Standing outside his condo door, Blake heard the unmistakable voices of his childhood ringing through from the other side. He dipped his head and closed his eyes, and with a deep breath, he reached for the handle and pushed the door open.

"I don't care what you think. I want to see her now. I've waited long enough." Olive's voice slammed through the kitchen.

"You can't just walk up to her and say, 'Hi, I'm your mom! Nice to meet you!'" Porter barked back, mocking his mom. The two of them hovered over the island, neither backing down.

Feet planted firmly at the threshold, his hand still on the doorknob, Blake cleared his throat.

"Oh, Blake! You're home." Olive rushed to him, her voice strained as she forced a smile. Lifting her hands to his face, she kissed him on the cheek while he gave her a questioning hug. "We wanted to surprise you. Your place is lovely."

Porter shook his head. "You wanted to surprise him because you knew he wouldn't have agreed to this. I'm sorry, man, but she was in her car already. She would have driven out here on her own if I hadn't come with her."

No sooner had the door closed behind Blake than a quick knock startled him.

Lifting his arms, he dragged his hands down his face. "This is probably the worst timing ever," he grumbled. With a whole lot of hesitation, Blake opened the door, positioning his body to block out Olive and Porter. With one glance into Sasha's hazel eyes, Blake squeezed his shut. "Please don't hate me right now," he whispered to her.

She stood there for a moment before dragging her lower lip between her teeth. "Hate you? Don't tell me you don't eat sushi." She smirked, lifting her hand as she displayed a bag with two poke bowls and a tray of sushi.

Blake couldn't tear his gaze from Sasha. He wanted to brush his lips across hers. He wanted to feel her skin against his, but every second he didn't speak was a second closer to her shutting down. If he didn't tell her soon, Olive or Porter might walk up behind him. They might show their faces and catch Sasha off guard. And the last thing he wanted was to cause her any more distress.

"Are you going to let me in?"

"No. Come with me." He took Sasha by the arm, leading her down the hall in the opposite direction of the elevators.

"Where are we going?" Her voice was laced with confusion.

Within seconds they were in the stairwell.

"Blake," she tried again, but before the rest of the question could form, Blake was grabbing the bag of food from her hand

and placing it on the ground. He leaned down and watched as her round eyes swirled with uncertainty.

"Do you trust me?"

When she nodded, he took her hands in his and pressed her to the wall. She gasped loudly, thrown off by the sudden force. He leaned in until his nose was brushing the side of hers. Their lips were close enough that he could feel the air escape her mouth. She stood on her tiptoes and tilted her chin in response, keeping her gaze on his.

Anticipation and desire filled him. When she inhaled, Blake swept his lips across hers, breathing in the scent of coffee that floated through her hair. Instantly, her chest heaved, and a soft moan escaped her mouth as her body reacted to his touch. Her hips moved closer.

She wanted this as much as he did. That thought was all he needed. His hands began moving. Unable to stop. He couldn't get enough of this girl. One hand moved to her rib cage while the other swept up the side of her neck until it was threaded into her hair.

When she moaned again, he drew her close and crushed his lips to hers. Smooth and soft. Warm and moist. Sasha returned the kiss, ravenous for more. She bit down on his lower lip, sending a wave of pleasure throughout his body. As his heart rate accelerated, she reached for his face, dragging her fingertips over the stubble that lined his cheeks. He knew he must have groaned. Maybe even growled. Because she smiled and pulled him toward her. She took the lead, her lips exploring his.

It only lasted a few seconds, but in those moments, it was as if nothing else mattered. It was just the two of them, just like the other day. Right now, she wasn't a missing girl. She wasn't found either. She was just a girl he was incredibly attracted to.

When he paused to catch his breath, he pulled away and looked at her. Loose strands of hair covered her eyes. Her lips, red and puffy.

"Do you still trust me?" he whispered into her mouth as they leaned against the wall.

"This wasn't it," she said between breaths.

He shook his head. "Don't be mad."

"What do you mean?" She dropped her hands from his face before placing one on his chest, forcing distance between them.

Looking down, Blake sighed loudly. "Porter and Olive are here. They kind of ambushed me."

"What? Like here, here?" she asked, pointing in the direction they'd just come from, her eyes terrified.

Squeezing his lips tight, Blake nodded solemnly. A knot formed in his stomach. "Porter is probably calming Olive down right now, but I don't know how long he'll be able to hold her off. If we walk back through that door, I can't guarantee she won't be on the other side, ready to pounce. She's pretty insistent."

He watched Sasha's eyes shift from him, to the door, and then to the stairs going down. She was probably planning her escape.

"Do you want to leave?"

Shaking her head, she responded. "I don't know." Her eyebrows crinkled and her nose scrunched. "I mean. I'm not ready to face them. But...I don't know. There's a part of me that's...curious." Her voice cracked.

"I don't want you to do anything you're not comfortable with. Please know that. But if you do stay, I'll be there the entire time. The second you're ready to leave, I'll take you home."

Blake was still holding Sasha when her hand fell from his chest. Biting her lower lip, she nodded.

"Okay."

"Okay? You're ready to meet Olive?" His jaw dropped in disbelief.

"Yes. And we should go now before I change my mind. But what about Porter? Will he be as intense as he was at the hospital?"

Releasing his hold on Sasha, he ran his palms over his face. "Intense? Porter is like a lamb compared to Olive."

CHAPTER NINETEEN

Sasha

Standing beside Blake in front of his door, Sasha listened to the yelling that came from behind it. Blake squeezed her hand, tightening his hold on her. Then he grabbed the knob and turned, pushing the door inward. The voices halted.

Blake led her inside and toward the kitchen, where Porter and a woman who bore a great deal of resemblance to him stood quiet and wide eyed. One look at Sasha and the woman's hand shot to her mouth.

"Olive. Porter. This is Sasha," Blake announced.

"Oh my God," Olive whispered under her hand. Disbelief covered her face. "I can't believe it. It's you." She shook her head, and tears instantly pooled in her eyes.

"Mom," Porter grunted, warning edging his words.

"Don't you 'mom' me!" she snapped without taking her eyes off Sasha. The veins in her neck bulged. "Can I come closer? Can I see you?" she asked, already moving forward.

Biting her lip, Sasha nodded. Her heart raced and her throat tightened. Blake squeezed her hand again, letting her know that he was still there, reminding her she could still change her mind if she wanted to. A part of her *did* want to change her mind. A part of her wanted to turn and run. She felt foolish for being there, for not saying anything. She just stared at the woman who everybody believed was her mom.

But Sasha didn't have time to backtrack, because in the next moment, Olive was standing before her, a mere arm's length away. Like Porter, she had soft features. Pale skin and a lot of freckles. Her hair was red, with a touch of warmth. Not nearly as vibrant as her own, though it was very possible it could have been when she was younger. Yet, it wasn't warm enough to be strawberry blond like her sister's hair. There was a familiarity about her, though she was sure she'd never seen this woman before. Maybe it was the same thing she'd told Blake. Maybe it was that all redheads looked the same.

Holding her breath, Sasha stood utterly still, unsure of what Olive would say. What she would do. The room was silent, and it seemed as if they were all holding their breaths too, waiting on Olive's next move.

"Can I…" Olive asked before dropping the question. Instead, she lifted her hand and reached toward Sasha's face. Her fingers brushed a lock of hair behind her ear. In doing so, her eyes grew large, and her chest rose and fell sharply. "Oh my God. It is you. That scar. That's your scar. I can't believe it. My baby girl." Olive let out a cry. Tears poured down her cheeks. Then, as if she didn't know what to do with herself, she fell into her.

Sasha's fingers slipped from Blake's hold as Olive clutched her tightly.

"My baby girl," Olive repeated.

The words and sudden touch caused Sasha's own eyes to betray her, and the tears escaped quickly. This woman was so certain she was her daughter. But she couldn't be. Sasha had her own mom and dad. Didn't Olive know that?

"Mom, let her breathe," Porter finally said, pulling Olive off Sasha. "You're scaring her. You know what they said."

Glancing up, Sasha caught sight of Porter's eyes. They glistened in the light. She swore she saw tears as he turned his head, avoiding her gaze. She looked from him to Blake as Olive took a step back. Confusion ripped through her soul. And then his words registered in her head. *You know what they said.*

"Who?" Sasha asked, not bothering to wipe her eyes. "Who are you talking about? And what did they say exactly?" Her voice cracked, but it held a bite. She ignored the feeling she had in the pit of her stomach.

Porter turned back to face her and cleared his throat. "The detective. He warned us not to push too fast. He told us we'd scare you away, which could make things harder." He scowled.

"Harder?"

"Yeah. Harder. You don't believe us. You don't remember us. So we're the enemies. Isn't that some shit?"

"Porter!" Olive snapped. "This isn't her fault."

"Yeah, well, it's not *our* fault either. And we have to tiptoe around her like *we* did this. Like *we* caused the problem. All while that man gets to sit at the hospital when he should be in jail."

"That *man* is my father!" Sasha burned with rage at his words.

"Porter!" Olive yelled again. Her eyes pleaded for him to knock it off.

"No. This whole thing is a bunch of shit!" Porter argued back. "That man you think is your father is nothing more than a criminal."

Sasha opened her mouth, ready to give a verbal attack, but before she could utter a word, Porter threw his hand up in truce and apologized. "I'm sorry. I shouldn't have been so obtrusive." Then he pushed back from the island and let himself out the sliding glass door to the balcony.

"Don't listen to him, sweetie. He didn't mean anything malicious by what he said. He's just overwhelmed." Olive wiped a stray tear. She didn't add anything else. Instead, she turned and walked toward the couch and sat down.

When Sasha felt Blake's hand on her shoulder, she looked up.

He gave a wry smirk and then whispered, "This is only the beginning. Do you want to stay? Or are you ready to leave?"

Sasha searched his eyes, unsure about how to respond. She wanted Blake to say something else. To offer advice. She trusted him, which suddenly surprised her. She hadn't put too much thought into it when he'd asked her in the hallway. But she did. *Shit.* If she trusted him, did that mean she believed him? Did that mean she really was Paige? If Porter was overwhelmed, then where did that leave her? None of this made any sense.

"Will you come sit over here? Can we chat?" Olive patted the cushion next to where she was sitting, interrupting Sasha from her thoughts.

Blake nudged her. "Go ahead. She won't bite. I'll go check on Porter."

After Blake stepped outside, Sasha made her way to the couch and sat beside Olive, quietly sinking into the cushion.

"Sweetie. I can't imagine what is going through your head right now. And I won't pretend to understand. But please accept my apology. I shouldn't have reacted that way. It's just, well…that scar. It looks just like my Paige's scar. Except it's lighter. Aged. Not as defined."

"My mom said it's from falling off my bike when I was little," Sasha said.

"My Paige fell off a bike too. Y'all were riding those bikes up and down the sidewalk. Blake said he ran into you, and you fell off. Said you didn't even cry. You simply got right back up and started pedaling down the sidewalk again. It wasn't till later that he noticed you were bleeding. Bless his sweet little heart. He tried taking the glass out of your forehead, but it only dug deeper. That's why the scar gets crooked right there." She paused and pointed at her temple. "He tried so hard to pull it out, but it just ripped at your skin."

Sasha brought her hand to her face and trailed the tip of her index finger across the rough line as she looked out the glass door. She watched Blake's mouth move as he talked to Porter. Porter laughed, and his arms relaxed. She wasn't sure what they were talking about, but she knew Blake must be calming him down. He was good at that. He was good at making people feel comfortable. Her mouth curled upward and then she looked back at Olive.

"He's smitten with you," she said. "I can see it in his eyes. The way he guards you. Still trying to protect you after all these years."

Dropping her hand from her face, Sasha flushed.

"Porter had it rough. But Blake. There were days I didn't think he'd ever smile again. He blamed himself for your disappearance. He still does."

Sasha suddenly felt uncomfortable. Olive kept referring to her as the girl who'd disappeared. And while she figured that would happen, it made it difficult to stay focused.

"My mom. You worked with her?" Sasha asked, changing the subject.

"I did." Olive looked away again, her voice laced with pain.

An awkward pause sat between them. Sasha felt guilty because she knew the mention of her mom was a stab to her heart. But *fuck*. Her mom *was* her mom. She had to find something that would convince this woman she had it all wrong. Something to convince herself.

"Can you tell me about her? Were you two friends?"

Olive looked up, but not in Sasha's direction. Tears edged the corners of her eyes. "Sharon Cohen moved to Cocoa Beach the year before you disappeared. She said she was from Virginia. Told us all that she moved to Florida to escape her life. That she'd been in a car accident. And that she needed a fresh start."

Olive reached for a Kleenex, but she wouldn't look at Sasha. "We were friends. She came over a few times. She took a liking to you. I didn't see it then. I had no idea. Before the end of the school year, she said she'd been offered another position at a school in Tampa, so she'd be moving again. I invited her to yours and Porter's birthday party right after school got out for summer. That was the last time I saw her."

CHAPTER TWENTY

Blake

"How did you guys get into my apartment anyway?" Blake asked Porter as they stood outside on the balcony.

"Your mom may have given her the spare key," Porter chuckled.

"You could have called first. I mean, you had three hours in the car with her. You could have warned me."

"And ruin the surprise? Not a chance." Porter snorted, a phlegmy sound that wasn't quite a laugh. "She still doesn't believe it, does she? Even with Mom here, she doesn't remember." A sadness covered his face. "I was hoping she'd remember Mom."

Blake shook his head. "I don't know. The fact that she doesn't remember anything is making it hard for her to believe she could be Paige. But a lot of things aren't adding up, and it's confusing her too. She just needs time. She has to figure this out on her own."

"I just don't get it. I tucked Carter into bed the other night, and when I watched him close his eyes, I couldn't possibly imagine a world in which he couldn't remember me." Porter turned away, shoving his hands into his pockets. "I just wish she'd remember something. Anything."

Blake knew the feeling. He wanted so desperately for Sasha to remember that she was taken away from her family. To make this all easier on everyone. He knew she'd never remember the details. She was too young. He could barely remember things from age seven, let alone when he was four or five. He turned and looked at Sasha through the glass. She was sitting next to Olive, although she left space between the two of them. He smiled. It was a good first step.

"Are you going to tell me what's going on?" Porter asked, interrupting his thoughts.

Blake raised his eyebrow.

"Don't look at me like that. You know exactly what I'm talking about." He nodded toward the glass door at Sasha.

"I can't tell if something already happened or if you're preparing for something to happen. But either way, I don't like it. Twenty years, Blake. Twenty damn years. Keep Mr. Casanova at bay, because that's my fucking sister in there."

Just then, a muffled yell interrupted them. Blake's head snapped back to the door in time to see Sasha leap to her feet. Blake hurried and slid the door open.

"No. That's impossible," Sasha said. She turned to look at him, her eyes pinched in disbelief. Then she looked at Porter, who stood behind him.

"Sweetie. I'm sorry. I can't force you to believe anything I'm saying. But that woman did not have any children when I knew her. She lived on her own. She wasn't even dating anyone that I'm aware of. She took you from me. She took you from our family."

Now both of them were standing up. Olive tried to reach for Sasha. To embrace her. But Sasha took a step back.

"I have a family. I had a mom who loved me. Who took care of me. A dad who protected me. And a sister who probably hates me, but still needs me. They're my family." She paused and turned to face Blake. "I'm sorry, Blake. I can't do this. You all want to believe I'm this Paige girl. But I'm not. I don't know what happened. I don't know why. But this is all a big misunderstanding. You'll see."

"Sasha," Blake said, but she put her hand up to stop him from continuing.

"No. Please don't. I just need to leave." She grabbed her keys from the island, and without turning back, she let herself out.

Before anyone could say a word, before anyone could move, Blake's phone rang.

"Good evening. Is this Mr. Blake Ryan?" a thunderous voice echoed through his speaker.

"Yes, but—"

"My name is Warren Thomas with Channel One News. I have a few questions for you regarding the missing girl you found. I believe her name was—"

"I think that's her!" Another voice shouted in the background, interrupting the man on the phone.

Blake turned around and bolted to his balcony. "Shit! The news is here!" Blake clicked End and ran to grab his keys. "Whatever you do, do *not* answer any phone calls from reporters and do *not* leave. I'll be back as soon as I get Sasha home safe." Blake ran down the stairs as fast as his feet would take him, ignoring the elevator that was older than he was. When he reached the front lobby, he saw a crowd of reporters cornering Sasha outside the glass doors, cameras surrounding her from all sides.

With one quick shove, Blake was outside, clasping Sasha's hand.

"Ms. Knight? How do you feel now that you've been found?"

"Have you been in contact with your biological family?"

"Did the man who took you hurt you?"

The questions shot off like rapid gunfire, but Sasha didn't respond. Instead, she looked frozen in place.

"Follow me," Blake said in Sasha's ear, loud enough to compete against the incessant questioning. Then, turning to the side, he tugged her hand and squeezed himself between two women with cameras, throwing them off balance.

"Are you Blake Ryan?" a tall man in a black suit and blue tie yelled over the crowd.

Blake didn't respond, but he didn't need to; someone else was answering for him. "That's the firefighter!"

Quickly, Blake and Sasha pushed past the rest of the people who'd gathered around and ran into the parking garage.

"Jump in. And keep your head down," Blake said as he opened the door to his truck, allowing her to get in first.

Sasha did as she was told and folded her body in half once she was buckled. Then she laced her fingers together against the back of her head, keeping it as low as possible.

"They're gone," Blake whispered once they were out of the parking garage and on the road.

But she didn't move, nor did she acknowledge him. She stayed in the same position, unmoving. Blake placed a reassuring hand on her back, wishing away her pain. Then, as if reacting to his touch, she trembled beneath his palm.

He felt terrible. Everything was moving quickly, and there were surprises around every corner. He should have told her that reporters had gotten a hold of the story, that it was just a matter of time before they showed up.

"Shit," he said aloud. Stomping on the brakes, Blake swerved into the closest parking spot along the side of the road and came to an abrupt stop.

Sasha released her fingers from behind her head and threw them against the dashboard as she rocked in the seat from the sudden jolt. "What are we doing?" she asked.

"You need to call your sister. I just realized if those reporters were at my place, then they're definitely at your place."

Her eyes went wide, but she didn't hesitate. She picked up her cell phone. "Margo. Thank God you answered the phone. I'm fine. Are you home right now? Can you look outside? Are there people out front?" Sasha's shoulders dropped. "Whatever you do, please do not leave right now. They're reporters. I'll have to call the detective to find out."

When Sasha dropped her phone to her lap, she looked defeated.

"What can I do?" Blake asked.

Sasha shook her head, avoiding his gaze. "Take me home. There's an entrance in the back."

The ride was short, even with Blake driving below the speed limit. He wasn't even sure why he was going so slow; there wasn't any traffic. As he neared Sasha's condo, his heartbeat quickened, and not because of the reporters. From the back entrance to the parking lot, it didn't look like too many people were camped outside, but he couldn't be sure.

"Just pull up to that door over there." She pointed.

"Sasha—" he pleaded, wanting to ask her when he could see her next, but Sasha cut him short.

"Please don't." Unbuckling, Sasha turned to look at him. Her eyes were full of tears. "Whatever this is. Whatever you want from me. I can't give it to you. I appreciate your help and you driving me home. But this ends here."

CHAPTER TWENTY-ONE

Sasha

Margo bombarded Sasha with questions before her condo door had even shut behind her.

"Why are there reporters out there? How did they find any of this out if our DNA results haven't come back yet? What do we do? Do we need a lawyer?" Her voice pitched at the last question.

Sasha winced at the thought of a lawyer. "Honestly, I don't know. I think we need to wait till we hear back from the detective." She kicked off her shoes and sat on the couch. Releasing a breath, she smoothed a spot next to her and continued. "We need to talk."

Margo made her way over and curled up next to her. "What do we do in the meantime? We can't hide in here. Drew's mom said we should have a lawyer release a statement, or they won't leave us alone."

"You talked to Drew's mom about this?"

"Of course. You've been busy, and I needed to talk about it to someone. Plus, Drew's dad is a lawyer."

"Isn't he a corporate lawyer though?"

"Yeah, but she said he could help us find someone."

Sasha didn't think her spirit could be crushed any more, but then there it was. Margo was the one person she'd been trying to protect in all of this, and somehow, she'd managed to be absent when she needed her big sister the most.

"I don't think they're going to leave us alone for a while."

Margo didn't bother to look up. She remained silent while Sasha filled her in on the events she had failed to share with her earlier. Announcing that the real Sasha Cohen died should have been the difficult part, but it was minuscule in comparison to the mountain that sat in Blake's living room.

Margo asked questions. Sasha answered them. They danced around the subject in different directions, careful not to discuss what it meant for their dad.

"So, you have a whole other family out there," Margo finally said when there was nothing more to add. She curled in closer and laid her head in Sasha's lap.

"No. You're my family, Margo. *You* are my family." She leaned in and kissed the top of her head.

"Sasha. Wake up." Margo shook her from her sleep. "Wake up. The detective is on the phone."

"What time is it?" Sasha asked, rubbing her eyes as she looked out at the night sky.

"It's almost nine. Here." Margo flung the phone toward Sasha.

"Hello?"

"Ms. Patterson? This is Detective Spencer."

"Is everything all right? Is my dad okay?" Sasha asked. Her eyes darted to Margo, who was sitting on the arm of the couch, biting at her nails.

"Yes. Your dad is doing well. He's still recovering. But that's not what this call is about."

Sasha should have seen it coming. She should have prepared herself. But how does one prepare themselves for news that could destroy a person's entire existence?

"Ms. Patterson, did you hear me? Your father is going to be appointed a public defender. And this is going to be a bit tricky since you're an adult. If you were a minor, we'd have no choice but to reunite you with your family. However, we understand this is a delicate matter."

"What about Margo?" She cut him off. "Did her test results come back too?" Sasha asked, desperation bleeding through her words.

She remembered Margo being born. She remembered the hospital. The smell of rubbing alcohol. Her grandma's hand as she walked her to her mom's hospital bed. *There she is. Your baby sister.* Those had been real memories.

"Yes. We just received them. Margo *is* the biological daughter of Mr. Patterson."

Relief washed over her. "How much time do we have before he's arrested?"

"Technically, we have to read him his rights at the hospital. But I can't tell you when he'll be brought into the station. That all depends on when his doctor releases him into our custody. Can I give you some advice?" He exhaled and continued before Sasha was able to respond. "Get yourself a lawyer too. Media is going to be all over this. You'll want someone to make a statement on your behalf, and you'll want it done right."

When Sasha got off the phone, she noticed five missed calls and a text from Blake.

Blake: *Please call me when you get this.*

He probably found out too, Sasha thought to herself.

Ignoring the message, she dropped her phone and lifted her face to look at Margo. Tears poured down her sister's swollen cheeks. Reaching for her, Sasha held her sister in a tight embrace, smoothing out her soft strawberry-blond hair.

"Can you call Drew's mom and dad?"

The next morning, Drew Zimmerman arrived with his mom, Dawn, his dad, Jeffrey, and a woman Sasha had never seen before.

"Girls, how are you two holding up?" Mrs. Zimmerman asked sympathetically.

She reached in and hugged Margo and Sasha, kissing each of them on the cheek. Then she placed a tray of pastries on the table and peeled back the plastic wrap. Dressed in a pink suede pencil skirt and a simple white top, she was the epitome of casual chic. As the daughter of a wealthy congressman and the wife of a corporate lawyer, Mrs. Zimmerman had spent years in the public eye, perfecting her smile and composition. Looking at her in those four-inch Valentino heels, one would think all she cared about was her appearance, but the truth of the matter was she used her sense of style to boost her lucrative fundraising efforts. Anyone who was anyone in the fashion industry could be found doling out hundreds of Benjamins at her sold-out charity galas. She knew her way around people. Connected with them. And because of that, Sasha had always liked her.

Mr. Zimmerman, the quieter of the two, nodded. "Girls, I want you to meet Pamela Walsh. She's a criminal defense attorney. And she's the best."

Sasha didn't know what to say. She'd thought Drew's parents would come over so she could ask them for advice, not hire them a lawyer.

"Mr. Zimmerman, I…we don't have money for a lawyer. Not yet, at least. I mean…"

"You must be Sasha," Pamela said with a curt nod and extended hand. "I don't know anything other than what Jeffery and Dawn told me over the phone last night, but it's obvious you need legal advice. Can we sit? I can't promise you anything. And I don't take all cases. But I'd love to hear the details, and we can go from there."

Margo tugged at Sasha's arm. "Please. We need help."

She was right. They couldn't even leave her condo. Reporters had camped outside overnight, waiting to be the first to capture their image. To get a statement. Anything. They were vultures.

Sasha nodded. "Thank you for coming. Please have a seat." She gestured to the table, which housed five chairs.

Each of them took a seat, except for Margo. She sat on Drew's lap, which made Sasha smile. It was such a teenager thing to do. In the midst of all the chaos, she was glad Margo had Drew on her side. They'd been together since they'd started high school. He was the yin to her yang, as Margo often claimed. Both were more mature than either of them needed to be at such a young age. It was nice watching them act their age for once.

"Let's start with the facts." Pamela placed a yellow legal pad in front of her. Clicking her pen, she wrote Sasha Patterson/Knight on the top line.

Sasha frowned. Knight didn't settle right with her.

An hour later, Pamela shook Sasha's hand. "We'll schedule a news conference for this afternoon. I'll get in touch with the detective and find out when the Knights plan to release their statement, if they haven't already done so." She paused, and for the first time, her expression softened. "Are you absolutely sure this is how you want to proceed?"

Sasha looked at Margo, who was now lying on the couch next to Drew.

"Yes."

CHAPTER TWENTY-TWO

Blake

"I'm going to tell you the same thing I told Sasha," Detective Spencer said. He stood in the kitchen, in the exact spot Sasha had the day before. He looked worn down.

"Her name is Paige." Olive glared at him across the kitchen island, her eyes as sharp as daggers.

Detective Spencer dipped his shoulders and exhaled before he continued. "Legally, her name is Paige. However, we aren't working with a child. She's been missing for two very long decades, and the only name she knows is Sasha. So, to make this easier on her, we should all continue to respect that and call her Sasha."

Blake leaned in and hugged Olive from the side.

"But like I was saying. I already told Sasha that this is going to be incredibly tricky. There have only been a few cases in which a child has been found after such a long period of time. And even fewer in which the child wasn't abused or exploited."

"What does that mean? What are you trying to tell me? He still held her captive. He took her from me. I know the law. There is no statute of limitations with kidnapping cases." Her voice shook with anger.

The detective let out another slow exhale. Running a hand through his dusty brown hair, he frowned. "Ma'am, I cannot begin to imagine what you and your family have gone through. But as lead detective on this case, I wanted to explain that Mr. Patterson *is* being arrested on charges of kidnapping due to his relationship with the woman we *believe* kidnapped her. However, that woman is no longer living. We are still investigating their relationship from the time Sasha went missing."

With arms crossed, he continued.

"I suspect the district attorney will take this case, and you'll hear from them in a matter of time. This is already all over the news. Every news reporter is begging for a statement. They're going to be watching your actions as well as your reactions."

Just then, Porter walked out of the bathroom, rubbing his wet hair with a towel.

"Porter," Olive called to him.

Porter turned, and his eyes went immediately to his mom and then the detective before finally landing on Blake.

"The test results came back. It's Paige," Blake said. There was no glee in his voice. No excitement. No running down the hall to embrace his friend because they'd found the girl they'd so desperately looked for all those years ago. Instead, he felt desolate and empty. Full of sorrow. Sadness. He'd known she was Paige all along. But she wasn't the same Paige. She wasn't the little girl they all hoped would come home one day.

"Does she know?" He dropped his hand to his side, letting the water drip down his face.

"I gave her the results late last night. Gave her some time to process. Her sister, Margo, *is* Mr. Patterson's biological daughter. I'm heading over to the hospital now. Mr. Patterson will be read his rights, but he won't be taken to the county jail until his doctor releases him," Detective Spencer said.

They all stood silently, letting the news sink in.

After a few moments, the detective cleared his throat. "Do you have any questions before I leave?" When they all shook their heads, he added, "I've worked a few other kidnapping cases over the years. And in all cases, the child just needed time to process. Even when they were returned to their parents within the first few days. Allow her that. She's healthy. That's the important thing."

After the detective left, Blake contemplated going for a run. Olive and Porter needed some time to decompress from the news. They needed to talk about their next steps. But there were still reporters outside, waiting for someone, anyone, to appear. Going out there was out of the question. Instead, Blake took another shower.

He let the hot water run down his back, allowing thoughts of Sasha to invade his mind. To the woman who sat on his lap at her dad's house while they dug for evidence to prove him wrong. To prove she wasn't Paige. Her fingertips, as she traced the tattoos up his arm, momentarily forgetting everything that surrounded them. Her lips meeting his. Her eyes staring at him, sweet, yet seductive. The way she'd let him push her against the wall in the stairwell. The feel of her soft skin under his touch. How her hips moved against him. The way she moaned in his mouth.

Shit. What am I doing?

Blake turned the handle until the water cooled. He scrubbed the soap from his hair as new memories swirled in his head. He was treading dangerous waters, but he couldn't stop himself. There was something about her. Something he'd never quite experienced. He'd had women throw themselves at him in the past. Confident women. Attractive women. And for the most part, he'd let them. But they'd all had the intellectual and emotional capacity of a shallow puddle. Sasha was different. She was tenacious and driven. She spoke her mind and did what she wanted. And she was vulnerable.

Blake pulled back the shower curtain and stepped onto the white shower mat. He let out a slow breath and shook his head as he caught his reflection in the mirror. He had to get Sasha out of his mind. He needed to stop thinking about her lips. This was Paige. This girl was Porter's twin, and Porter needed him as a friend right now, not a guy chasing after his sister.

"So, what are *our* plans?" Porter asked his mom as Blake walked into the kitchen.

"I should call your father," she replied.

"After that. Are we staying? Are we leaving? I need to let Tina know." They sat at the kitchen table, next to one another in physical space, eons away in every other way.

"Porter, what do you want from me? I don't know what to do. I want my baby girl back. I want to see her." Olive spoke with trepidation.

"Yeah, well, I need to get back to work." He stood up and shoved the chair under the table.

"Hey, listen, you can stay here as long as you—" Blake began.

"What the *fuck*?" Porter interrupted him. His eyes narrowed, but they weren't directed at him.

Olive spun around in her chair. Her eyes went wide, and her mouth dropped open.

Blake followed their gaze. There she was. Sasha. And Margo. And two other women he didn't recognize. They were plastered on the large television screen that hung on his wall just a few feet away.

"Turn it up," Porter yelled; his feet rooted to the floor.

Olive pressed her hands to the table and stood. Then she inched her way closer.

The three of them stood side by side and listened.

"Good afternoon. I want to first thank you all for coming out." A tall woman in a gray business suit stood in front of a podium outside what looked to be Beach Brew. Her short blond hair was pulled to the side, away from her face. She turned her head, looking behind at Sasha and Margo and then back at the camera. "Almost twenty years ago, five-year-old Paige Knight was abducted from the home of Ned and Olive Knight in Cocoa Beach, Florida while celebrating her fifth birthday. Late yesterday evening, my client, Sasha Patterson, was positively identified as that girl. Unfortunately, the woman who allegedly abducted her is no longer with us. She passed away eight years ago.

"My client is twenty-four years old today. She has a life. A job. A sister and a father whom she adores. She is requesting that the media give her some space. There are absolutely no winners in this." She paused and cleared her throat.

"Is it true there was an arrest made today?" a reporter asked above the noise.

"Yes. There was an arrest made. And the state's attorney will have you believe that her father, rather, the man who raised her, played a role in her abduction. I'm extremely confident, however, that all charges will be dropped."

"Will Paige Knight be reunited with her family? We heard they're here in St. Petersburg, waiting to see her," another reporter yelled out.

"Paige has already met with a few members of the family. However, she is asking everyone involved to give her space. Her priority is her immediate family."

The crowd went nuts. Blake watched as reporters talked over one another. The cameras shifted to Sasha, who stood solid, avoiding all expression and emotion. Margo stood beside her with another woman at the other end, holding her in a tight embrace.

"Immediate family? Aren't the Knights her immediate family? How do you think they feel now that their daughter was found and wants nothing to do with them?"

The woman at the podium leaned into the microphone. "Let me be very clear. My priority is not the Knight family. What happened to them is a tragedy. However, my priority is to protect the innocent.

"My client has one statement to make. After that, there will be no further questions."

Blake watched as the camera shifted its attention to Sasha. She rested her hand on Margo's shoulder for a second before releasing it and turning toward the podium. She licked her lips and then brushed her long red hair behind her shoulder.

Unfolding a piece of white paper, Sasha looked down and began to read. "The last few days have been incredibly difficult for both myself and my sister. We ask that you give us privacy as we figure out how to move forward. Please do not come to my home, where we live, and bother us."

Olive's breathing suddenly picked up.

Blake clasped one of his hands on to hers and squeezed it.

Sasha stopped and licked her lips again before continuing. "To the Knight family. I am so very sorry for the loss and grief you endured over the last two decades, but I am not that little girl anymore. I don't think I will ever be the girl you want me to be. I already have a loving family. I hope you will grow to see that."

"What the actual fuck?" Porter asked once the press release was over.

Tears fell from Olive's eyes.

Blake pulled out his phone. He saw the end of the news coverage. He saw what Porter and Olive had overlooked.

CHAPTER TWENTY-THREE

Sasha

Sasha peered at her phone after the Zimmermans left, taking Margo with them. There were ten missed calls and dozens of messages. All from Blake. She couldn't open them. She couldn't bear reading anything from him right now. There was something kind and gentle about him. The way he was always helping her in times of distress. Protecting her and yet protecting Olive and Porter at the same time. His heart seemed so pure. She knew if he was watching the news conference, he and the Knights would have been crushed by her words. She felt bad. She did. But they couldn't be her priority.

Ignoring the messages, she shoved her phone back into her pocket and yelled out to Rebecca. "Hey, Becks, I'll be in the storage room taking inventory today. If you need anything, just yell for me."

"Don't you worry. Dominic said he'd come by to help," she replied from the front. "He just texted me. He'll be here in five minutes."

Dominic was another part-time employee. He typically only worked weekends but agreed to help in the afternoons for the next week. Longer, if necessary, if business boomed with all the media coverage.

Having the news conference in front of Beach Brew had been her idea, and it had worked out perfectly. It allowed Sasha to draw in more business while also slipping away without anyone knowing she was right under their noses. Once her statement was over, she'd climbed into a black SUV, followed by Margo and Drew's mom in a second identical SUV. Then, their lawyer, Pamela Walsh, drove away in the third. As they all drove off, one following the other, a swarm of journalists and reporters tried to tail them.

Fortunately for Sasha, her SUV went unnoticed as it circled back to the café. It was then that she secretly slipped through the back entrance and told Rebecca she'd be in the office for the remainder of the day.

She had a lot of work to catch up on, but most importantly, she needed to call the bank. She had to put a halt on her small business loan application and request a personal loan instead. She also needed to call Mitch and break the news to him. There was no way she could buy him out now. Not with having to pay for her dad's lawyer.

Sasha scrolled through her contact list. When Greg's name appeared first, she hesitated. Greg was her ex-boyfriend. He was also her ex–drug dealer. She'd met him when she was sixteen. When she was young and naïve. Full of hope and desire to fit in with kids her own age.

One night, after persistent pleading, Sasha's mom finally agreed to let her go out. "Be back by ten. And if Bridget's mom can't pick you up, call me and I'll come get you girls," she'd said.

Bridget, not quite sixteen, was her neighbor and the only friend Sasha had. Neither of the girls had their licenses, and so they walked to the movie theater like most kids their age. They would have gladly walked home, but her dad would never have gone for that. "I don't care if it's only three blocks away; no girl needs to be walking the streets at ten o'clock at night," he would say.

As they walked inside the theater, Bridget tugged at her shirt. "That's Greg. He's eighteen. He's the hottest guy at our school. Isn't he amazing?"

Since Sasha had been homeschooled, she didn't have much to compare Greg to, but he was attractive. She noticed his smile first. Then his eyes and his shaggy brown hair. When he turned in their direction, he caught her staring at him. She'd been so lost in his presence she didn't even notice he was staring right back.

"Hey, Bridget, who's your friend?" he asked as he walked over.

And that's how it started. Greg and his group of friends convinced them to purchase tickets to the premier of *Now You See Me*, but Greg hadn't been interested in Bridget; his eyes had been on her.

Bridget got over it quickly though, when another boy asked her to sit next to him.

During the movie, Greg laced his fingers between Sasha's and grinned at her. That pull-you-in type of smile that makes a girl feel special, like she's the only one in the world. And then he dug in his pocket and asked if she wanted the white oval-shaped tablet that sat in the palm of his hand. Without knowing better and wanting this new boy to like her, Sasha took the pill and popped it into her mouth. Then she washed it down with her soda.

Greg's smile grew large. "Do you always take random pills from strangers?" he asked, his brown eyes swirling.

She didn't know how to respond, so she didn't.

It wasn't until halfway through the movie that she began to feel different, calmer, at ease. Maybe a bit euphoric, but that might be taking it too far.

When they left the movie, Briget told her Greg had given her a Vicodin.

"Vicodin. Isn't that like a pain medication?" Sasha laughed, still feeling a bit dizzy.

Over time, Sasha introduced Greg to her parents, which turned out to be a huge mistake. They hated him.

"He's too old for you, and he always looks like he's high. You can do better than that, sweetie," her dad told her.

But that didn't stop her from seeing him. Some nights, when her parents and sister were sound asleep, she slipped out her bedroom window to be with him. To marvel at his smile, his touch, his endless supply of pills. He had white and yellow pills, round and oval. You name it. He had them all. Not once did she ask what she was taking. She didn't need to. They made her feel happy. Wanted. Loved.

Then one day, Greg and his pills were gone.

"Oh my God, Sasha! Greg is in jail," Bridget cried. A look of sheer worry crossed her face.

And that's how her addiction started. Rather, that's when it became clear she'd become dependent on those pills. Though the lies she told herself were woven so deeply into her core that she didn't see it. Not the way one thinks of an addict.

That same night, desperate, Sasha raided her mom's prescription drawer. She found a bottle labeled Xanax and ripped off the lid, popping one in her mouth before she could change her mind. She begged Bridget the next day to get her into contact with anyone who could help her find more pills, but when she did, she didn't have enough money to buy more than a few at a time. So she went back to her mom's Xanax bottle and took another. And another. And another. And then they were gone.

When her mom took her own life just weeks later, Sasha felt hollow on the inside. Her dad didn't seem to notice since he'd been wrapped in his own grief. She knew she needed to get her hands on more pills, anything to keep her afloat. But she had no one to turn to. By then, Bridget's mom had put a halt to their friendship, only allowing Bridget to attend the funeral under her watchful eyes.

Then, as if the world heard her self-loathing cries, Greg was there. Again. He'd been released from prison under some sort of technicality. She didn't ask; she didn't care. After he handed her what she wanted, she slipped the three tablets into her mouth and ran away to be with him. The rest was…well it was something she didn't want to remember. All that mattered was that four years later, Greg landed back in jail, and Sasha finally got the help she needed.

"You know you'll need me again. One day you'll come back to me," Greg said, smiling his gorgeous smile at her through the plexiglass that separated them.

"No. I'm happy now. This is my goodbye," she'd said. Then she pushed the stool in under the counter and walked out, promising herself that she'd never look back.

Now, looking at his name again, Sasha thought about those pills. How easy it would be to click on his name. To hear his voice. To ask him for just *one* Vicodin or *one* Oxycodone. He'd been out of jail for the past year. This she knew.

Her hands shook again. No. She didn't need a damn pill. She needed to save every last penny for that expensive lawyer.

She scrolled past Greg's name and found Mitch. She pressed Call. The phone rang four times before his voicemail picked up.

"This is Mitch. Leave a message."

"Hi, Mitch. It's Sasha. I'm not sure if you've been following the news, but it looks like I won't be able to secure a loan to buy you out. If you're willing to wait a bit longer, I can try to figure something out once everything settles, but I can't promise how long that will take. I completely understand if you want to look for another buyer."

She clicked End and flopped back into the metal chair, the heaviness from the past few days weighing her down. *What the fuck do I do now?*

Manual labor was exactly what Sasha needed. At least, that's what she'd told herself three hours earlier, before the room looked like a tornado had swept through. Sasha had only intended to take inventory and run purchases, but that didn't take nearly as long as she'd anticipated. Once she finished, she still had pent-up energy begging to be unleashed. She needed something to take her mind off her mom and dad and the lies she'd been told. She needed to forget Blake and Olive and Porter.

So, she pulled down all the old boxes that littered the back room. Boxes Mitch had left there since he first opened the café ten years ago and had said he'd clear out the next time he was in town. But Mitch rarely came back, and Sasha didn't for a second believe he'd ever get rid of them. It was the perfect distraction.

Lifting the lid to the first box wasn't terrible. Maybe because it was on top. Newer. Less dust and grime. Sasha peeked inside and found bank statements from before she started working there. She placed the lid back on and tossed the box up against the back wall. Then she blew the dust from the second box and coughed as it engulfed her. This one held what looked like old ledgers and receipts. She stacked that box on top of the first. She did this again and again for two hours. Her hair was a tangled mess. Her hands were crusted with dust and dirt. Spiderwebs hung from her shirt. She was about to stop and wash her hands when a spot of color amid the dull cardboard boxes in the corner caught her attention. Something yellow was sticking out of one of the boxes she'd just tossed to the floor. The one she'd been too tired to fully go through.

She leaned over and flipped the lid. Her eyes immediately fell to the manilla envelope that sat at the top. Dan Patterson's name was sprawled across it in black marker. Her hands shook as she reached in and pulled it out. Why in the hell did Mitch have a file on her dad?

Peeling back the tab, Sasha opened it. Pictures of her dad spilled onto her lap. A young version of him in his dress blues. The small wedding ceremony he and her mom had at city hall. She'd seen it before. Her parents had it hanging on the living room wall.

Only this one had her in it, sitting on the floor to the side, keeping herself busy with flower petals. That was her, wasn't it? Or was it the other Sasha? How could she be sure now? How could she know when this was taken with all the lies she'd been made to believe? If what Detective Spencer had said was true about her dad meeting her mom after he got out of the Marines, then this had to have been her, but the memory was forgotten.

Sasha was lost in thought, confused and frustrated, when another picture caught her attention. Mitch. Mitch and her dad. The two of them stood side by side, arms wrapped around each other's shoulders like they were buddies. With her tiny toddler frame between the two of them, clinging to her dad's neck.

Sitting alone in the quiet confines of the back room, Sasha struggled to catch her breath. How the hell did her dad and Mitch know each other? Why did Mitch have all these pictures?

Suddenly, her phone rang, causing Sasha to drop everything. It was Margo.

"Hello?" she said.

"Hey. Are you still at work? You okay?" Margo asked.

"Yeah. I was just cleaning out the back room. I kind of lost track of time," she lied.

She didn't dare tell her sister what she'd found. She couldn't tell her that Mitch and their dad had known each other and never told her. *Known each other?* Sasha hadn't known Mitch even existed until she started working at Beach Brew.

"I just wanted to see if everything was okay. You don't have a way home and you've been there for hours."

Sasha rolled her wrist to glance at the time on her watch. Shit. It was after seven. Rebecca and Dominic were long gone by now.

"I'll be okay. I shouldn't be too much longer. Just sorting through some stuff," she said.

"Okay, well, there's something else," she muttered.

"What is it?"

"The news. It's been on all day. They're making it seem like Dad kidnapped you. They're saying there is enough evidence to put him away for life." Her voice broke, and Sasha knew she was fighting back tears.

"I'm not going to let that happen. Remember what the lawyer said. Turn off the TV. Stay low. I'll call you when I head home. Ask Drew not to keep you out too late." When she clicked End, Blake's name appeared. Again. And she ignored it. Again.

She turned to face the stack of boxes, and an overwhelming urge to scream tore through her chest. To throw the pictures. To destroy everything in her sight. Her chest heaved as each breath grew more ragged. She wanted to fix this. Not make it worse. She'd firmly believed her dad was innocent in all of this. He had to be. But now? With what she'd been told? And these pictures?

She didn't scream. She didn't throw anything. Instead, she scrolled through her list of contacts and clicked on the name of the one person she knew could make all of her feelings go away.

CHAPTER TWENTY-FOUR

Blake

Blake paced his living room floor. It was exactly twelve steps if he started next to his television, walked straight through to his kitchen, and stopped at the sink. Twelve steps one way and twelve steps back. He'd been pacing ever since he'd tried calling Sasha the first half dozen times after Porter and Olive left. He tried to understand what was going through Sasha's mind. What she must be feeling. Was she shocked? Scared? Angry? He could get behind those feelings. But to not answer his calls? That worried him.

He'd seen her hands on his television when she spoke to the camera. They were shaking. Hell, even her arms were shaking. And while it might mean nothing at all, he had a dull ache in the pit of his stomach. He dialed her number again, halting his steps, and listened. It rang. Once. Twice. Three times. Four. Voicemail.

"Shit," he muttered under his breath.

With nothing else to lose, he grabbed the keys to his truck and left. Avoiding attention, Blake snuck out the back entrance, just as he'd done with Sasha the day before. Just as he'd done when he hugged Olive and Porter goodbye.

"Please watch over her," Olive had told him solemnly. Then she raised a finger to her eye and wiped away a tear before climbing into the passenger seat.

Blake nodded. It was a goodbye and a promise.

It was dark and the roads were empty, so it didn't take long before Blake neared Sasha's condo. But instead of turning into her parking lot, he changed his mind and kept driving. She wouldn't be upstairs in her room sulking all night. He hadn't known her for long, but that much was a no-brainer. She'd be trying to distract herself. And what better way to distract oneself than with work?

He drove past Sasha's place and turned around at the next light. Then he turned right onto Gulf Street, where tourists were more active, enjoying late-night dinners and walks along the beach. He kept driving until the road narrowed, where it was darker. Less traffic.

Within minutes, Blake was pulling into Beach Brew's tiny lot. A black sedan he didn't recognize sat along the side, just feet from the entrance of the café. There were no other cars, but there was light coming from inside. He closed his eyes and took a deep breath. Then he unbuckled and stepped out of his truck.

Pushing his way inside, Blake instantly heard voices coming from the back. One belonged to Sasha, that he could tell. But there was a man's voice too. They weren't visible, but he could tell by their tones that they were arguing. He doubted they'd heard him come in, because they didn't pause. Instead, their voices grew louder. He didn't want to startle anyone, so he took a few steps and tried clearing his throat, hoping they'd come out and see him. But that didn't work either.

"What the fuck are you doing? Do you know how much money you're flushing down the fucking toilet?" a raspy voice cried out. "Holy shit, Sasha, Rickie is going to flip out. I don't run the show anymore."

"I don't care. This was a mistake."

"I'm not taking the fall for this one. You need to get in the fucking car." Intensity rang in the strange man's voice.

"Let me go!" Sasha screamed.

At the fear in her voice, Blake ran to the back. There, a lanky man with long brown hair stood with his back to Blake. His hands clutched Sasha's wrists.

Neither of them noticed him at first, not until Blake spoke.

"Get your hands off her. Now."

Their heads snapped up at the same time. Sasha's eyes held surprise but sparkled under the fluorescent lights.

The stranger glared. "We're closed. Don't you know how to fucking read?"

His hands were still wrapped around Sasha's wrists, his fingers digging into her flesh. White impressions indented her pale skin. That pissed Blake off. What kind of man hurts women? He was just about to lunge at the guy when Sasha twisted out of his hold. She grabbed the empty coffeepot sitting on the counter and threw it. The guy didn't even see it coming. One second, he was glaring at Blake, and the next, blood was oozing from his skull.

Blake ran to Sasha. "We need to get out of here."

She stopped and tugged away from him. "No."

"Sasha. You need to call the cops." He pointed at the guy, who was shaking himself out of his own stupor.

"No," she said again, shaking her head, not meeting his gaze.

She turned her attention to the guy on the ground. "This was a mistake. *You* were a mistake. You need to get the fuck out of here." Then she took a step back.

Blake did too.

The guy reached for his head and laughed, as if he found Sasha's words to be funny. But he stood up and walked toward the door anyway. As he neared the exit, he looked at his blood-covered fingers. Then he lifted his head and looked at the two of them. His eyes pooled with darkness.

"This bitch." He nodded toward Sasha. "She's about to be in some serious shit. Rickie doesn't play games."

"Get out!" Sasha screamed. She picked up a mug and launched it at him. It barely missed his face.

"What the fuck, Sasha?" the man growled.

"Get out! Get the fuck out!" she screamed again, grabbing another mug off the countertop and raising it in the air.

"Okay. Damn. I'm leaving," he grunted, raising his hands in a truce before reaching for the door handle.

"You'll be sorry about this. Don't think I didn't warn you." His eyes darted from her to Blake. And then he shoved the door open and disappeared into the dark.

"Sasha," Blake said once they were alone. He was ready to go to her. Hug her. Ask her what that was all about. But she wasn't having any of it.

"I want you to leave too." Her voice was cold and sad, like she was doing everything in her power to stay strong.

He didn't want her to cry. He didn't want her to feel alone. "Sasha, can we talk about this? I want to—"

"Help? You want to help? Haven't you done enough? Please. Just get out."

And there it was. He was the enemy. He was the one who had done all of this. Twenty years ago, he'd been the one to let her slip by. He should have been watching Paige, not closing his eyes. It was dark. They shouldn't have been playing hide and seek. And now, here he was again, destroying her life by being there. Finding her. His heart sank at the realization.

"Sasha." His words were nothing more than a whisper. A plea.

"Blake, I need you to leave," Sasha repeated, this time softer.

All the pain he'd felt in the past, all the agony, the loss of his childhood friend, the loss of a carefree childhood, it all came bubbling to the surface. Nothing in this moment would change that. Not for her. Not for him. So he chose the only three words he could find. Three words that felt meaningless because they couldn't fix a damn thing.

"I'm sorry, Sasha."

CHAPTER TWENTY-FIVE

Sasha

Sasha took a few minutes to break down before she told herself to stop and suck it up. She'd never been a big crier, but ever since she'd met Blake, her eyes had somehow betrayed her. Her emotions were all over the place. It made her think of her mom and when she died. She'd numbed her feelings to avoid crying. And that scared her now. It made her want things she knew she shouldn't have.

Looking at the back room, Sasha released a heavy sigh. There were so many boxes. So many unanswered questions. What if there were more pictures? Did it even matter anymore? Should she call her lawyer? Let her know what she found?

And what about Greg? Shit. What had she gotten herself into?

Sasha dragged her hands over her face. She was mentally and physically exhausted. All she wanted to do was to go home, get in bed, and sleep the night away. So, with that in mind, she grabbed her phone and keys, turned off the lights, and locked up. However, Sasha hadn't made it past the front entrance before she caught sight of a tall shadow leaning against the side of the building.

"Blake? What are you still doing here?" Uncertainty wove through her words.

He turned toward her, but he didn't move from his spot. "I couldn't just leave." His voice cracked.

Though the darkness encircled them, Sasha could see his face. He looked forlorn and dejected. His eyes were red-rimmed, and the corners of his lips were pulled down into a frown.

She didn't know how to respond, so they stood like that for a few moments. He'd been crying—or the male version of crying, at the very least. She could hear it in his voice, the way his words came out tight and unsteady. In the way his shoulders sagged and how he rubbed his jaw over and over again with the same hand. And then, for the first time, she recalled what Olive had said about him. That he'd blamed himself for her disappearance.

"Why do you feel the need to protect me?"

His eyes went wide in surprise, but she held his gaze with determination. She needed answers for once, not a hug.

"I don't. I mean. I…" he stammered.

"I don't know what caused you to feel like you're the reason Paige went missing, but I doubt you were to blame. You were just a boy. You don't have to repay any debts. You don't owe society anything." Once the words escaped her mouth, she felt a twinge of guilt for being so straightforward. But that's who she was. She wouldn't sugarcoat anything for him.

"Is that what you think? That I'm merely repaying my debts?"

She'd hit a nerve. Good. She wanted him to get angry; to feel an ounce of what she'd been feeling. And yet, she knew this wasn't his fault. She was misdirecting her feelings, which wasn't fair to him.

"You do realize some asshole was trying to drag you out of your café, right? Or did you forget that? You have no car. You have no way home. And that guy said someone named Ronnie was going to flip out, and that you were about to be in some shit. Doesn't sound very safe to me. I couldn't just leave." His hands were in the air, animated and angry.

"Rickie," she corrected him. Then she smiled because correcting him right now was kind of funny. Though, he didn't see it that way.

"Ronnie. Rickie, Ricardo. I don't give a shit what his name is. You're missing the point."

"No, I get it. But I took care of Greg. I didn't need your help." Blake huffed, clearly frustrated with her.

"Let me take you home. I can't let you walk by yourself when someone is out there, pissed at you. For all I know, he's waiting around the corner, ready to hurt you."

"Fine," she said. Part of her agreed with Blake. It wasn't so much about being scared of Greg. Hurting people wasn't his style. But she wasn't sure what he had meant about Rickie running the show now. He'd always been a nobody. Scary, yes. But a nobody in terms of seniority. And she did just dump a crap ton of pills down the toilet.

Blake walked around to the passenger side of his truck and opened the door for her. Then he closed it after she climbed inside. Even in all his anger, he was still a gentleman.

They drove in silence until they reached a red light. She was looking straight ahead at a group of women as they walked through the crosswalk when she felt Blake turn his attention to her. There was a tiny part of her that wanted to acknowledge it. Okay, there was a big part of her that wanted to return the look.

But what was she supposed to say? *Hey, I'm mad at the world and blame you for bringing everything to light? And yet I want your mouth on mine?* Because if she were being brutally honest with herself, that's all she could think about. His soft lips capturing hers the way he had in the stairwell. The force and magnitude behind it. Like he couldn't get enough of her.

"Can I ask you something?" He broke the silence.

She closed her eyes. She didn't want to look into his gorgeous green eyes.

"Mm-hmm," was all she could muster.

"That guy…was he…did he give you pills?"

Sasha didn't respond. Not right away.

The light turned green, and he eased off the brake, slowly accelerating through the intersection. They drove like that for a while longer, down the dimly lit road, until the mood shifted.

"Yes. But it's not what you think. I didn't take any."

Her answer seemed good enough for the rest of the drive. But she doubted it pleased him. She doubted he even believed her. Why would he? She'd already told him about her addiction, and there he was, smack dab in the middle of an attempt to throw her life down the toilet.

They pulled up to her condo only minutes later, parking in a spot behind the building. It was the same place he'd parked when they were avoiding the reporters the night before. Blake shut off the engine and unfastened his seatbelt like he planned to stay, but he didn't reach for the handle. He just stared out his windshield. He looked lost in thought as he studied the brown stucco exterior of her building complex.

Sasha wondered what he was thinking about. What would cause him to grow so quiet? A huge part of her felt guilty. But she didn't have the energy to care. At least, that's what she kept telling herself. In another life, she'd just be Sasha. And he'd just be Blake. And maybe they might like one another. But this was messy. And she had too many other things on her plate to take care of than kissing a man she so desperately wanted to kiss.

"Thanks for the ride," Sasha whispered and quickly unbuckled before Blake could say something to change her mind.

But he didn't. He didn't say a word. When she turned around to shut the door, he wasn't even looking at her. So she did the only thing she knew how to do. She turned and walked away.

And then she instantly regretted it. Her brain tried to reason with her body, but her body wouldn't listen. She turned back toward Blake's truck and climbed back inside.

When he looked at her, his eyebrows arched.

"I found some stuff at the café. In the back room where we keep all the supplies." She looked down at her hands. "There were some old photographs, pictures of my dad."

She wasn't sure why she was telling him, but the second the words escaped her mouth, she couldn't stop. She knew she was Paige. He knew she was Paige. Hell, the public even knew she was Paige. But her sister only knew her as Sasha. She, too, only knew herself as Sasha. How was she supposed to reconcile that? How was she supposed to carry the weight of that on her shoulders to appease everyone? This afternoon, she hadn't cared about anyone except her family. But her dad? She was trying to protect her father. The man who'd always been there for her. And he'd lied to her.

Blake was the only person who seemed neutral when it came to her identity. He was willing to let her be Sasha while the rest of the world wanted her to be Paige.

"I don't know how to do this. I don't know what to believe."

Blake covered her hand with his. "You believe the facts."

He said it so matter-of-factly. Like she could snap her fingers and just be Paige now and let her dad rot in prison for being involved in her kidnapping. But then he surprised her with his next sentence.

"Your DNA might have come back as Paige, but look at the other facts too."

He removed his hand from hers and reached up to rub his temple. "You told me your dad helped you with your…addiction, right?" he asked, tiptoeing around the obvious.

"Yes…"

"Then it's a fact that he loved you. He moved to St. Pete to be closer to you. He took care of you. That's love."

She thought about it for a moment. He was right. But the dad she knew didn't line up with the dad in the pictures. That dad was a liar.

Sasha reached her hand into her bag and pulled out some of the pictures she'd found. She handed them to Blake.

He turned on the interior light and looked down, examining each one. "I don't understand. Who are they?"

"That's my dad when I was little. I'm pretty sure that's me. Like the real me." Sasha pointed. "And that…that's Mitch. He owns Beach Brew." She paused. "I think he was involved."

Blake looked up. Confusion spread across his face.

"After rehab, my dad compiled a list of jobs that were hiring in the area. Beach Brew was on that list, but it wasn't my immediate choice. I filled out a few applications across town. I received a few calls back and went on a handful of interviews. The whole shebang. My dad never mentioned knowing Mitch. But he also never pushed for me to work there. Mitch ended up offering me—by far—the highest wage. I couldn't turn it down."

"Does your dad even know Mitch owns it?"

"I don't know. I've talked about him before. There was a part of me that thought, you know what, Sasha? Maybe, just maybe, he hasn't put two and two together. Maybe he doesn't realize it's his friend Mitch. Maybe he doesn't think his friend Mitch is the guy who owns Beach Brew. But these pictures? I'm right there. Next to the two of them. And Mitch has never mentioned my dad either. It's like the two of them clearly knew each other. And then…then they stopped communicating altogether."

Blake flipped through the pictures again. "Your mom isn't in any of these."

"I noticed that too," she said. "There are more pictures at the café. And honestly, I'm afraid to open more boxes. I'm afraid I might find more."

Blake looked at her. His eyes were liquid. Dark and warm. He didn't have to ask. She knew what was on his mind. What he wanted to know.

She dropped her gaze to the truck seat. Shame washed over her.

"That's why I called Greg. I didn't think I could handle my dad being a part of this. We hired a lawyer for him. Now I'm not even sure if it'll be worth it. If he deserves it."

CHAPTER TWENTY-SIX

Blake

It was still dark when Blake's alarm went off the next morning. Heavy clouds blanketed the sky, dark and dull and gray. A perfect depiction of his mood. He closed the curtains and reached for his phone. There was one new message.

Sasha: *You really don't have to come today. I mean, you can. But don't feel obligated.*

Last night, Blake promised Sasha he'd help her go through the boxes. All of them. Which meant he would pick her up before the café opened so they could avoid reporters.

Blake: *I don't feel obligated. I want to. I'll be there in half an hour. Meet me in the back again.*

Half an hour later, just as the sun began to rise, Blake found himself pulling up to Sasha's condo. But the plan to fool the reporters didn't go exactly as they'd hoped. Instead, a young woman spotted his truck as he pulled around the corner. She jumped to her feet and locked eyes with him. Then she barked orders to her cameraman and ran, determined to catch him. To be the first in a line of reporters to nab an interview.

Blake winced when he realized just how fast the woman was, as if nailing this story meant surviving another day. He wanted to text Sasha, to tell her not to come out yet, but it was too late. She was already pushing the glass door open when the reporter spotted her.

Blake rolled down the window and motioned for Sasha to hurry.

Then, in a flash, the reporter flipped her hair and grinned. "I'm here this morning, in St. Petersburg, Florida, where Paige Knight and Blake Ryan are about to meet for the first time since Ms. Knight's public statement."

Sasha's eyes widened, but she didn't stop. Instead, her feet moved faster.

Blake unlocked the door, ready for her to jump in, but more reporters had now gathered around. All standing between his truck and Sasha.

"Ms. Knight, does this mean you've changed your mind about your biological family? Have you spoken to them yet?" she asked, sticking the microphone in her face.

"Have you spoken to your dad yet?" another reporter yelled over the crowd.

"How does it feel to know the man who claims to be your father abducted you?" a third woman jumped in.

Sasha ignored them all. She pushed past them and climbed into the truck.

Blake was rolling up the window when the last question caught them both off guard.

"Ms. Knight, is it true you're an addict?" the first woman said, casual and cool. Like it was perfectly planted so everyone could hear.

"Drive," Sasha whispered, staring straight ahead.

So he did. He pressed the accelerator and drove. But he didn't turn toward the café. And Sasha didn't ask him why. He just kept driving. And then, they were pulling up to the fire station just as the rain released from the clouds above.

"Throw this on." Blake handed Sasha a gray hoodie.

She did as she was told. Didn't even question him. Once her hands were through the sleeves, he jumped out of the truck and ran around to open her door. He offered his hand to help her out, and she took it. Together, they ran as large drops of water collided with their clothes.

Jay was standing in the main hall when Blake and Sasha opened the door. A gust of wind followed behind.

"Came out of nowhere," Jay said, referring to the downpour outside.

Blake was still holding Sasha's hand when he noticed Jay's eyes fall between them. But he didn't let go. Instead, he tightened his fingers.

"I need a favor," Blake said.

"Hey, have you seen the news? Blake is on there with…" Marcus said as he came around the corner. "Oh shit. Sorry, I didn't know you two were here." He stopped in his tracks when he caught sight of the two of them next to Jay.

"I need one of you to loan me your car. The reporters know what my truck looks like now. I need something we can get by in. At least for today."

"Blake, can I talk to you?" Jay nodded behind him. "It'll only take two minutes."

He looked down at Sasha. She gave him a wry smile and let her fingers slip from his hand.

"Hey, Sash! Is Rebecca working today? Do you think you could put in a good word for me?" Leave it to Marcus to be completely normal, to not treat Sasha differently than he would anyone else just because of the news.

"Blake. Do you know what you're getting yourself into?" Jay said as he shut the door to his office.

Blake narrowed his eyes.

"I didn't tell you this before because…well, because I didn't think anything would come of Sasha," Jay continued. He tugged at the collar of his shirt and paced the small room. "Hell, even after you two slept together, I figured that'd be it. Nothing more. But that girl out there is trouble. And she's going to drag you into it." He pointed to the door as if Sasha were right there.

Blake held out his hand and interrupted him. "First off, I didn't sleep with Sasha. Second, the trouble I think you're referring to is none of your business. There's history with us. She's like family." He suddenly felt annoyed. That Jay, of all people, would warn him about Sasha. As if neither of them was in the occupation of helping people.

"It is my business. You work here. You don't want to get caught up in anything she has. You don't want—"

"If you won't lend me your car, that's fine. But this conversation? You don't know what you're talking about." Anger rose in his voice.

"The hell I don't. I've had to use Narcan on that girl. When I was working in Tampa. To save her fucking life. Her fucking boyfriend used to be the puppet master in Tampa. Started selling to all the teens. Got them all fucking addicted."

The admission caught him off guard, but it didn't matter. Her past didn't matter. It was her future he was worried about. "That was years ago, Jay." He turned to leave. He didn't want to hear any more.

"She's responsible for getting my brother addicted. Ask her about him. Ask her about Rickie. I'm telling you, she's fucking trouble."

CHAPTER TWENTY-SEVEN

Sasha

"Use my car. It has tinted windows. They'll never see you." Marcus tossed the keys to Sasha as Blake rounded the corner.

"Thanks," she said. Her lips flattened into a fine line. She held her hand up and jingled the keys toward Blake.

"Just be nice to Brooke," Marcus crooned.

"You named your car?" Sasha laughed.

"Damn right. After my first girlfriend. She was fine!"

"We gotta go." Blake's voice was firm, full of tension. He grabbed the keys and then reached for Sasha's hand.

"Remember what I said. Be nice to her," Marcus called out just as the door closed.

Within minutes, they were back on the road, driving through the storm. Blake turned on the windshield wipers, but even those couldn't keep up with the relentless rain. Dark clouds loomed across the sky, blocking out every inch of daylight.

"I didn't take Marcus for a Tesla guy," Blake said, breaking the silence.

"No? What type of car did you imagine him driving?" Sasha said, relieved to be talking about something other than herself. She could tell something was bothering Blake. But for once, she was glad he'd chosen not to bring it up. She was content talking about something entirely different from her mess of a life. Though she knew it wouldn't last long.

"I don't know. I guess when I think of Marcus, I think of meat and potatoes. Big bones. So maybe a truck."

"Like yours?"

"Oh, God no. He's too flashy for something like mine. Maybe something more like the Hennessey Velociraptor. With big-ass tires."

She grinned in agreement. She could see Marcus behind the wheel of something like that.

They laughed and smiled as they continued the conversation, discussing the types of cars that matched their personalities. "You are definitely a simple car type girl, but you have such a strong personality. You don't take crap from anyone. I can see you in a Jeep Wrangler. It's perfect for weathering any type of terrain."

She liked the sound of that. That Blake knew who she was, even though they'd only met six days ago. She moved her arm to the middle console, where Blake's hand was resting. Her elbow brushed against his. The touch was soft and warm. They were so close she could almost feel the air getting trapped between them. He looked at her, those green eyes swirling as his lips curled up into a small smile. She could get lost in those eyes.

They pulled up behind Beach Brew and sat silently for a few moments, letting the rain fall. Letting the air circulate between them. Her heartbeat quickened and temptation crept through her chest. Suddenly, she wanted nothing more than for him to lean over and kiss her and to feel the warmth of his lips. She knew he wanted it too. But today was different. He didn't budge. He didn't reach out. Something held him back. So, to avoid that conversation, she unbuckled. He followed. Then they ran through the rain.

"Shit!" Blake said once they walked into the back room. "I didn't expect so many boxes."

"Not all of them belong to Mitch. These are supplies and inventory." She gestured to the shelves with an open palm. "Those are the ones I still need to sort out." She pointed toward the wall.

"Where do we start?" he asked.

She sighed and rolled her neck. "I guess it doesn't matter." She moved through the mess and sat down on a stack of boxes. Blake followed.

She lifted the lid to the box closest to her. Stacks of old bills and supply receipts fell out. She put it to the side and opened another. Rusted tools. Blake bent down and helped her move that one next to the first. Sasha pointed at another box, and Blake handed it to her. Junk. Old magazines and newspapers. "Maybe that's all there was. I mean, maybe I jumped the gun. I just feel like—" She stopped when Blake said her name.

"Sasha. You need to look at this." He turned to face her, pictures fanned out in both of his hands.

"These are kids. All of them. The whole box." His forehead creased with worry.

Sasha grabbed one of the pictures from his hand and studied it. A little girl wearing a yellow dress smiled back at her. She took another picture. The same thing. This time it was a boy. Possibly the same age. But he wasn't smiling. She looked into the box. Stacks of pictures bound by rubber bands lay inside.

"I don't get it. Why does he have all these pictures? Who are they?"

Blake didn't respond. Instead, he moved on to the next box and opened it. He let out a deep breath. Then he brought his hand to his forehead and rubbed at his temple. "There's more."

She peeked into that box as well and shook her head. "Do they say anything? On the backs of them? Names? Dates? Anything?"

Blake shook his head. "No. We could go through all of them though. If you want."

But before Sasha could respond, she was lifting the lid to another box. Letters. Full of letters. No return address. No names. Only an address to where they were delivered. Sasha leafed through all of them. Each one in different handwriting. Each one like the one before it. She pulled a single sheet of paper from one of the envelopes on top and read it aloud.

"Hannah is a great fit. Thank you for your help." Sasha stared at the paper. "There's no signature."

Blake looked at her quizzically.

She dropped the letter and reached for another. "It took Tony a while to come around, but he is doing great. I couldn't have asked for a better kid. He'll be loved for sure."

She dropped that letter too. Instinctively, her hand shot into the box and retrieved another envelope. "Kenya is the sweetest little girl and has adapted so well. Thanks for arranging this."

Her eyes bulged as realization hit her. "Oh my God! All these kids?" She flipped the lid to another box. More letters. Her breathing picked up. Her body tensed. "No. No, this can't be." She shook her head. Her hands were trembling as she stared at Blake.

Before either of them could say another word, there was a loud bang at the back door. Sasha jumped.

"Hey, open up! You locked the door. And it's pouring out!" Rebecca yelled from outside.

Sasha ran and opened the door.

Rebecca stepped inside. "Doesn't look like we'll be busy today. Not if this rain doesn't let up," she said. "Oh. I didn't know you had company." She flashed Sasha a grin. "I'll start opening up front." She raised her eyebrows and strode toward the door. Then, before she slipped completely out of sight, she mouthed, "He's so hot!"

"There have got to be hundreds of pictures. Hundreds of letters. And there's nothing identifiable. Nothing to suggest who they are. Except for an address in Cocoa Beach. Didn't you say..." Blake's eyes shot up.

She nodded. "Mitch has a house there." She sat down and shuffled through the letters absently. "What do I do? Do I call the cops? Do I tell my lawyer? I can't sit here and do nothing. This...this is crazy, right?"

He sat in silence, as if contemplating what to say. Then he stood, dropped the letters, and pulled out his keys. "Let's go for a drive."

CHAPTER TWENTY-EIGHT

Blake

Sasha didn't hesitate. It was like she instinctively knew what he was thinking, knew where they were headed. And she trusted him. With one of the letters in hand, the two of them found themselves back on the road, back in the rain. It was still gray and gloomy, but fortunately, the wind had died down, and he didn't need to keep the windshield wipers on full blast.

By the time they crossed the bridge into Tampa, the rain downgraded to a light mist. And by the time they passed Orlando, it had stopped completely. Somewhere after that, the clouds dissipated, and the sun made its first appearance of the day.

The ride was smooth in the Tesla. Conversation flowed easily, though Blake avoided tough topics. In the three hours that it took to reach Cocoa Beach, he'd learned that Sasha attempted college a few years back but dropped out during her first semester because she hadn't considered herself very studious.

"I don't believe that for a second. I think you're incredibly smart," Blake said.

She shrugged. "Thanks. But I was right out of rehab. I couldn't sit in an hour-long class without getting myself into trouble. I guess I didn't trust myself. So I decided to get my yoga and meditation certification instead."

"You teach yoga?" he asked.

She nodded. "*And* meditation. It helps ground me. I teach both classes on the beach every Wednesday, as long as it's not raining."

"Tomorrow?" He narrowed his eyes. "Do you think you'll be up for being on the beach with reporters on standby?"

She pursed her lips as she contemplated his question. "I know," her eyes lit up, "I can dress up. I can pretend to be someone else. Maybe wear a costume or something." She got giggly and adjusted her position in her seat. "I can wear a wig and big round sunglasses."

She was smiling. Damn, did she look good smiling.

"I think you might need more than a wig."

She placed her finger to her chin to think. Then her eyes grew large. "A sombrero. And a tutu!"

They laughed and poked fun at one another. It felt so casual, and yet he couldn't deny the flirtatious undertones. At one point, Sasha even ran her hand through his hair, asking if he'd ever had long hair. It was nice, more than nice. He wanted to do the same to her, to run his fingers through her hair. Maybe he would. Later.

As soon as they pulled off the expressway, the mood shifted, neither really knowing what to expect or what their plans were. And it lingered between them.

"Where do Porter and Olive live?" Sasha's tone turned serious.

"Porter and his wife live that way, maybe fifteen minutes from here." He pointed to the left. "Olive, Ned, and Penny still live in the same house, next door to my parents in the same direction, but closer."

"Do they know we're here?" she asked, her voice suddenly soft.

"No. And I don't plan on telling them either."

She nodded and then turned to look out the window.

"Go past this light and turn right at the next intersection," the GPS announced.

"What do we do when we get there?" Sasha asked, rubbing her palms up and down her thighs nervously.

"I was hoping you'd have a plan," Blake said playfully. He reached over and placed his hand on top of Sasha's. She didn't turn to look at him. Instead, her focus remained out the window. But she acknowledged his touch by relaxing her hand, which allowed him to slide his fingers between hers. Once each finger was laced with hers, she squeezed them back, almost as a thank you.

Blake turned down a quiet street and slowed. It was a beautiful residential area, with modest homes much like the one he'd grown up in. Most of them were cream, white, brown, and tan. All similar in style.

"It's that one. Right there." He pointed to the left. "There are two cars in the driveway."

"Let's get out and walk," Sasha said. "Do you have a hat?"

He handed her a Tampa Bay Rays baseball cap. She pulled her hair up high into a messy knot and stuck it under the cap. Then she opened the door and stepped out into the sunshine. Blake met her on the sidewalk, and together they walked on the opposite side of the street slowly, eyeing the house. Mitch's house. A large For Sale sign came into view as soon as they were parallel to it.

"Should I call to see if we can get a showing? Maybe we can check it out. See what we find?" he asked.

"I have a better idea." She grabbed his hand and led him across the street.

A tall brunette held the door open while a young man and woman followed behind. "Oh, it's beautiful. I love the floors, and the windows let in so much light," the younger woman told the man.

"It is exceptional. And it was just listed yesterday. We don't expect this to stay on the market for very long, especially since the seller is offering to pay for all closing costs," the brunette said, smiling in their direction.

"Excuse me. Are you the realtor for this home?" Sasha called out.

The woman looked up. "I am. Can I help you with something?"

"Yes, actually. I'm so incredibly sorry that I'm interrupting you, but my husband, Dr. Ryan, and I have been wanting to look at this house since it went on the market." She squeezed his hand.

"You'll have to call the office. I don't make the appointments, and I'm actually with clients right now." She looked at the man and the woman, who were clearly annoyed.

"We've tried calling the office all morning, but it keeps telling us the number has been disconnected. And since we're here, we'd really love to look around."

The woman narrowed her eyes as she pulled out her phone. "I'll have to check with my office staff to see if someone can help you. I'm afraid I'm busy." She turned to the couple. "Are you ready to see the next house?"

"No, I think we want to put in an offer on this one," the man said. The girl smiled and kissed him on the cheek.

"That's wonderful. We can draft up the paperwork, and I'll let the seller know he can expect an offer by the evening."

Blake saw the panic in Sasha's eyes, and suddenly, his mouth was moving. "Shannon? Shannon Parker? Is that your name?" He nodded to the sign where her name was sprawled in big block letters. "I'm not sure what your clients are about to offer, but with the way this market is right now, I'm willing to beat their offer and pay in cash. No loan needed."

Shannon tilted her head. She smoothed out her tight red blouse and pursed her lips. "What was your name again?"

"Blake Ryan. Dr. Blake Ryan."

"Is that your car?" she asked, referring to the Tesla parked down the street.

"It is."

Shannon turned to her clients. "I'll draft your paperwork in case this doesn't work out. But if you two would like to get going, I don't want to keep you all day. You can go through the list of other homes, and I'll book showings for those next weekend."

The young woman shot daggers at Blake, but she walked away, her husband at her heels.

"It's nice to meet you, Dr. Ryan. Right this way," Shannon said, waving the two of them inside. "How long have you two been married?"

"Newlyweds," Sasha said, rushing her words.

"So this will be your first home together?" Shannon asked as she typed something into her phone, too busy to care. "Have you looked at any other homes yet?"

"Nope. We're pretty set on this one. The location is great, and we both have family nearby. I guess this is more or less a formality. Can we look around? We want to see what kind of remodeling it would need."

"Absolutely. But it won't need much work. The seller has been living in the Bahamas and has a cleaning service that comes out every few weeks. It has hardwood floors throughout the entire home. Marble countertops. Double ovens. The seller wants to move quickly, so cash will work perfectly. He has movers coming in the morning, so it will be empty by tomorrow afternoon, but all the appliances will stay."

Blake followed Shannon into the kitchen and released Sasha's hand, allowing her to slip away.

CHAPTER TWENTY-NINE

Sasha

The house was larger than it looked from outside. The oversized front door opened to a grand entrance and hallway, which led down to the kitchen. Rather than follow Blake and the realtor through the lower level, Sasha sidestepped toward the staircase, which led to three giant bedrooms. Each one was picturesque, like it had just been featured in a home décor magazine. No picture frames on the walls. Nothing personal. It was as if Mitch had never even lived here.

Determined to find something, Sasha poked her head into the master bedroom and opened the closet door. It was smaller than she'd imagined for such a room. It was wide, but half the depth of the master closet in her condo. Rows of clothes lined both sides. Menswear on the one, women's on the other.

She'd never met Mitch's wife, but she'd seen pictures. She was tall, blond, and beautiful. Seemingly perfect from head to toe. Sasha dragged her hands across the clothes as she looked at the boxes stacked neatly on the shelf above. She wanted to look through them, to see what lay inside, but there wasn't enough time. Shannon would likely make her way up, and Sasha couldn't afford to be caught.

She stepped out and walked around to the master bathroom. Again, it was stunning. Nothing suggested anyone was even living there. She let out a deep exhale. She didn't know what she'd hoped to find, but there wasn't so much as a hint of Mitch in the house. The other two rooms held exactly what she'd expected. More seascape furnishings with beach and antique glass hues, the standard for beachside living decor.

Walking back down the stairs, Sasha was greeted by a smiling Shannon. "It is gorgeous, isn't it?" She flipped her hair to the side and lay a hand on Blake's wrist.

Was she flirting with Blake? Sasha wasn't sure what Shannon had been referring to. What she'd walked in on. But the way Shannon was eyeing Blake didn't sit well with her. She didn't like it one bit.

"What's gorgeous, sweetie?" Sasha said, announcing herself. She moved toward Blake and brushed a soft kiss on his lips as she simultaneously reached her arms around his waist. She had to play the role of a loving wife, right?

He looked down and cocked his head to the side, amusement dancing in his eyes.

"The dock out back. It has two boat slips. That means I can buy another boat after we move in," Blake said. His grin was wide and inviting. He hugged her back, squeezing her ever so gently. His touch reminded her of when they were in her condo. When he'd held her up against the wall, her legs wrapped around his waist. Before Margo came home and walked in on something she desperately wanted to happen. At least, she wanted it to happen the other night. But definitely not now, not anymore. There was too much history between them, too much confusion. Sleeping with him would make a bigger mess.

"You should go check it out," Blake said, interrupting her thoughts.

"Hmm?"

"The outside. You should really go check it out. There's a beautiful wrought-iron fence with two gates. One leads right onto the canal."

Why did Blake want her to go outside? Maybe for formalities? To keep from making it completely obvious they were full of shit? So she did as she was told while Shannon took him on a tour of the rest of the house, which pissed her off. Shannon was supposed to show them this house, not toy with a married man—okay, a pretend married man. She was probably a home-wrecker.

Outside on the newly varnished wood deck, Sasha took in the surroundings. It was pretty, and the wrought-iron fence *was* gorgeous. Rose bushes climbed the front gate while shrubs and bushes ran along both fence lines, offering privacy to an otherwise open landscape. She didn't care enough to go down to the dock. She trusted it was just as nice. She turned around to go back in when the house next door caught her eye. It was a one-story ranch home, as was the house on the other side of Mitch's, now that she took a moment to study it. And from the looks of it, neither of his neighbors were home. She paused and then looked behind her. No. There was no way Blake was thinking the same thing she was thinking. Blake didn't strike her as the type to break laws. Or was he?

"Here's my business card. I'll need to send over some paperwork so we can get started on the offer, but if anything comes up, please don't hesitate to call me," Shannon said as they exited the house. She handed Blake her business card and then closed the padlock to the front door. "It really was a pleasure meeting you both today."

Sasha and Blake held hands as they walked back toward the Tesla. Sasha could only hope Shannon would notice and take a hint.

Once they were out of earshot, Sasha leaned in and said, "If anything comes up, please don't hesitate to call me," in a high sing-song voice, mocking Shannon.

"Do I detect jealousy?" Blake stuck a finger in her side, making her squirm.

"Jealous? Me?" she laughed. She wasn't jealous. What was there to be jealous about? It wasn't like she actually liked Blake. Sure, he was hot. And his lips tasted great. And he was charming. But that was it.

He opened her door, allowing her to get in first. As soon as he closed it for her, she blushed. It was a delayed reaction. *Shit.* She *was* jealous.

"So?" Blake said once he got in.

What was Sasha supposed to say? She was just now figuring out how she felt, but she didn't want to say this stuff to Blake. How could he be so open about it, so direct?

"I just can't believe she was so obviously ogling you, knowing that you were a married man. I mean, it was pretty ballsy for her to act that way, don't you think?" Sasha sputtered, the words coming out quick.

Blake clenched his jaw and smirked. "That isn't exactly what I meant by 'so.' I was wondering if you unlocked the gate and window. But now that you mention it, Shannon was pretty damn hot. I'm sure her grandkids wouldn't mind if I borrow her for a night. What do you think?"

Sasha's face grew warm. "Grandchildren?"

"Yes. Grandchildren. If you had been walking with us, you'd know she is happily married with twin grandsons. She was friendly because she thought she was about to make a handsome commission, and I'm not talking about me here."

Sasha smacked his arm, completely embarrassed.

"So, did you get the hint and unlock the gate and window or what?"

Hours later, after Sasha and Blake walked barefoot through the warm quartz sand and across the thousands of shell fragments that stretched along the shore of the Atlantic, they found themselves once again in front of Mitch's home.

It was dark now, but the sky was full of stars.

"I can't believe we're about to do this," Sasha said, trying to hide her nerves. The last time she'd broken into a home, she was high, and it had been her own house.

Blake shook his head. "I didn't see any cameras, and there wasn't an alarm system. So we just need to keep an eye out for the neighbors."

Sasha looked around. The street was deserted. No cars in any of the driveways. No lights inside any home. From her viewpoint, they were alone. Anyone who lived around here was either out of town or enjoying the nightlife that Cocoa Beach had to offer. Either way, it worked in their favor.

Silencing her phone, Sasha led the way across the lawn to the fence. She bent down and moved the rock that blocked the gate from latching shut. When she stood back up, she whispered, "Last chance."

Blake pointed his chin forward, as if showing her he approved. He reached out and pushed the gate open, just wide enough for them to squeeze through. Then he took the rock from Sasha's hand and placed it back on the ground to keep the gate from moving in the wind.

Sasha's heart pounded as she inched her way closer to the utility window closest to where they stood. She pushed her weight against it until she heard the pop from the plastic casing and then slid it open, feeling the cool air from inside rush out and hit her in the face. She peeked her head inside to find total darkness and then turned to look at Blake.

He nodded and bent down, threading his fingers together. Sasha placed her hands on his broad shoulders, using them to steady herself, then climbed into his makeshift cradle. The ledge was low enough she probably could have climbed up on her own, but touching Blake, letting him lift her, was an opportunity she wouldn't pass up.

Blake climbed in after her, and together they tiptoed through each room. They opened every drawer they could find. Every closet in the house. It was just as they had seen earlier. Too clean. Too perfect. Staged in every way imaginable.

"It's odd that Mitch just put the house up for sale, but it already looks immaculate. At first, I figured the realtor staged it, but there wasn't time for that. It had to have been like this before," Sasha said as they walked into the master bedroom for the second time that day.

"Did he rent it out?" Blake asked, playing devil's advocate.

"No. Last summer I asked him about it. I was looking for a place that my dad, Margo, and I could all go. Somewhere close but far enough away that we could relax. He said he didn't like strangers in his house."

She opened the master closet and walked inside. "Can you flash your light over here? I want to check out those boxes," Sasha said. It was her last hope. She still wasn't sure what she thought she'd find. More pictures? Letters? An explanation for what was going on? Who all those kids were?

She shuffled through the contents of all four boxes. Nothing. Just an assortment of women's lingerie. She held one up. It was red and strappy and complicated looking.

"I think you have it upside down," Blake said, flashing the light on her.

Sasha flushed. "How would you know?"

"I'm just saying, it looks like these straps go here." He placed the long black straps up to her shoulders. "And that strap, it goes down there." He arched his eyebrows and pulled his hand away, letting it hang down in front of her body.

When his fingertips grazed her shoulder, her heart rate accelerated. She should have been nervous about breaking into Mitch's house. She should have been worried that they'd be caught. Instead, she was anxious. Anxious because of the way Blake was looking at her. She couldn't deny the way her body responded to him, the way it pulsed and throbbed. Maybe it was his physical presence. Or his ability to get her, to understand her emotionally. Maybe it was his eyes. The way he was staring at her in that moment—was he imagining what she might look like under her clothes? Maybe it was everything. They'd been spending so much time together; it was inevitable. Sasha tried to think of anything but Blake, but it was useless. She wanted to feel his lips on hers, and she wanted them now.

Just as she was about to lean in—she was pretty sure he was leaning in too—he flinched. He directed the flashlight beam behind her.

"Holy shit. I can't believe I didn't notice this before."

She furrowed her eyebrows and turned. "What?"

He knocked on the wall. "You hear that?"

She shook her head, feeling slightly disappointed. "What am I supposed to be hearing?"

"The bathroom is over on this side." He knocked on the wall where the woman's clothes hung. "And the hallway is over here." He knocked on the opposite wall. "But back here…" He knocked again.

She sucked in a breath. That did sound different. Harder, not as hollow. She bent forward and knocked on it next. It bent, giving way toward the center.

"Help me move this," Blake said, grabbing on to the stand-alone shelf that ran along the back wall.

With the little room they had, they wiggled it back and forth until they were face to face with a sheet of plywood that was painted white to match the wall.

"Tell me why your boss would have a fake wall in his bedroom closet," Blake breathed, his hands on his hips as he lifted an eyebrow.

Her heart pulsed erratically, hyperaware that they were up there alone and that anything could be behind that wall.

"Blake. What happens if there is something back there that we shouldn't find? Shannon said the movers were coming tomorrow to clear out the house. If there is something back there, something Mitch is hiding, he'll be back before then to clear this out himself. Right?"

CHAPTER THIRTY

Blake

Sasha was probably right. He hadn't thought about what they could find. But if the pictures and letters at the café were any indication, then someone might be by to collect, to wash away anything incriminating. That is, if anything was behind that wall.

"If you want to leave, say the word. I'll put this back, and we'll pretend we were never here."

Sasha pressed her lips together but shook her head. "No. We came all this way. We need to find out what's back there."

Together, they pulled the loose nails that held the oversized plywood firmly in place. With a quick tug, the board fell off with a muffled thud. Blake and Sasha crouched down, both shining their flashlights into the dark hole. At first, Blake couldn't see anything. The cutout was roughly three feet by three feet, and it looked like any other empty opening. But once the light filled the small room and their eyes adjusted, everything came into view.

His breath caught as shadows bounced across shelves. Rows and rows of shelves. Each one with a dozen picture frames. All displaying a mother and child. Bronze plated, black, wood, metal.

Blake was too shocked to say anything, too shocked to move. But once Sasha let out a rugged breath, he snapped his head toward her. She ignored his gaze and climbed through the small opening.

"It goes straight up," she said, lifting the light upward, her ass now in his face. "There've got to be hundreds of pictures in here."

"But why the secret room? What's the purpose?" Blake said, unable to see much now that Sasha took up the majority of the opening. "Those numbers? What do you think they mean? Can you see how many there are?" he asked, noting a small dot in the corner of each frame.

But Sasha remained quiet.

"Did you find something?" he asked, concerned when Sasha still hadn't responded after several seconds.

She turned around and met his gaze finally. Then she stuck her arm out and handed him a frame. He looked at it, at the two people in the picture. And then he looked back at Sasha. Her chest was heaving and her eyes were wide.

"That's you."

He remembered that day. Every fucking detail was ingrained in his memory. That pink dress her mom made her wear for the party. The fit she threw because she didn't like the way it felt when she was playing. He ran his finger across the dusty glass. And there was Mrs. Cohen, his first-grade teacher. The woman Sasha had been referring to as Mom. They stood next to the tree. The same tree Blake had stood under as he closed his eyes and counted. The tree he returned to when no one could find Sasha. The tree he refused to leave when Sasha's real dad picked him up and carried him inside, kicking and screaming.

Sasha cleared her throat, probably not consciously, but it was enough to pull Blake's attention back to her.

She was looking at him. Like something else was on her mind. But he couldn't ask her, because in the next second, a car door slammed somewhere nearby.

His eyes grew wide. "Did you hear that?"

Another door slammed shut.

"Sasha, we need to get out of here. Now."

Sasha didn't respond. Instead, she turned around and ignored him.

"Sasha. We need to get out of here. If they catch us…" His voice trailed off. Fuck. If they were caught, he wasn't sure the cops would be called. Not with what they'd just found. He imagined the consequence would be far worse. His heart rate accelerated. Panic tore through him.

"Okay. I'm ready," Sasha whispered as she crawled out backward, her voice shaking as she spoke. She took the frame from him and clutched at it tightly.

Blake reached for the plywood and quickly leaned it against the opening of the hole once Sasha stood back up.

"The back window. We left it open. We have to get out or they'll know we're here," he said.

Just then, he heard keys rattling in the front door.

Sasha bolted from the closet. "Hurry," she said.

He followed her down the stairs, taking them two at a time. At the bottom, Sasha didn't even look; she just darted across the kitchen floor, leaving Blake alone. If he ran and that door opened, he'd be caught like a deer in headlights. But he had to risk it. They had to escape. He let out a deep breath before changing his mind, and then he ran, praying the door wouldn't open.

The hinges creaked just as Blake slid past the island.

"I finally got the damn padlock open," a man's voice boomed just as Blake made it to the utility room, Sasha on his other side.

"Flip on the lights out here. I can't see anything," a woman's voice demanded.

Blake turned to Sasha. He laced his fingers together again, like he did earlier. She stepped into them and lifted herself onto the window ledge. He winced when her heel banged against the wall. He paused and listened, hoping it hadn't been loud enough to alert the people who'd just entered the house, but they were too busy bickering at the front door to notice.

He held his finger to his lips, then he flicked his hand at her, reminding her to hurry up. She flipped to her stomach and lowered herself out the window and onto the grass below.

It was Blake's turn now. Shit. He was bigger. Bulkier. If he wasn't careful, his feet would bang against the wall too. Quietly, he hoisted himself up, and with his core tight, he managed to rotate inside the windowsill without so much as a peep. He could hear Sasha breathing hard, waiting, wanting to run.

Just then, lights flickered on in the hallway. Fuck. He jumped, not caring if he could be heard or if they'd seen him. They just had to run. He'd call the cops once they…what the hell? Sasha was running toward the back gate, not the front. Not the way they'd come in. He ran after her, chasing her across the yard without looking back to see if they were being watched. If anyone knew they were there. He just kept running.

"What are you doing? They're going to see that window open and know someone was here. We should have run the other way," Blake said once they slipped through the back gate.

They inched their way along the canal behind the fence. Hidden behind bushes and vines.

"No. They won't come looking for us," she said. She showed him the frame she'd taken. "They'll know someone was there anyway. We didn't put the shelf back either. They're going to pack up as fast as they can and run."

"What do you want to do now?" he asked.

She let out a slow breath. "I think it's time to call the police."

CHAPTER THIRTY-ONE

Sasha

The air was dry, and Sasha was suddenly thirsty. Though her hands shook, she held out her phone and dialed 911.

"Nine-one-one, what's your emergency?" a woman's voice asked after the first ring.

Sasha froze. What was she going to say? That *she'd* just broken into someone else's house. That the owner was home and there were pictures of random people in a secret room? Shit. They wouldn't believe her. They'd think she was crazy. She hadn't thought this through.

Blake must have realized the same thing because he remained silent, then he reached his hand out and let his fingers hover over her phone before he clicked End. The voice on the other end disappeared. He pulled her into a tight embrace. One arm stretched across her back while the other smoothed out her hair. Then, as if he knew exactly how much time she needed, he pulled her away and looked into her eyes. "Do you want to call your lawyer first? See what she says?"

Did she? Sasha had hired Pamela Walsh to help her dad, but now she wasn't sure he deserved the help. Everything was happening so fast; she hadn't had time to process those feelings. Getting the lawyer's advice would be a smart move, but it still made her nervous. She'd have to tell Pamela about the pictures. What she speculated about them. And while it was obvious to her, she wondered what Pamela would think. She didn't even know what Blake thought or what was going through his head.

Before she said anything, she looked back at the house. The lights were on upstairs. It was just a matter of time before Mitch would find that his hidden room had been compromised. Before panic set in and they'd be packing up and back on the road. She wondered where he would go. Would he go back to the Bahamas? Would he head for Europe? Or did he have another place to hide?

"Let's walk that way. I don't want to be over here anymore." She pointed away from the house. There wasn't a lot of room between the fence and the drop-off into the canal, and because the vegetation was so plush and hadn't been maintained very well, they walked one behind the other.

"Be careful of the roots," Blake warned, his voice low.

But just as the words left Blake's mouth, Sasha stumbled over some sort of mesh netting. Jagged wire dug into the flesh of her leg, causing a sharp, searing sensation. The pain caught her off guard, and she lost her footing. She threw her hands out in front of her to break her fall and landed on the ground hard, losing her hold on her phone and the picture frame and sending them flying into the air. Her ankle twisted, and she heard a sharp crack. Instantly, pain radiated throughout her lower leg, and heat rushed to her face. A muffled scream escaped her lips.

"Sasha." Blake reached for her, assessing the gravity of what just happened. "Don't move."

She didn't. She couldn't. It was too painful. She could feel the wire still attached to her leg, and nausea rose in her throat.

"We have to call an ambulance," he said, his voice rushed.

"Can't you just pull it out?" she begged, holding back tears.

She waited for his response. But he remained silent. Instead of speaking, he lifted his hands and climbed around her. He pulled out a Leatherman multi-tool—one of those gadgets men carried that had a multitude of functions. "Don't move. Not an inch."

On impulse, she snapped her eyes shut, as if the action would help her remain still. But she suspected it was more out of fear. She knew whatever was coming; she had to hold still, which meant she should close her eyes and hold her breath.

Then, what felt like eons later, Sasha heard the clink of metal and then…sharp stabbing pains shot through her leg again as Blake clipped down on the wire. She bit back the bile that formed in her throat. The pain was excruciating. She laid her head down on the earth below her. Sweat began to drip down her face. She forced herself to breathe again, slow and calculated, as she tried to bear through the agony.

"My girlfriend needs an ambulance. I'm off Merdock Drive. In the back, along the canal. Broken leg and a deep laceration."

Sasha heard Blake talking, saw his lips move as he looked down at her, but she couldn't focus on his words. Her surroundings blurred as she focused on her breathing. Her belly expanded with each inhale, sending air down toward her feet. Then, on each exhale, her diaphragm relaxed. She did this over and over until a hand touched her forehead.

"I'm Callie. What's your name, sweetie?" a soft voice asked.

Opening her eyes, Sasha watched as an older woman kneeled beside her. She had dark brown hair pulled back into a slick bun and a bright smile, still visible in the darkness, that seemed to be swallowing her up.

"Sasha," she panted.

"Looks like you took a bad fall, Sasha. I'm placing all bets on it being broken. And you have a pretty nasty laceration on your thigh. There's still a section of wire in there, but it doesn't look like you lost much blood, so that's good. My friend Porter and I are going to give you something to help with that pain once we get you inside the ambulance. How does that sound?"

Sasha pushed her hands to the ground, ready to lift herself, when Callie stopped her.

"No, no. Stay right here. Porter will be right back with the stretcher. Don't put any weight on that leg, you hear me?"

Sasha closed her eyes again and nodded, resting her head against the hard ground. She continued to listen as Callie talked to her in that soothing voice. "I'm going to clean this up a little though. It might be uncomfortable at first, but the dressing will add some pressure, which might make it feel a little better before the morphine kicks in."

Sasha's eyes popped open. "Morphine?" I can't have morphine."

Just as she said it, her eyes landed on Blake. And right behind him was Porter, carrying a stretcher. Shit. That Porter. How had she not put two and two together? How many Porters were there in the world anyway?

"Oh, are you allergic? We can see what else we have in there."

"No. I can't. I'm not allergic. I'm an addict. I can't take any pain meds." She winced as the pain propelled up her leg.

Callie turned to look at Porter.

Porter stopped in his tracks and looked at Blake.

"Get her some anti-inflammatories. She'll need that," Blake said.

ell

Half an hour later, Porter pushed Sasha through the emergency room doors. He hadn't said a word since they'd left. Not to her. Not to Blake.

"Room four," a small man with an olive complexion and navy-blue scrubs barked from behind a counter in the middle of the room. "My name's Ben. I'll be your nurse," he said, rushing behind them. He took the clipboard from Porter and flipped through the pages. "Looks like they didn't give you any pain medication." His eyes shifted to Porter, but Porter didn't pay him any attention. "We'll get that started right away. You'll be comfortable in no time."

"I don't want anything," Sasha protested.

"You're going to need—"

"I don't *need* anything!"

Blake came around and stood at the side of her bed, grabbing her hand and giving it a gentle squeeze as she remained flat on her back. It was nice and offered her a sense of comfort, but it didn't help with the pain. Nor did it help with the asshole nurse who was still rambling on about the benefits of opioids.

"Honey, you're in a lot of pain. Between the laceration and the possible broken leg, you should've had a morphine drip by now. And you'll probably need surgery, which means anesthesia," Ben added dryly, unamused.

"Don't fucking *honey* me. You aren't listening. I don't want, nor do I need anything. I'm a fucking addict. I've been clean for four years. I am not throwing that away for a little bit of relief."

Tears begged to be released at the thought of surgery. While the pain had been excruciating, it'd been manageable. Surgery was another story. She couldn't be put under. Anesthesia was filled with an assortment of opioids, and she wasn't willing to risk going backward. She'd rather cut off her hand than allow them to inject her with that hell.

Porter cleared his throat. "This hospital has a few nonopioid anesthesia options. Once you talk to the doctor, ask him or her about your choices. But that leg is definitely broken." He looked back at Ben. "Make sure she gets an X-ray of the ankle too."

Ben looked annoyed. He turned around and typed something into his tablet and then placed a tag around Sasha's wrist. "Someone will be by to take you to X-ray in a few minutes. Do you need anything in the meantime?"

Sasha shook her head, gritting her teeth. Sweat continued to pour down her face, and her body shook.

"Can she get some ice and maybe a blanket?" Blake asked as Ben opened the curtain to leave.

Ben paused. "I'll have it ready for when she gets back."

Sasha could have sworn she saw him roll his eyes. "Asshole," she muttered.

Blake squeezed her hand. "Shh."

"Sorry, did I say that out loud?" Her teeth chattered, but she didn't give a shit. She was tired of people like him, people who thought they were better than people like her.

"Okay, you two need to start talking. What the hell is going on here?" Porter asked. His hands were on his hips and a sharp scowl crossed his face. "What are you two doing out here in the first place?"

CHAPTER THIRTY-TWO

Blake

"**G**et me a laptop. I'll show you," Sasha said, sitting up in bed. Her leg was casted from the knee down, propped up on a white hospital pillow. "I don't need my phone. Everything on it saves to the cloud."

It had been hours—too many to count—since they'd arrived at the hospital. Blake was exhausted but relieved they were finally in the recovery room. Sitting on the edge of Sasha's bed, he watched as the police officer excused himself to go in search of a laptop. Blake knew Sasha had dropped her phone in the water when she fell. He'd heard the splash as it echoed in the silence of the night. He even tried to search for it once Porter arrived, but the sky was too dark and the water too deep.

Now, however, it didn't seem to matter that she'd lost her phone.

"Honestly, I don't need it. I can get a new one," she reassured him. Her hand rested on his arm, and he warmed at her touch.

Sasha had managed to break both her right ankle and her fibula when she hit the ground. And the wire that cut through her thigh had awarded her fifteen stitches. Blake wasn't sure how she had managed to handle the pain. How she'd made it through the surgery without morphine. But when it had gotten out that a young redhead was refusing it, word spread fast. She became a celebrity among the nursing staff, a mythical creature that only came out once in a lifetime. Everyone wanted to see her for themselves. Everyone except Ben, which suited Blake just fine. He knew the less they saw of Ben, the better Sasha would feel. And he just wanted Sasha to feel better.

A few moments later, the officer returned with a laptop, followed by Porter, who was two steps behind.

Sasha clicked away while Blake tried to avoid Porter's death stare. He knew Porter had seen Sasha's hand the second he walked through the door. She hadn't pulled it away. Instead, she tightened her grip and squeezed it. She hadn't known there was a need to move it. Porter hadn't told her to stay away from him. It was the other way around. The reference to Casanova made it clear that Porter wanted Blake to keep a distance from her, romantically speaking. And while he wanted to respect Porter's wishes, Blake found it harder and harder to do so as the days wore on. The more time he spent with her, the more he felt like she'd been the air his lungs had been missing.

"The first two rows. Those are the pictures I took inside the room," Sasha said, interrupting his thoughts. She flipped the laptop around on the portable table. A gallery of images filled the screen.

Porter's eyes went wide in disbelief.

Before Sasha had gone into surgery, she'd tried to explain everything to Porter. She told him about the boxes she'd found at Beach Brew. The unidentified pictures. The vague letters. The unexplainable connection between her boss and her dad. But the words had come out harsh, causing Porter to grow impatient and angry.

Typically, Porter worried and obsessed over everything, and he was pessimistic by nature. Maybe it was due to his life experiences. But the one thing Blake knew was that Porter's dad had insisted that the two of them grow up to be good men. That what mattered most in life was a person's character. Porter was compassionate and empathetic. He was thoughtful and unselfish. He faked nothing. Because at the end of the day, Porter was a good person.

But he was also human. And his anxiety mixed with the concern he had for Sasha put him on edge. The fact that the sister he'd missed all these years wanted nothing to do with him probably made it all the worse.

So Blake had stopped Sasha and continued the story for her. He told Porter about breaking into Mitch's house and the hidden room in the closet. He even told him about the picture frames. "I think this Mitch guy is behind Paige's abduction."

He turned and looked at Sasha, worried she wouldn't like being called Paige. But she didn't seem to mind. That, or she hadn't noticed.

"I also think we're looking at the possibility that he abducted more children. Lots of them." The words felt foreign to his lips. He'd been thinking it in his head, but to hear them spoken aloud felt wrong. Like saying it meant he was involved in some way. And now he had an obligation to fix it all.

Before Porter could respond, before Sasha could add more details, two new nurses had whisked her away. First for X-rays and next, for surgery.

That's when the police showed up. Two men dressed in black uniforms. The older man, the one with a head full of chocolate brown hair, did all the talking, while the younger one, who was, ironically, bald, sat back and took notes. "We have some questions, if you'd like to come with us."

"No, actually, I wouldn't," Blake said, unmoving.

"You were with the young lady who was taken into surgery, were you not?"

Blake said nothing.

"Listen. We're responding to a call about someone trespassing on a personal property off Merdock. We know that young lady was delivered here by the paramedics." He looked to Porter, who had been standing against the wall, still in uniform.

"Am I under arrest?" Blake got up from his seat and faced the officer.

"No, but if—"

"It's my constitutional right to remain quiet. And I don't like being threatened." Blake glared at him.

Porter cleared his throat. "The woman who was taken into surgery is Paige Knight. My sister. The one all over the news. I'm sure she'll talk to you once she's out of surgery."

Now, here they all were, before sunrise, stuffed into a small recovery room, looking at the images he'd seen the night before. He felt a dull ache in the center of his stomach as Sasha enlarged each of them, one by one, for everyone to see.

"What is it we're looking at?" the bald police officer asked. He tapped his fingers on the table.

"These women. These women are responsible for taking those children." Sasha pointed at the screen.

"How do you know that? They can very well be their own children. There's no proof to say otherwise."

Sasha turned her head to face Blake. "Do you still have it?"

Blake nodded and walked over to the bag that held Sasha's clothes. He reached in and pulled out the frame she'd dropped earlier. Then he set it on the table.

Both officers looked down at it, questions circling in their eyes.

"That's me." Sasha jabbed at the picture. "And that woman, she's my mom. But according to DNA results, she isn't my biological mother." Sasha's voice was unwavering, but her tone softened and her eyes shifted toward Blake when she continued. "That's the day I was taken."

Blake locked eyes with her. Did she remember? Had the picture jogged a memory?

Sasha slowly peeled her eyes away and then brought them up to Porter. "There were so many pictures. I don't even know how I noticed this one. But the second I saw it, I remembered our birthday party. Or at least I think I remember it. I remembered not wanting to wear that dress. I remembered crying until you gave me something. I don't know what it was. I don't even know if the memory is real or if I'm imagining it."

"Your blanket," Porter let out a whisper. "It was your blanket. Anytime you cried, that damn blanket was the only thing that calmed you down."

Blake rested his hand on Sasha's good leg. She remembered. He wanted to be happy for her. Happy that she was remembering something that linked her to them. Happy that Porter could finally feel a connection. But there was nothing to be happy about. There was nothing but pain and misery in this room.

"This picture. It's a trophy. They are all trophies." Sasha's attention turned back to the officer.

Thirty minutes later, Blake was alone with Sasha. The officers had thanked them for their time and left with their report, promising they'd get in touch with Detective Spencer, the one leading the kidnapping investigation.

Porter had left too. He said something about going home so his wife could get to work on time. But before he left, he'd turned to look at Sasha. "I'm sorry. I'm sorry I wanted you to remember me so bad. Last week, when I heard Blake had found you, all I could think of was getting to you. I just wanted to see you with my own eyes. But now...I can't imagine how confusing it must be. To be told something you can't make sense of."

Sasha opened her mouth, but without speaking, she closed it again and bit her lower lip.

Porter turned to head out the door, but then faced them once more. "Thank you for taking care of her." The statement was directed at Blake. Then he was gone.

It was just the two of them now, lying on the hospital bed, next to one another, scrunched up and exhausted. For the first time in days, Blake relaxed.

"Thank you for calling Margo last night and staying with me," Sasha sighed.

"Staying with you? Did I have any other choice?" Blake laughed. "I mean, if I would have known I had a choice..."

Sasha smirked and then elbowed him.

Blake grabbed his stomach and laughed. "I deserved that." Then, leaning over, he brushed her hair away from her face and kissed the top of her head. She tensed but relaxed again quickly, as if giving in to the rightness of the gesture. He lay his head on hers, nuzzling his nose into her hair. He felt her body sink back into the pillows. Then he slipped his arm around her waist, and before he knew it, he was asleep.

CHAPTER THIRTY-THREE

Sasha

Blake was asleep. It was cute. One second, he was snuggling into her, and the next, his warm breath was brushing against her neck in slow, even intervals. He needed the rest. She could see the exhaustion in his eyes, so she let him sleep.

It wasn't until Sophie, the nurse, came in to check on her hours later that Blake stirred. Lifting his head from her shoulder, he looked handsomely disheveled. His hair crinkled in the front, poofed in the back, and flattened on the side where he'd fallen asleep against her.

"Okay, sweetie, I'll go find those crutches, and then we'll get you on your way," Sophie said as she pulled the IV from her arm.

"How long was I asleep?" Blake asked, slipping his arm out from under her.

"Long enough for all of us to know you need to see an ENT." Sophie grinned. "I'll be back as quickly as I can."

When she was out of sight, Blake whispered, "Was I snoring?"

She smirked. "No, but you were really tired."

"Is that code for 'you were snoring a little'?"

"I have something crazy I want to throw at you," Sasha said as Blake came back from the bathroom. He paused, then he eyed her suspiciously as he ran both hands through his hair, slowly combing it with his fingers. Once he let his hands fall to his sides, several strands of his hair stood right back up.

She laughed. It felt good to laugh. He looked so silly, but so damn hot it didn't even matter. All of his hair could be standing on end and he'd still have that crazy sex appeal she'd seen him wear when he'd first walked into Beach Brew last week.

"I can feel it." He smirked. Then he tugged at his hair until a few more strands lay flat.

"This crazy thing, does it involve eating? Because I'm starving." At that, his stomach growled. "You hear that? Don't get me wrong. I'd sit here all day long with you, but I won't pretend not to be happy we're leaving this place." He laid his hand on her good leg. When his focus landed on her, Sex Eyes was back, his irises swirling with darkness. He sat at the edge of her bed, unmoving. The moment stretched, neither of them saying a word.

Her heart raced, like it wanted to escape her chest. She felt heated with his hand there, with his eyes searching into her soul like he knew her, like he'd known her all along. And then she remembered what he'd said last night. He'd called her his girlfriend when he was on the phone with 911. Or had she imagined that?

"I'm hungry too," she admitted, changing the mood.

"Does that mean we can get food?" He raised an eyebrow.

Sasha laughed. "Yes, we can absolutely grab food."

"Oh, thank God." Blake flopped onto the bed.

"I'm back," Sophie said, carrying two silver crutches beneath her arms. "The doctor wants you to follow up with an orthopedic in two weeks to make sure it's healing correctly." She handed Blake some papers. "Okay, let's get these bad boys adjusted for you, shall we?"

After Sasha hobbled back and forth a few times, grimacing in pain, Sophie helped her back to the bed. "Okay. Mission one complete. You can walk. Mission two…" She paused and turned toward Blake. "There's an Uber waiting out front for you. No one will be there bothering y'all. We told those reporters y'all left after the police left." Sophie looked pleased with herself. "Now, let's get you two out of here."

"Okay, so this crazy thing you wanted to tell me earlier. What does it involve? Because I don't think I can handle another hospital visit. I mean, between rescuing you from a fire at your dad's house and you breaking your leg, I'm pretty exhausted from saving your life," Blake joked.

They were sitting in the back seat of the Uber, on their way back to where Blake had parked the Tesla the night before. Their bodies were close. His leg leaned against hers.

The fact that Blake had said "your dad" wasn't lost on her.

Sasha took a deep breath and ran her sweaty palms together. "Well," she said nervously, "since everyone thinks I'm headed back to St. Petersburg, I was thinking, maybe we should stay here for a little bit. I'm waiting on the lawyer anyway. And Margo is already mad at me for being here in the first place…"

Her voice trailed off. She wanted to see Olive and Porter again. She wanted to meet Olive's husband and their other daughter, Penny. But more importantly, she wanted to see something else. To see if it triggered any other memories. Something she knew Blake wouldn't understand.

She pulled the frame from her bag and pointed at the tree. "I know this sounds crazy, but that tattoo on your arm…when we were at my dad's house last week, going through all those papers, I saw your tattoo. And this picture. That tree. I—" Sasha stopped, unsure of how to say what she was thinking. She felt silly the minute the words left her mouth. Insinuating that his tattoo was the same tree was ridiculous.

She shook her head, ready to apologize for rambling, when Blake slipped his hand into hers. It was soft and smooth, except for the small calluses at the base of his fingers.

"It's a maple." His voice was soft.

She scrunched her nose, confused.

"That tree. It's a maple tree. Like this one." He pulled up his sleeve, exposing the black ink. A long trunk with branches clustered around one another, split near the top. It was divided into two sections, one with red leaves, the other without. Roots cast downward. "It's the same tree. At least, that was the inspiration."

Sasha touched his arm. She traced the ink like she'd done the last time she'd seen it. A part of her doubted it meant anything to her then. Though she'd been drawn to it the same way she was being drawn to it now. This was why she wanted to see it for herself, the real tree, to see if it would bring back a memory like the picture had. Maybe she'd have more. Maybe there were more memories locked up under the maple.

"You don't think I'm being foolish?" Sasha asked, dropping her hand.

"Absolutely not. But do you think you can handle it?"

"What's the worst that can happen? I make everyone hate me even more than they already do and then break my other leg?" She grinned.

"That's not even funny." He squeezed her hand. "Let me text them. Maybe we'll grab some food first and then head over there. They'll be excited."

She snorted. "Doubtful."

"They will, trust me. But I should also call Jay and Marcus to let them know you're all right. Maybe I'll take tomorrow off too."

Sasha was about to open her mouth to protest, to tell Blake she didn't want to intrude on his life any more than she already had. That they could just turn around and head back to St. Pete. Then it hit her. She'd been so wrapped up in her own life, in her own confusion and denial, that she hadn't realized Blake was carrying around his own weight of uncertainty. His own shock. His own pain.

She'd pretended she already knew it, pretended like she understood. But she didn't. He was only a little boy when she disappeared without a trace. He'd carried that around with him his entire life.

She looked up at him, and instead of saying anything, she smiled. It felt like a sad smile. A smile you'd give to someone who'd just lost their pet.

He looked back at her. And in that moment, her heart didn't race, it crushed her.

How could she have forgotten everything? The first five years of her life. Her real mom. A dad she still couldn't put a face to. Porter. While she wanted so desperately to remember something, there was still an overwhelming chunk of her that felt like she was betraying her dad and Margo by just being in this car. And yet, she needed answers.

After a quick bite to eat, Sasha and Blake pulled up to a mustard-color two-story Spanish-style home with a terracotta roof. It sat smack dab in the middle of smaller ranch homes of varying shades of creams, browns, and yellows.

Looking out the window, Sasha almost turned to ask Blake if they were at the right house. This one couldn't be where Porter grew up or where Olive still lived. It was too perfect, too glamorous, and too over-the-top with its manicured landscape. She didn't know what she'd expected, but it sure wasn't this. Olive hadn't struck her as ritz and glitz. Then she realized there wasn't a single tree in the yard. She inched her head forward, trying to look around Blake.

There it was, the maple tree, standing tall, full of red leaves, casting a shadow across half the lawn.

Next door.

"This is my house. Rather, my parents," Blake said, correcting himself. He shut off the engine and opened his door. Sasha's heartbeat quickened. Crap. She'd forgotten he lived next door. She'd been so hyper focused on Olive and what she'd say to her today that she hadn't thought about Blake's family.

Worry set in. What had she been thinking? Was she biting off more than she could chew? Again. Her mind and body wanted answers. They wanted to know everything. Even if the answers were going to hurt. Her heart, however, told her to hold back, to wait. If she had answers, she might crumble and fall.

Then, as if he'd read her thoughts, Blake continued. "Don't worry. My parents aren't home." He gave her a tenuous smile and then relaxed. "Don't move. I'm coming over to help you."

He climbed out of the Tesla and made his way around to her. Opening the passenger side door, he paused. "Okay, how much pain are you in right now? If I helped move your leg, would it hurt?"

Sasha let out an exasperated breath. "Oh my God. Do not touch my leg. I'm at a seven right now, but if you touch it…I can get out by myself. Just grab the crutches for me, will you?"

"Okay, Olive is the only one home right now. She said Ned is at work and will be home in about an hour. Porter and his wife will probably be by any minute with their son. His name is Carter."

"How old is he?" Sasha asked. She swung her leg around the edge of the car and hoisted herself from the seat.

"He'll be five next month."

"What about Penny?"

Blake handed Sasha one crutch at a time. "Olive said she was doing something for school. I don't know what that means or when she'll be home."

She walked along the sidewalk ahead of Blake, carefully placing one foot in front of the other. By the time they reached the driveway next door, the front door was wide open.

A wide-mouthed Olive stood with her hands on her hips. "What in the world happened?"

CHAPTER THIRTY-FOUR

Sasha

The sun warmed Sasha as she sat with her back to a large bay window in Olive's living room. It overlooked a beautiful wooden deck and a backyard full of flowers and bushes and wind chimes. Lots of wind chimes. A small peanut-shaped pool hugged the property line. Beyond that was the Banana River. The same river that Mitch's house overlooked a few miles away.

But Sasha hadn't wanted to stare outside. Instead, she glanced around the room, wanting to look at the interior. To see if it offered any hints about who she was before she had become Sasha. Seeking a connection to this place, to these people. She scanned each wall, where vibrant abstract paintings hung in perfect rows. Sasha didn't know anything about art, but seeing them that way felt like a contradiction to their purpose. Her focus drifted to the coffee table and then the bookshelf in the corner of the room. Aside from books and a few blown glass figurines, there was nothing else. No pictures. Nothing that linked Sasha to this family.

"Here you go." Olive pushed the coffee table closer to Sasha and placed a glass of water on it. Then she hesitantly moved to the other couch. Sasha knew she should have spoken up. She should have told her it was okay to sit there, next to her. But she couldn't seem to find the words. Blake had left her alone with Olive, offering no advice. "I think it'll be good for you to have some one-on-one time with her," he had whispered in her ear before heading out the door to go shower at his parents' house.

While she had agreed, she hadn't anticipated the awkward silence that came with it. She knew she should apologize for what happened the other day, for getting angry and storming out of Blake's condo. And for completely disregarding the Knight family in her very public statement the next day. She opened her mouth, but the words got lost. Instead, she reached for the water and took a gulp.

"Blake mentioned you were homeschooled. Both you and your sister," Olive said, breaking the ice.

She was going for small talk. Taking the easy route. Sasha didn't blame her. Olive was probably just as nervous as she was, too afraid to say something that would scare her away again.

"Yes. I was homeschooled my entire life. But my sister went back to school once my mom passed away."

Olive's forehead creased with concern. "Was it hard? For your sister, I mean. Going into public school after so many years of being homeschooled? I'd imagine that'd be difficult."

Sasha wasn't sure. She hadn't been around for Margo during the first few years after their mother's death.

"I don't know how much Blake told you. Or Porter. But I kind of rebelled during my teen years." She stopped and looked down at her hands. She bit the inside of her cheek.

Sasha was an open book. She didn't lie about her addiction. She didn't hide from the truth. Hell, she didn't even care what others thought about her. However, it had been nice to rarely have to explain her past since she'd moved to St. Pete. If it did come up, it was often to people she knew she'd never see again. But Olive wasn't just a stranger. Not anymore. And while she still wasn't sure what she expected from Olive, she suddenly had a strong desire to be accepted.

"I got addicted to pills," she blurted out. "I wasn't really there for Margo. She had to grow up too quickly. She took care of me instead of the other way around. I wasn't much of a big sister. And now I feel like I'm letting her down again. I should be there for her. Aside from my dad, who is still in the hospital, I'm her only family." Sasha let out a loud exhale.

"I feel selfish for wanting to learn more about you. For wanting to know what happened." Hot tears suddenly streaked down her cheeks. She reached up and tried to brush them away, but they kept coming.

"Oh, honey," Olive cried. She pushed herself off the couch and kneeled in front of Sasha. She stared straight into her eyes. "None of this is going to be easy. Not for anyone. I feel selfish too. I think we all want to be selfish. But you caring so much about your sister, that means your parents raised you right. And for that I am so incredibly grateful. We all rebel in some way. Don't let that define you."

Olive smoothed her hair. "I'd like to meet her. Maybe one day you'd like to bring her over? Maybe we can all rip off the bandage together?" A few tears strayed from her eyes, but she didn't attempt to hide them.

Sasha nodded. She liked that. She liked that Olive was being rational and understanding. Involving Margo hadn't occurred to her. Keeping everything separate felt like protecting Margo in a bubble wrap sort of way.

"Grandma!" a tiny voice yelled from the front, interrupting their cry fest.

Olive beamed. "You are going to love this little boy." She placed her hand on Sasha's good knee, patting it for reassurance, then she stood up.

"In here!" she called out.

"Grandma, look what I made." A small boy with dirty-blond hair ran into the room and jumped into Olive's arms. "It's a dinosaur!" he growled as he showcased his green and blue clay creation for Olive to see.

"That's the scariest dinosaur I've ever seen."

Porter walked in next, still in his uniform. He hugged Olive and gave her a kiss on the cheek. He glanced over at Sasha and smiled. "How are you feeling?"

Sasha was just about to answer when a beautiful pregnant woman rounded the corner.

"You must be Paige. I mean Sasha. I mean crap. I wasn't going to say your name. I'm sorry. I'm so sorry. Let me start over. I'm Tina." She closed her eyes for a brief second, and when she opened them again, she pursed her lips. "Ignore the tears. I swear this kid is going to be a girl. I can't do anything without crying."

Sasha smiled and wiped her cheeks with her hands. "It's okay. But please, call me Sasha." She shifted to stand when Tina cried out. "Oh no! Stay there! Porter told me everything. You poor thing."

Tina rushed over and wrapped her arms around her shoulders. It was a tender hug, soft and full of life, like she had been saving it just for her. Like she was afraid she'd hurt her if she squeezed too hard. Or maybe her baby bump had just gotten in the way.

Either way, the embrace was warm and welcoming, and it made Sasha melt.

When Tina pulled back, Sasha immediately saw the resemblance between her and the little boy. "Wow. You can see where Carter gets his looks from." She looked at Porter. "Sorry, it's not you."

Olive and Tina laughed. Porter shrugged, and then he, too, let out a small chuckle. The atmosphere lightened, and before she knew it, the four of them were talking. Smiling. Having a good time. They meshed so well that it didn't take much effort on anyone's part. It was nothing like she'd expected. And yet, it was everything she'd hoped for.

Before long, Blake appeared in the living room. She'd been laughing when she looked up and saw him standing there. There was a small curve to his lips, and his eyes sparkled. He didn't look away when she met his gaze. Instead, his smile grew, and his eyes swirled with darkness. She liked that look. It made her feel both wanted and appreciated, a combination of desire and contentment. No one had noticed him yet, and it felt like it was just the two of them in the room.

"Uncle Blake!" Carter was the next to see him and went running into his arms. Blake scooped up the smiling boy and rustled his hair, inciting a round of giggles from Carter before he begged Blake to go see his new dinosaur. "It's a T-Rex!"

Sasha watched as Blake interacted with Carter. It was adorable, and not once did Blake turn around to check to see if she was watching.

"That's as real as it's going to get," Tina whispered, leaning into Sasha's ear. "I don't have any brothers or sisters, so it's been comforting to be part of this family, to know Carter has people who love him. I know Blake isn't blood related to Porter and

Penny, but I don't think I've ever been thankful he wasn't until now." She winked.

Sasha bit her lip as a wave of warmth rushed to her cheeks at Tina's implication.

"I've never seen him look at a girl like he looked at you when he walked into the room. Never." Tina patted Sasha's knee and then placed her hands on the cushion. Pushing herself up, she announced, "This baby is hungry. Porter, help me make sandwiches for Carter and me. Olive, grab those pictures."

The room grew silent as they all disappeared into other rooms.

Sasha kept her attention on Blake as he walked over and sank into the seat next to her. Her heartbeat picked up speed as he reached for her hand, looping his fingers between hers.

"I have good news."

CHAPTER THIRTY-FIVE

Blake

Blake let himself into the Knights' house without knocking. He'd been doing it for so long he didn't think twice when he pushed open their door. Taking off his shoes, he inched his way down the hallway but stopped dead in his tracks when he heard a loud snort, followed by a long stream of continuous laughter. His lips curled up in surprise. Laughter was good. It meant they were getting along.

Moving closer, Blake paused at the entrance to the living room. Everyone was looking at Porter, who had his head tilted back in an uncontrollable fit of laughter. Blake couldn't help but wonder what was so funny, but before he could say a word, Sasha caught his eye. Her smile was like a sudden ray of sunlight. She brought her hand up to her mouth, trying to cover it, but there was no use. She was beaming.

"Uncle Blake," Carter yelled, running into his arms.

Just then, Olive, Porter, and Tina turned to him, smiles still pressed to their faces.

"Blake, you missed it. Tina was just telling Sasha the story about how she and Porter met," Olive laughed, wiping the tears from her eyes. "How he thought she was drowning and jumped into the pool at the YMCA to save her. How he pulled her out but lost his shorts in all the commotion."

"In my defense, I did feel a draft, but I thought I'd just torn my trunks," Porter mused.

"Not to mention I was fully awake when you tried breathing life into my lungs," Tina said, trying to keep a straight face. "He was too busy concentrating on my mouth to realize my eyes were wide open, staring at his balls dangling in my face." She lifted her hand in the air as if to grab Porter's imaginary balls.

Sasha snorted again and then giggled at Tina's words.

Blake shook his head and chuckled at the memory. "Your daddy sure knows how to impress the ladies," he said, ruffling Carter's hair.

After playing a round of dinosaurs with Carter, and after everyone excused themselves from the living room, Blake sat next to Sasha. Clasping her hand in his, he watched as her eyes danced and her chest rose with each breath she took. He wished he could keep this moment locked up in a bottle. Keep it for when she needed it again. There would be tough days ahead, but he would sacrifice just about anything to get her through them.

"I have good news."

Sasha raised her eyebrows. "I like good news." Her smile widened, and she tightened her fingers around his.

Blake opened his mouth, ready to speak the words, when a deep voice echoed through the hall.

"Do we have a full house today? Are Carter and Tina here too, or is it just Porter?"

Blake felt Sasha's body tense. Her smile disappeared and was replaced with a look of concern. When her fingers went slack, Blake slipped his hand out from her grip. "It'll be okay. Just breathe."

"You're home early." Olive reappeared just as Ned's giant frame came into view.

"Porter said you needed help with something." He kissed Olive on the cheek.

"Help?" Her face twisted in thought. "Oh, yeah." She turned and stole a glance at Blake before turning back toward her husband. But before she could say another word, Carter came barreling down the hallway.

"Poppa, look what I have!" Carter squealed. "Roooarrr. It's a T-Rex. I made it myself!"

"Oh no, a big, bad T-Rex." No sooner had the words escaped his mouth than his focus shifted to Blake and Sasha. His arms fell to his sides in mid-dinosaur attack mode. His jaw dropped. And then the room went silent.

"Honey. Blake is here with…" Olive began, but stopped mid-sentence. Her eyes shot to Blake, and a plea for help crossed her face.

"Sasha." Blake finished her sentence.

Ned lifted a hand to his face, dragging it down his cheek and across his neck. Uncertainty and disbelief washed over him.

Blake stood and met him at the entrance. He gave Ned a hug, patting him on the back. Up close, he could see the pain etched in the rugged lines of his face. Lines caused by years of worry and stress. It was painfully clear in that moment that neither Olive nor Porter had told him Sasha would be here.

"Oh man, would you look at the time? It's getting late. We need to get Carter home for a bath and bedtime. It was really nice meeting you, Sasha. I hope I'll get to see you again soon. Your sister too," Tina said. She and Porter gave everyone a quick hug, and then they were gone.

"Ned, come have a seat." Olive ignored his silence and walked back to the couch. She dropped a plastic container full of pictures on the table and began pulling them out. "Here. I was never good at organizing all of your baby pictures. But these are from when you and Porter were little."

Blake, still standing next to Ned, nudged him with his elbow and nodded toward the living room. The two of them sat, sinking their weight into the small cream-colored loveseat at the same time.

"Look at this one. You and Porter were inseparable. Always clowning around. Always at full speed while awake and then zonked out the minute your heads hit the pillow." She held a picture of two tiny kids, no older than three. The quality was bad, and their faces were fuzzy, but it was most definitely Porter and Sasha, sharing a pillow, fast asleep on a couch Blake had seen in this house years ago.

"Oh, and this one. This had to have been when we bought the house. Right, Ned? We had a housewarming party and invited everyone we knew."

Ned nodded. "The twins had just turned two." His words were slow and calculated, as if he knew he'd scare Sasha away if he spoke any faster.

Blake could see the moisture building in Ned's eyes, which surprised him. He'd only seen him cry once in the two decades he'd known him. It was after the police had left the night Paige had gone missing. After he carried Blake into their house, kicking and screaming.

"This isn't your fault. Do you hear me? You did absolutely nothing wrong." Tears had streaked his face, keeping pace with Blake's. "We'll find her. She'll be home soon. Everything will be okay."

But things weren't okay. Paige had never been found. Ned built a wall so high that no one could scale it. He became the strength everyone needed to get through each day.

"I know this isn't much, honey. But does any of this jog your memory? You were so little. I know you can't possibly remember things like this." She held up another picture. This one included Blake. He, Sasha, and Porter were on the swing set.

"I remember that swing set. Didn't you tear it down in order to install the pool?" Blake asked, surprised at his own memory.

Olive smiled at him. "Yes. Of course you'd remember that. You were devastated when we took it down."

Sasha sighed. "I'm sorry. None of these things look familiar. I know you can't understand, but it's almost as if I'm looking at someone else's life. These don't feel like me." She flipped through the pictures. A smile crossed her face every so often, but it slipped away as she reached in for another stack.

She was almost to the bottom of the box when her demeanor changed. She stiffened, and her eyebrows crinkled. For a moment, Blake thought maybe Sasha remembered something. She held a picture in one hand and looked at the one behind it. That's when Blake saw it happen. Her eyes widened and her mouth dropped. She took the two photos and held them out in front of her.

"How do you know him?"

Olive tried to look first, but Sasha wasn't facing them toward her. She was holding them so Ned could see. While Ned was squinting to get a better view, Blake took a double take. It couldn't be. Could it? They were old, and like the other pictures, the quality was poor, but from where he sat, it looked to be the one person he least expected to see. His eyes shot to Sasha, who was seething.

"Oh, I can't remember his name. Maybe Michael? He was our realtor. Sold us the house. Do you remember his name, Olive?" He scratched his head, as if he were really struggling to recall the guy's name.

"His name was Mitchell. He was such a sweetheart. Got the sellers to pay closing costs. Connected us with a bunch of people when we wanted to do renovations. Don't you remember at our housewarming, his wife was so drunk, she kept saying, 'Call him Rich Mitch'?" Olive wasn't looking at anyone when she said this, not until she snorted. She covered her mouth, trying not to laugh when she caught Blake's expression first. "What? Do you know him?"

Blake watched as Sasha struggled with her words. "That's the guy whose house we were just at. He's the one with all the pictures," Blake said for her.

The pictures fell to the floor. In one, Mitch was standing next to Ned, his arm around his shoulders. In the other, Mitch and some woman stood next to Paige and Porter. It was probably Mitch's wife, but he couldn't be sure.

Ned stood up. "This guy? There's got to be a mistake. You were only two in this picture. We never saw that guy after the party. You went missing almost three years later." He paced the living room, rubbing the back of his neck. "I thought you said that woman was involved. The one you worked with." His words were directed at Olive.

Olive didn't respond. The color drained from her face.

How did Mitch seem to be everywhere? He knew the Knights. He knew Sasha's mom and her dad. There were so many pictures in that hidden room. How many other people had Mitch known? How many kids were taken because he'd interacted with their parents?

Time seemed to stand still, and everyone but Ned—who was still pacing—froze in shock.

"What do we do? What did the police say about the pictures when you told them? Are they trying to find this guy? We can't just sit here and do nothing." Ned shot off question after question, his feet continuing their path back and forth across the room.

"This guy." Sasha took in a deep breath before continuing. "He's also my boss."

Ned's feet stopped moving. Both he and Olive turned to face her.

"I work at a café. I planned to buy it from him. But all of this happened. I don't know what to make of any of it. And none of these pictures help."

Blake finally got up and lifted the pictures off the floor. "We need to call the detective back."

Olive adjusted in her seat, and then she cleared her throat. "Ned. Oh my God. This is all my fault. It's all my fault." Her face was white, and a tear trickled down her face.

CHAPTER THIRTY-SIX

Sasha

Nothing surprised Sasha anymore. How could it when everything new was compared to finding out she was abducted as a five-year-old? To not knowing who her own mom and dad were. So when Olive told them that she'd been friends with Mitch's wife, Sasha hadn't flinched.

"Her name was Joanne. We lost touch after you went missing. I lost touch with a lot of people back then. It's just, well, that's how it was. No one could understand what we were going through." Her eyes shifted to Ned. She gave a half smile. "Joanne was at the birthday party when you disappeared. Mitch wasn't. Only Joanne. She stayed after the police arrived. She talked to them. She even helped me create the list of people who had come to the party."

Olive's hands trembled, but she continued. "I introduced them. Sharon said she was on her way to Tampa. She'd already said goodbye. But I asked her to stay longer. Convinced her to have a drink with me. That's when Joanne came by. She sat down, and things got weird. It felt like they already knew each other, but neither of them said anything. And I didn't ask. I was too busy making sure everyone was having a good time."

The air grew heavy around them. Sasha tried to imagine how the night had unfolded. Where Olive might have sat with her mom and Joanne. Had she gone willingly with Sharon when she left? Had Joanne been a part of it? Who took the picture of them by the tree?

Blake reached into his pocket and pulled out his phone. "I was going to save the good news for later, but I'm not entirely sure this is good news anymore," he sighed. "Your lawyer called while I was at my house. She arranged for you to meet with her and your dad at the county jail tomorrow. He'll be discharged from the hospital and then transported first thing in the morning. She hired a private investigator, and from his findings, she was hopeful he'd be released based on lack of evidence."

"Lack of evidence?" Ned scoffed. "She's been living with him this entire time." He stood up and walked out of the room.

"Call the police. They need to see these pictures." Olive laid a hand on Sasha's. "We'll find the truth in all of this. Ned is…" she sighed. "Ned took it pretty hard. You were his little girl. We know you love this man…your dad. We can see he's taken good care of you. And I think that makes it that much harder. We know we can't compete with a stranger's love. Someone who's loved you from your first memory. We won't do that to you. We won't compete. But we do want to love you, if you'll give us a chance. Ned will come around." She stood up. When she pulled her hand away, Sasha quickly grabbed it back.

Olive turned in surprise.

"Thank you," Sasha said.

Olive bent over and took her face in her hands. "Oh, baby girl, we'll go to the ends of this earth for you. Whatever happens with your dad, we'll be right here, supporting you."

Sasha wished she could say that being at their house brought back a flood of memories from her childhood. But she couldn't even visualize herself in the pictures Olive had shown her. Sure, they looked like her, but ever since she'd found out the real Sasha had died, she had seen herself as a fraud. Or maybe it was Paige who'd been a fraud. She couldn't be sure, and reconciling the two made it impossible to believe anything was real.

Even the maple tree had turned out to be a dead end.

"It's useless. I don't remember a damn thing." Disappointment laced her voice as she slumped down against the dry brown bark of the tree's trunk.

"Don't be too hard on yourself. Trauma can be tricky when it comes to how we store memories." Blake leaned against her.

"If you and I experienced the same thing, why is it that I don't remember anything, but you remember so much?"

Blake sighed. "For one, our trauma wasn't the same. You were the one taken. I only saw the aftermath. And I'll be honest, sometimes I'm not entirely sure I'm remembering everything the way it happened. I have intense fragmented visions, but they feel more like snapshots. Kind of like when someone draws a cartoon and flips the pages really fast. I see some things moving from picture to picture, but not everything catches my eye all at once."

"You speak like you know what you're talking about."

Blake cleared his throat. "Therapy. Lots of therapy."

By the time they pulled up to her condo later that night, Sasha could barely keep her eyes open. She couldn't wait to crawl into her own bed. To snuggle up beneath her sheets and fall fast asleep against Blake's bare chest. Just as she was daydreaming of sleep, Blake was at her side, rousing her from her thoughts.

"Here, grab my arm." He leaned in to pull her out of her seat.

He smelled so good, like cedarwood and citrus. It hovered between them, and she wanted more. She was positive she didn't smell nearly as good. Strike that; she knew it to be true. She hadn't showered in two days. She groaned.

"You okay?" Blake asked, worry forced from his throat.

She nodded, trying to hold down a smile. There was something so endearing about him, so sweet and straightforward. It made everything he said sound so passionate.

They made their way into the elevator and down the hall to her condo. Sasha was about to dig for her keys when the door swung open.

Margo stood in the entrance. Her lips were in a tight line but curled at the edges the second she saw her casted from the knee down. "Why do you always have to be so dramatic when we fight?" She laughed, but a few tears escaped her eyes. The two of them were a sight: one sister in a cast and the other in a boot.

"Margo Marie. Are you crying?" Sasha asked.

"No. I do not cry. Especially when I'm still mad at you." She turned around and walked back inside. Sasha and Blake followed behind.

"Oh, hey," Drew said, lifting himself off the couch. "I just came up to drop Margo off. My mom made you some food. I stuck it in the fridge."

"Thank you for hanging out with Margo these last few days. I really appreciate it. And tell your mom thank you."

Drew nodded. "Oh, I almost forgot. Margo said you lost your phone. If you want, you can have this. It's my old phone. You can activate it so you have something until you get a new one."

"Thank you, Drew. What would I do without you and your family?" Sasha let out a deep breath as relief washed over her. She hadn't even thought about a phone until now.

"I should get going. I have work in the morning," Drew said.

"I'll walk you down," Margo replied.

When the two of them were gone, Sasha hobbled to her room and sank onto her bed. The crutches fell to the floor.

"I should get going too. I also work in the morning," Blake murmured.

Sasha frowned. "I was hoping you'd stay." She rotated to her side.

A second later, Blake sank onto the bed, his focus intent on her. He brushed her hair from her face, his fingertips rubbing against the skin behind her ear. "I'd like nothing more than to stay here with you tonight. But if I do, I won't be able to keep my hands off you."

His words caught her off guard. His soft voice, mixed with blunt honesty, pulsed through her body. No one had ever been so direct with her. How was she supposed to respond? *Yes, please?* It sounded fine in her head, but if those words actually came out of her mouth, she'd probably embarrass herself.

"Plus, you need sleep. Real sleep, not in a hospital bed or in my car. When Margo gets back, I'll help her set up the phone so you can text me if you need me. And remember, you're meeting your lawyer at noon tomorrow." He leaned in and kissed her on her forehead and then pulled back her blankets. "Now get under these covers."

His voice turned demanding. She couldn't help but crack a smile.

When he was gone, she couldn't stop thinking about his words. The way he made her feel. He was charming, compassionate, and sexy, all wrapped up in one gorgeous package.

Then a thought crossed her mind. What if he was having some sort of survivor's guilt? Maybe none of this was actually about her.

He could be so blinded by the fact that he'd been the one to find her that day at the café that this could all be infatuation. She didn't want that to be the case. Blake was the first person she'd felt attracted to since Greg. And Greg didn't hold a candle to Blake.

Somewhere in the dark, Sasha heard Margo return. She heard Margo's voice coupled with Blake's soft whispers but couldn't make out what they were saying, but it didn't matter. She was too consumed with sleep.

The next morning, Sasha rolled over to find an iPhone on her nightstand. Next to it, a glass of water, a white pill, and a letter. She inched her way into a sitting position, pulling the heavy weight of the cast with her as she moved. With one hand extended, she reached for the letter and flipped it open.

Sasha,

Take the ibuprofen when you wake up. Drink the entire glass of water. Text me afterward so I know you're awake. I programmed my number.

Blake.

A smile formed at the edge of her lips. Leave it to Blake to think about everything. She grabbed the pill with one hand and the water with the other. When she was done swallowing the ibuprofen, she took the phone and found not only Blake's number, but Olive, Ned, Porter, and Tina were stored in there as well. So were Margo and Drew. She shook her head and laughed. Instead of texting Blake right away, Sasha pulled herself out of bed and made her way into the kitchen, making sure not to wake Margo, who was sound asleep on the couch.

On the counter lay the picture frame that held the photo of her and her mom. The one she'd taken from Mitch's house. She wondered if Blake had talked to Margo about it. What details had he shared and what had he left out? She ran a finger over the glass. Shame caught in her throat. She missed her mom. Margo missed her too. Sasha wanted to protect her sister from all of it. She knew that if her dad had been involved in any of this, she might not be able to shield Margo from the truth of it. Sasha could very well be the only family Margo had left.

Sasha was deep in thought when the phone buzzed on the kitchen counter. Blake's name appeared on the screen.

Blake: *Are you awake yet?*

Sasha: *Yes.*

Blake: *You didn't text me?*

Sasha: *You didn't give me a chance. I'm texting you now.*

Blake: *Did you take the ibuprofen?*

Sasha: *Yes. Don't you have work today?*

Blake: *I'm already here. I stopped at Beach Brew. Rebecca was there. She said Greg came by a few times looking for you. I told her if he came by again, she should call the cops. I hope that's okay.*

Crap. The café and Rebecca. Beach Brew was Sasha's second home. She thrived off the stability it offered. What was she going to do? She couldn't buy it now. And where was Mitch? Had the police found him? She didn't know what to make of any of it. Greg, however, was the least of her worries.

Sasha changed the subject.

Sasha: *Did you tell Margo everything that happened? Does she know about our dad's possible involvement?*

Blake: *No. She asked a lot of questions though. She's worried about you, but I think she's mostly scared.*

Sasha exhaled. A piece of her was relieved Margo didn't know yet. Another piece felt disappointed. If Blake *had* told her, she wouldn't have to be the one giving Margo the bad news.

Blake: *You should tell her. Talk to her today. Bring her with you to see your dad. You need each other.*

Just then, Margo cleared her throat. She sat up and pulled the blanket tightly around her shoulders.

"How long have you been awake?" Sasha asked.

"Long enough to see you texting Blake."

Sasha felt the hurt in her sister's words. And that's when it hit her. Margo wasn't just scared about their dad being in prison. She was scared she was losing her. To Blake. To the Knights.

"Can I sit with you?" Sasha asked as she made her way to the couch.

CHAPTER THIRTY-SEVEN

Sasha

Pamela Walsh walked into the county jail like she owned the place. Dressed from head to toe in black, she looked like she was on her way to a funeral. But her facial expression wasn't mournful. Instead, it was stern. Her lips were tight, and her eyes were pitched. Like she was ready to pounce on anyone who got in her way. She was a woman on a mission. Sasha felt envious.

"I'm here to see my client, Dan Patterson," she demanded, dropping her briefcase on the counter for added emphasis.

The man behind the counter looked up for a second, not bothering to make eye contact. "Sign the log." He pressed a button and spoke flatly into the round speaker next to him. "Patterson's lawyer is here."

Moments later, the three of them were escorted into a tiny square room.

Finally, after they'd waited what felt like an eternity, watching the second hand tick by, the door opened, startling Sasha from her thoughts. Her dad entered the room, flanked by two officers, and was dressed in an oversized orange jumpsuit. His hands were cuffed to one another in front of him.

"Oh my God. What happened to you two?" her dad said, immediately noticing the cast on Sasha's leg and the boot on Margo's.

"Daddy," Margo cried out. She tried to hug him, but one of the officers stopped her before she made it around the table.

"No physical contact." He pointed at the seat.

Her dad sat first.

"Mr. Patterson, I'm Pamela Walsh. I was hired by your daughter," Pamela looked at Sasha before she continued, "to represent you. You've been charged as an accomplice in the abduction of Paige Knight. We don't have much time to talk, so let's get the obvious out of the way. Anything you say to me is confidential. I work for you. Our goals are the same. Therefore, it's critical that you tell me everything. Anything you can think of from the moment you met Sharon Cohen."

Sasha watched as her dad brought his hands to his eyes. He wiped the tears that sat at the corners. She tried to read his mind, to understand what was going through his head. Would he lie to them? Or was he finally going to expose the truth? Her heart raced in anticipation.

"When did you meet Mom?" Sasha finally asked, starting the conversation.

He shook his head, burying it in his hands. "You don't understand. You were so little. Times were so different."

"When did you meet her?" she repeated herself. Then she slid her hand over Margo's as they waited for him to respond.

He lifted his head. Sad, swollen eyes stared back at her. "You were five. I already told the police everything. I should have told you, Sasha. But you *are* my daughter. I've always loved you like my own. Your mom didn't want you to know. I wanted to respect her wishes."

"Mr. Patterson, I am fully aware that you've spoken to the police. But I want to hear this for myself." Pamela flipped open a notebook and clicked her pen. "Please tell me more about the friend who introduced you to Sharon."

Her dad let out a sigh and continued. "Zeke. He was from Tampa, like I was. Got out of the Marines before I did, and we reconnected when I moved back there. I met up with him for a few drinks one night. His wife was there, and so was Sharon. I'm pretty sure I fell in love with her the moment I saw her. We connected right away. She was a teacher, and I'd just been hired on at the high school for the upcoming school year."

He paused and looked Sasha in the eye.

"I met you a few weeks later. Your mom was still new to Tampa, and the only sitter she had was the teenage girl who lived in the apartment above her. She asked me to come over one night. Said if I wanted to see her, I had to be okay with meeting you."

Sasha's heart pulsed erratically, and her chest tightened. She couldn't believe what she was hearing. Was any of this the truth? Sasha considered interrupting him but decided against it. She would let her dad finish his story. Then she'd ask her own questions.

"Honestly, I kind of freaked out. I'd never dated anyone with kids. I had no idea what to do. But I knew I'd already fallen head over heels for your mom. There was no turning back. I brought pizza. What kid doesn't love pizza?" He dipped his head and rubbed his eyes.

"When I got to her apartment, your mom didn't answer the door. I heard you crying from somewhere inside, so I knocked again. I waited awhile, even called out to her, thinking maybe she couldn't hear me. But your cries grew louder. I took a risk and checked the door handle. Thankfully, it was unlocked." He paused to lick his lips, as if struggling to get the last of the words out. "Your mom had overdosed. It was the first time I'd seen it."

Sasha clenched a fist in her lap. She wanted to yell and scream and tell him how screwed up this all was. But she couldn't. Not because she didn't believe him, but because she did.

Visions exploded in front of her. She was suddenly transported back in time. Her dad was wearing a pair of brown pants and a blue shirt. There was an alligator head above the left breast with some kind of orange circle around it. She focused on the alligator when he talked. "Your mom will be okay honey, I'm here."

"Mr. Patterson. When Sharon overdosed, what did you do? Why didn't the department of child and family services send a social worker for Sasha?" Pamela asked, looking up from the legal pad she'd been scribbling on.

"After the cops came, they asked me about you," he said. "I'd already called Zeke. Asked him if Sharon had any family close by. He panicked. He said she didn't have any family left. It was just her. His wife got on the phone. She begged me to hold on to you until they got back. They'd just left on a cruise, and they didn't trust the system to keep you safe. So I told the police you were mine. They didn't question it. And why would they? You wouldn't let me go. You clung to me like a spider monkey."

"Mr. Patterson, you are aware that Sasha is not actually Sharon's daughter, correct? They provided you with the DNA results when they arrested you, I hope."

He nodded. "I'm so sorry. I keep replaying that night in my head. If I hadn't opened that door, Sharon would have died. Sasha, I don't know what would have happened to you. Grandma Mary even said I made the right choice. You would have gone into foster care. That you might not be reunited with your mom and all because of a mental health issue. I agreed with her. But now? What would have happened if I told them the truth? Would they have realized you were someone else? That poor family. I can't even imagine…" His voice broke off.

"This friend of yours. You said his name was Zeke? What was his last name?"

Her dad scratched his head and let out another slow breath. "Zeke *was* his last name."

"What was his first name then? We'll have to corroborate his story. Do you have a phone number for him?"

"Oh no. I haven't seen him in years. His first name is Mitchell. Last I heard, he moved to the east coast. I think the Cocoa Beach area."

Sasha's head snapped in Pamela's direction.

Pamela tilted her head and narrowed her eyes. "Mr. Patterson. I'm going to stop you for a moment and give you time to think about this. Did you say his first name was Mitchell? As in Mitch?"

"Drew and his dad are out of town on a golf trip this weekend, so I'm going to stay at his place with his mom and aunt. Is that okay?" Margo asked as she pulled up to Beach Brew.

Sasha turned to look at her before she unbuckled. "That's fine. But make sure you have your phone on standby."

They both smiled, but Sasha saw the sorrow in Margo's eyes.

"He's still my dad, regardless of biology. We're still sisters. This doesn't change anything."

"You have another family. It changes everything," Margo whispered.

Sasha wanted to tell her she was wrong. That nothing would change. But that was a lie. She leaned in and gave her sister a quick kiss on the cheek. "We'll get through this. I promise you." Then she lifted herself out of the car, leaning her weight against her crutches. "Be safe. I love you."

Sasha pushed open the door to a very quiet Beach Brew.

Rebecca stood behind the counter, a broom in hand. She turned at the sound of the bell, and her eyebrows immediately shot up. "Sasha."

"The one and only."

"Oh my God, you had me so worried. I can't remember the last time you took a day off, and now…I understand. But I was still worried." Rebecca leaned the broom against the wall and rushed over. She embraced her in a deep hug. She was so close Sasha could smell the fragrance of coconut shampoo in her hair.

"Here, sit down." Rebecca pulled back and grabbed a chair from a nearby table. "What happened?"

Sasha wanted to tell Rebecca everything, but what was she supposed to say? "I broke into someone's house the other night. And not just anyone's house, but our boss's house"? Where does one even start a conversation like that?

Before she could respond, Sasha's phone rang, and Pamela's name flashed across her screen.

"Sorry, I have to grab this." She motioned to her phone. "Hello?"

"Sasha. Good news. Mitchell Zeke and his wife are in custody. It's already all over the news. Looks like the Coast Guard found them out at sea," she said dryly.

"That's great. I think." Sasha exhaled. But was it? She wanted answers, though she wasn't sure she was ready for them. Things were moving too fast, and she was too exhausted to keep up. She ended the call and dropped her head into her hands.

"What can I do to help?" Rebecca asked.

Sasha pinched the bridge of her nose before swallowing hard. She shifted in her seat. This wasn't going to come out right, but she had to start somewhere. "You're already doing so much. But I need to be honest with you about something. You might want to start looking for a new job."

And there it was. Shock crept up Rebecca's face.

"What? Why?"

"Mitch is in custody. They're going to freeze his assets. I'll do payroll now, but I can't guarantee anything after today."

Rebecca scrunched her nose. "Mitch? Why? What happened?"

Sasha gave Rebecca an abbreviated rundown of what she knew.

When she finished, Rebecca still looked confused. "You aren't going to buy him out of the café?"

It was Sasha's turn to scrunch her nose. "I don't know how I'll be able to after all this." Sasha wasn't even sure she wanted to anymore. The idea of buying something that was linked to Mitch made her physically ill.

They sat in silence for a few moments before Rebecca pushed the chair out and stood up. "I've got to use the bathroom, but don't leave yet. I still want to hear all the juicy details about Blake. Want me to lock up early?"

Sasha shook her head. "No. I'll do it. I need a minute to stretch anyway."

After Rebecca walked away, Sasha stood and took in the familiar setting she'd loved so much. Until now. Now her memories of this place were tainted. She shouldn't be wasting valuable time gossiping about boys. She should finish payroll so Rebecca and Dominic could get paid.

She should also make a to-do list. She needed to call the insurance company so they could get work started on her dad's house. That needed to be a priority, even if it was still part of an active investigation site. She shuddered at the thought. On second thought, gossiping about Blake sounded like a great plan.

The bell above the café door chimed. Sasha turned to let the customer know they were closed, but the words never left her mouth.

Greg stood at the entrance. He didn't hover there long, because in the next second, he was standing over her, his hand gripping tightly over her mouth. "Shh. This will be so much easier if you're quiet," he whispered into her ear.

Sasha shook her head. What was he doing? Greg didn't hurt people. If this was about the pills, she'd clear it up. She'd pay him. "Greg," she tried to say through his hands, but he clamped down harder. It was difficult to breathe. Her heart raced and her chest tightened.

Greg gripped her at the waist and moved behind her. He pulled her head up, and a full view of the front entrance came into focus. Standing there, dressed in black jeans and a grey flannel shirt, was Rickie. Even at a distance, she could see that his eyes were dark and full of rage. His lips, razor thin. He moved slowly toward her. One foot in front of the other.

"You've been avoiding me, Sasha," he said, dragging his gloved finger across her cheek. "Nobody gets away with taking my inventory and not paying." His eyes fell to her cast. "Greg. You didn't tell me she was hurt. You sure she didn't keep any of those pills for herself?" He spoke to Greg, but his words were meant for her.

Greg didn't respond. Instead, his hand slipped from her face momentarily. His palm was damp with sweat. He was nervous. *Shit.* Greg never got nervous. If Rickie was such a big deal now, then this wasn't about getting his money back. This was more.

Suddenly it all became clear. Sasha was face to face with a man who wanted to make a statement.

Rickie reached into his sweater pocket and pulled out a small white bottle. He flipped the lid and poured several white pills into his hand. "I love Russian roulette; did you know that, Sasha?"

Not waiting for a response, he continued. "It's all about the gamble. Not with a revolver though. My choice of weapon is pills. See these? There's a combination of opioids here. Pills that might take away some of that pain." He touched her thigh, pressing down until she felt the stitches tear from her skin. Sharp pain shot through her leg, and she muffled a scream behind Greg's hand.

He chuckled and then continued. "Some of these might help you sleep good tonight. So good you just might not wake up."

Sasha wanted to fight back, but they had her at a disadvantage. She wouldn't get anywhere with her leg this way. And Rebecca. *Shit.* Rebecca was in the bathroom. She didn't want to endanger her life. This was Sasha's fault. She didn't want to die, but she didn't want Rebecca getting caught in the crossfire.

Rickie was going to play Russian roulette with her life. He was going to try and make this look like an overdose.

With Greg's hand still covering her mouth, she tried to acknowledge the task at hand. A muffled "okay" poured from her lips as she nodded in agreement.

Rickie counted the pills aloud. "Lucky number thirteen."

Greg released his hold while Rickie slammed the pills into her mouth. He held his hand there, waiting for her to swallow them.

Then, without warning, Rickie pulled out a gun. "Fucking idiot," he said, and then he pulled the trigger.

CHAPTER THIRTY-EIGHT

Blake

"I had it washed and waxed," Blake said, dropping the keys in front of Marcus. "Thanks again."

"No problem. How's Sasha feeling?" Marcus asked.

Blake had called him the other night, while Sasha was in surgery. When he explained that he needed the Tesla a bit longer, he planned to leave it at that, but Marcus, whose curiosity had always surpassed that of anyone Blake knew, started asking questions. While Blake didn't make it a habit to share pieces of his life with others, it felt surprisingly cathartic to have a conversation with someone other than Porter and his family. Someone outside the circle of people who'd known him his whole life.

"She's okay. I plan to meet her after work." Blake tossed his bag into his locker.

"Remind her about Rebecca for me. Maybe we can double sometime." He smiled.

Blake laughed but promised to bring it up to Sasha. He didn't know Marcus very well, but in the short amount of time he'd spent with him, he knew he was a stand-up guy.

Over the next several hours, the fire station kept him busy. Call after call came in, sending him in all directions. It wouldn't have been so bad, but Jay had been with him on every call, which made for a long day.

Jay was a great leader. Demanding and focused, yet self-aware and empathetic. He'd been one of the reasons Blake took the position at the station in the first place. When they'd first met, they clicked, which was important to firefighters, who had to trust one another with their lives.

Today, however, Jay only barked orders. There was no compassion in his voice, no teamwork. His demeanor was one of a dictator, and Blake was painfully aware of the reason.

Blake tried to imagine what it would be like to lose a brother to drugs, creating images in his head of the people he'd seen. In his line of work, he'd seen those who were just dipping their feet into a new experience, as well as full-out junkies.

In his mind, he imagined Jay's younger brother starting off with one pill. Maybe two. Those probably turned into handfuls, until he was no longer recognizable. And Jay blamed Sasha. It was difficult to place Sasha in that role, but Blake hadn't known her back then. It was possible she had been a dealer. Though he found it unlikely with her story about Greg.

Then Blake dug deeper. Why had Jay's brother wanted the pills in the first place? And what about Sasha? Was it fair to blame someone else when it came down to drugs? This was what he didn't want to get into with Jay while they were driving back to the station. He wasn't experienced enough to have an opinion, and he hadn't wanted to make things worse. Maybe he'd talk to Sasha about it later. Maybe she could shed some light on it so he could talk to Jay about it too.

Just as the fire truck pulled into the station, red lights flooded the garage. An ambulance pulled out first, followed by another fire truck. Marcus ran out, waving his arms. "There was a shooting. At Beach Brew."

Blake wasn't sure he'd heard him right. He narrowed his eyes and then glanced at Jay, trying to process the information.

"Let's move. Quick," Jay said without hesitation. "You coming with us or not?" he asked Marcus.

By the time their truck pulled up to Beach Brew, there were cops everywhere.

Blake's chest tightened. His heartbeat quickened. A wave of heat washed over him, and his vision went blurry at the sight of two officers marking off the perimeter with yellow tape. That tape could only mean one thing…

"Blake." Jay shoved him. "Let's go!"

He turned his head, unable to process the words. He'd witnessed a lot of tragedy. He'd seen people get hurt. Some so bad it scared him. But nothing came close to how he felt now. He couldn't go in there. He couldn't see who'd been shot. That person hadn't made it.

Sasha had texted him earlier, telling him she was on her way there. That she had payroll to take care of. It was just her and Rebecca in there. The pulsing in his chest echoed in his head. "No. No. This can't be happening," he muttered. Sweat formed at his temples.

Out of the corner of his eye, Blake saw movement near the front entrance, and he held his breath. It was Rebecca. Marcus was running to her. She saw him and clasped one hand over her mouth. Then she buried her face in his chest.

"Blake," Jay called again.

Taking a deep breath, Blake climbed out of the truck, but the dread weighed him down.

In front of him, a cop pulled out his radio. "Two gunshot victims."

Two paramedics with a stretcher rushed past them.

The noises grew louder as he stepped into the café.

Jay yelled and ran toward the paramedics with the stretcher. A guy, a man Blake had never seen, was being lifted onto it, crying in pain.

A crowd of officers were gathered near the tables, drawing Blake's attention but also severing his line of sight. Looking down, he saw blood staining the hardwood floors. He brought his hands up to his mouth. No. No. It can't be her. It can't be. He fell to his knees, tears escaping his eyes. He'd just found her. This couldn't be happening. He wanted so desperately to hold her. To tell her he was sorry for not finding her sooner.

A tall man in a police uniform stood over him. "You okay, son?" He laid a hand on his shoulder, offering comfort.

Blake tried to respond, but his voice came out muted. The tightening in his chest overpowered everything else.

"Did you know the victim?" he asked, waving his hand in the direction of other officers.

"We need an IV over here," someone yelled from behind the crowd.

He glanced up as the words hit his ears. The crowd shifted just then, exposing a gap between an officer and a paramedic. Both bent at the waist. Both talking to someone. His breathing slowed as he adjusted his focus, trying to make sense of what he was seeing. In an instant, Blake pushed to his feet and through the uniforms, ignoring the friendly officer and the voices around him. There, sitting hunched over on the floor, sat Sasha.

He threw both hands over his mouth. Tears still slid down the edges of his cheeks. "Sasha!" he cried, fighting his way to her.

The paramedic looked up at him and then glanced at his uniform. She was rubbing small circles across Sasha's back. "Do you know her?"

He nodded. "Yes. Yes, what happened?" The words danced in front of him when he realized what Sasha was doing.

"I need you to tell her to stop. We can give her activated charcoal, but she needs to stop first."

He looked down at Sasha. A small brown wastebasket sat at her feet. She had a hand balled into a tight fist and one finger down her throat. She was dry heaving.

"Activated charcoal. Why?" Blake asked, confused. He knew what it was used for, but why did Sasha need it?

The paramedic gave him a sideways glance. "They drugged her. Russian roulette style. Not sure with what. She said there were thirteen pills. Probably opioids. We can't rule out fentanyl if they were trying to kill her."

Blake suddenly felt dizzy. "She's an addict. She doesn't want the pills to get into her bloodstream."

"Get her to stop," she said sternly.

Blake bent down just as another paramedic rushed in, carrying a bag of saline and a cup of activated charcoal. "Sasha. Sasha. I need you to look at me. These people are going to take good care of you." He placed a finger on her cheek. Her body stiffened under his touch. "You're doing more harm than good. The activated charcoal will help absorb the toxins before they get to your bloodstream. It'll work faster than this."

He moved his hand down toward her wrist and slowly pulled it away from her face. With his other hand, he tilted her chin up. Black mascara smudged across her cheeks as she finally acknowledged him.

"He's dead. Greg's dead. He died because of me." Her lip quivered. She shut her eyes, and fresh tears poured down her cheeks. She buried her face in his chest and sobbed as he threaded his fingers together behind her head.

An hour later, Blake and Sasha were in the emergency room, lying next to one another on a small hospital bed once again. Sasha had been silent since they left Beach Brew, and Blake had only picked up on bits and pieces of what happened.

From what he gathered, Greg and Ricki showed up while Rebecca was in the bathroom, and in that short amount of time, Greg held Sasha down while Rickie forced her to play a deadly game of swallow the pills. Shortly after, Rickie pulled out a gun and shot Greg for allowing Sasha to blow his inventory. At the same time, Rebecca shot Rickie. She'd heard the fighting and thought Rickie was going to shoot Sasha. If Rebecca hadn't been there, Sasha may have died too.

Blake smoothed Sasha's hair, pulling it away from her face. A cool, wet rag lay across her forehead. Her breathing was slow and steady, but her cold feet rubbed against his legs beneath the covers as she let out an exaggerated breath. Believing she was cold, he ran his hand down her arm, trying to warm her. He meant to do it in a comforting, consoling manner, but in the next instant, Sasha slipped her hand under his shirt and placed her palm to his abs. She rested it there for only a second before she dragged her nails along his side. Her breathing grew louder. Heavier.

She inched up, propping herself on one elbow, and leaned into him. Her lips touched his. They were gentle and warm. Soft and tender. One of her hands still lay under his shirt, and it took everything in him not to beg for more, but he couldn't. Not now, not here.

Blake reached for her face, forcing her to look at him. Her eyes were full of sorrow, full of pain.

"I want you to kiss me. To touch me. Fuck, I want to kiss you too. But not like this. You're using this to cover your pain," he whispered. "You have a right to be mad. To cry. To fall apart."

She dropped her gaze, and her shoulders slumped. "I've fallen apart more in the last few weeks than I did when my mom died." Her voice was small and deflated as she lay back down.

Blake's mind raced, searching for ways to comfort her, but nothing came to him. Words couldn't take away what happened today. Words wouldn't bring Greg back to life. Only time would lessen the pain. That, and smiling. Smiling was great for the heart and the soul.

So, instead of saying something cheesy like, "I'm here if you want to talk." Blake chose a different route. Something he'd never tried before. Something he hadn't told anyone, because it made him feel foolish. But now? Just thinking about it made him smile, and he wanted to make Sasha smile too.

"Can I tell you something?" He resumed rubbing her arm.

She nodded, but she didn't look up at him as he continued.

"I was engaged a few years ago."

Her eyes popped open. He knew those words would grab her attention.

"You were?"

"Yeah. I was in the Marines. I was stationed in California. Found myself a hot blond," he chuckled. "I was barely twenty, and she was a gold digger." He paused and cringed, as if he had just confessed to a crime. "Turns out, I didn't have any gold."

She smirked and her eyes lit up. "How did you end up engaged if she was only after your nonexistent money? You don't strike me as the type to lie about something like that."

"I didn't have to lie. She never asked. I think she assumed being married to a service member meant she'd have a cushy life. She put on a great show. Super sweet. I thought I was in love. Though, in hindsight, it's funny. I never did tell Porter about her."

"You've got to be kidding me," she said. Blake had her full attention now. "So?"

"*So…*" he said, exaggerating the *o*. "I bought her a ring. She said yes. And then one day, I told her I wanted to be a firefighter when I got out of the Marines. She got pissed. Said she didn't want to marry a nobody."

"A nobody?" Sasha's voice rose in amusement. Her nose scrunched in the same cute way it always did when she couldn't believe something.

Blake watched as the lines creased at Sasha's eyes and her lips curled up. She was beautiful beyond words. He wanted to take a picture of this moment, of her smile, of her happiness. This is what he'd hoped for. He'd do anything to brighten her day.

"Okay, but what happened? If you were engaged, what happened to Ms. Gold Digger?"

Blake shrugged. "We got into a fight. The next day, I found out she was screwing another marine in my shop."

Sasha's eyes widened. "Oh my God. I'm so sorry."

"Don't be sorry. It was the second best thing that's ever happened to me." His heart began beating quicker the moment the words escaped his mouth.

"The second?" Sasha's eyes sparkled. "What was the first?"

"The first time you kissed me," he admitted.

CHAPTER THIRTY-NINE

Sasha

"Hi, Sasha. How are you feeling?" A young nurse entered the room, interrupting Sasha and Blake's conversation.

Blake shifted on the bed and adjusted his focus to the woman.

Sasha gave a shrug but didn't verbalize a response. She was afraid her voice might crack if she did. Blake's words had surprised her, thrown her off course. She hadn't expected his confession. The words terrified her, though they melted her heart in a way she'd never experienced. Maybe it was the sincerity in his voice. The way his eyes pulled at her soul.

Blake wasn't a player. He wouldn't say something he didn't mean. She hadn't known him long, but with the amount of time she had spent with him, she knew he was genuine in just about everything he did. She'd watched him interact with others. A truly nice guy. He wasn't the boy toy she'd pegged him to be when he walked through Beach Brew that first day. Though he still had the most incredible sex eyes she'd ever seen.

Sasha was attracted to him. There was no denying it. And she loved spending time with him. He allowed her to be who she was at her core. Regardless of what name people wanted to call her.

"Well, I have a little bit of good news," the nurse said. "We're going to move you from here and admit you upstairs to your own room. This way you'll have more privacy. Unfortunately, poison control wants us to monitor you for another eighteen hours."

The nurse's eyes shifted to Blake, who was still lying on the bed next to her. "You ready to get moving?"

Blake didn't notice the subtle social cue, so Sasha elbowed him in the side. "Get up. She's about to move me."

Blake jumped to his feet. "Oh…no wheelchair?"

Confusion looked cute on him.

"No, we move the entire bed." The nurse smiled.

Sasha had been through this plenty of times in the past. First stop, the emergency room. Then, depending on how many hours poison control dictated, she'd either sleep off the drugs in the hallway, next to the nurse's station, or she was moved to her own room. Either way, this was the first time she'd be admitted with no security on standby.

They made their way out of the ER and down a long fluorescent-lit hallway.

"Can you press the button?" The nurse looked at Blake when they reached the elevator.

When the doors to the elevator opened, the three of them crammed in, the bed taking up most of the space. Blake stood against the back. The nurse in front.

Sasha glanced up and smiled when she caught Blake staring at her.

"Hold the elevator," a familiar voice sounded behind her.

Sasha was facing away from the door so she couldn't see who it was, but by the way Blake's face changed, she knew it couldn't be good.

"Floor three," the man said.

"We're headed there too," the nurse replied.

It didn't take long before the doors reopened. "You first," the man said.

Once the nurse had pulled her bed from the elevator and turned it to continue on, Sasha lifted her gaze to the man standing beside her. If looks could kill, Jay was murdering her right there. A shiver ran through her body, and she shuddered at the thought. Blake cast his head down and pressed his lips together. Something was wrong. What did he know that she didn't? Why was this guy angry at her?

"Stop," she said, but the words missed the nurse completely. "Stop. I need you to stop!" This time she practically yelled.

The bed came to a halt.

All eyes landed on Sasha.

"Are you okay?" the nurse was the first to ask.

She shook her head. "You two. What's wrong?" Sasha pointed her finger back and forth between Blake and Jay.

Jay opened his mouth, but it took a few seconds for sound to come out. "He didn't tell you?"

"Tell me what?" she demanded.

Jay huffed.

"It's not my place to say," Blake said calmly. Like whatever it was didn't pertain to him.

"Rickie. The guy who tried to drug you today. He's the same guy you got addicted to pills in the first place. He used to be a fun-loving kid with his whole life ahead of him. But now he's in surgery. He'll go to jail for the rest of his life. All because of you." Jay paused, his chest puffed out, anger rising in each word that came next.

"You're the reason he's an addict. You're the one who gave him his first supply. Then his next. How the hell do you think he got sucked into that life in the first place?" Jay shook his head. "You're the reason my brother's in this situation."

He glared at her and then turned to walk away.

The nurse turned the bed in the opposite direction and resumed her mission to get Sasha into a room.

"You're right," Sasha yelled. Her expression darkened at the word "brother."

The nurse stopped moving. Sasha was surprised she'd stopped again, but she seemed invested in the encounter.

"Rickie *acted* like a fun-loving kid when I met him. But he was also sad and depressed and incredibly angry."

Jay's feet stopped moving, but he didn't turn to look at her.

"Your brother made a stupid decision when he was fifteen years old. Just like I did. I didn't force him to take anything. He came to me. Do I regret giving him his first pill? Yes. Of course I do. But I was only sixteen. I was young and stupid and had my own set of problems. No one starts taking pills thinking they want to be an addict. No one pops one and imagines chasing a high they can never seem to recreate. And I didn't turn him into a killer. He did that on his own."

Sasha's voice grew hoarse as she yelled the words down the hall. When she finished, silence sat between them for what felt like an eternity. She wasn't sure what he was waiting for. There was nothing else to say. If he wanted to respond, he had the floor.

She watched as his shoulders lifted and sank with each breath. His feet slowly pivoted on the tile floor, and he met her eyes. "Just because you're this girl…Paige…just because you were kidnapped and whatnot, doesn't give you a free pass."

"I didn't ask for one," she deadpanned.

He gritted his teeth. "I became an EMT and a firefighter to save lives. To help humanity because of people like you. People who don't give a shit about anyone other than themselves. I did it because I watched my brother lose himself, and there was nothing I could do to save him. Figured maybe I could save someone else. But then I had to go and fucking save your life. The girl who started all this shit in the first place. I tried. I really tried to like you. I was glad you sobered up. That you got the help you needed. But…then you had to move to St. Pete. It's like I couldn't get away from you. And now this shit. And with Blake. I can't. You don't understand."

Blake moved toward him, but Jay pulled away and disappeared down the hall.

CHAPTER FORTY

Blake

Eighteen hours isn't a long time. Not when you're busy making phone calls and making sure the girl you like is feeling okay. *Shit.* Blake more than liked Sasha. He was falling in love with her. He wasn't sure if she felt the same way, but he couldn't deny his feelings any longer. Fuck. He told her the one thing he'd promised himself he'd never share with a living, breathing soul, and it hadn't bothered her. It was his once-upon-a-time mistake, and she hadn't so much as batted an eye. She hadn't judged him, nor had she questioned his intentions.

Then, to top it all off, he had told her that her kiss was the best thing that had ever happened to him. He hadn't planned to say that. Though he was happy he did. The confession made him feel lighter.

He was glad she'd made the first move that day at her dad's house, when they'd been sifting through papers and folders. He'd been so wrapped up in his own thoughts, he wasn't sure he'd ever find the courage to touch her in a romantic way. Lack of confidence had never been a problem for him.

It was just…Sasha was more than he'd ever imagined. She was the damn sun. And he wanted nothing more than to be near her, to see her, to feel her warmth. She was beautiful, assertive, strong, and resilient. And yet she was also honest and vulnerable. She hadn't hidden her past from him. She'd fallen apart in front of him, a virtual stranger, at the very beginning. Sasha was the air he'd been struggling to find his entire life. The thought of almost losing her again terrified him.

He said all of this to Jay when he found him in the hallway waiting for Rickie to get out of surgery. "You don't have to like Sasha. But you know she was right. She didn't turn your brother into an addict any more than that guy turned her into one. Everyone makes their own choices, and then they have to suffer the consequences of those actions. We're just here to ease the burden of those mistakes."

Blake laid a gentle hand on Jay's back. They sat on cold metal chairs. "You know as well as I do that prison may be the best thing for your brother. Maybe he'll get the help he needs."

"I don't hate her," he began. "I don't even dislike her. I'm just angry. My brother just took someone's life. I know she didn't do that. That was all him." Jay rubbed at his temples. "I feel like I should have done more though…"

"You know that's ridiculous, right? You did what you could. He chose the rest."

Jay sat with his elbows on his knees and his face planted into the palms of his hands. "I haven't told our mom yet. This is going to destroy her."

Blake didn't respond. He knew all too well how families suffered during times like these. He patted Jay on the back again and then stood.

"Wait." Jay looked up. "How is she? I should have asked sooner."

There he was. This was the Jay he'd grown to respect and admire. "She's okay. She's sleeping some of it off now. They should discharge her soon."

"What about her family? I heard they made an arrest. Did they let her dad go, or is he still considered a suspect?"

Blake dropped his weight back into the chair and sat shoulder to shoulder with Jay as he filled him in on all the updates. "Sasha's lawyer just called. Said she wanted to meet with her tomorrow. I'm not sure if it's good or bad."

Even in the early morning hours of the following day, the air was hot and sticky. There were no clouds in the sky, just a brilliant sun and a sea of blue as far as the eye could see.

"Thanks for picking us up. If we were just going to Pamela's office, we'd stick it out, but the police station is too far in this heat," Sasha said as they drove down the highway with the air on at full blast.

Blake hadn't planned to pick them up. He figured he'd give them some space and spend his day off hanging pictures. Maybe he'd even sort and shelve his books. But Sasha had called him in a panic. "I'm sorry for calling at the last minute. The air conditioner in Margo's car isn't working. And now Pamela wants to meet us at the station. Do you think you can pick us up?"

Half an hour later, the three of them pulled into a spot across from the main entrance of the police station. Blake unbuckled and reached for the door handle when his phone rang. Ignoring it, he let the call go to voicemail and helped Sasha out of her seat. When he handed her the crutches, his phone rang again. This time he looked at the screen.

"It's Porter. Why don't you two go ahead? I'll wait out here."

Sasha's face dropped. "You don't want to come in?"

"I do, but this is about you and Margo." He shifted his gaze to her sister. "They probably won't let me in anyway. I'll be out here waiting. Then I'll take you girls out for lunch. How does that sound?" He laid a reassuring hand on Sasha's back.

She smiled and nodded, her eyes glimmering in the light.

They hadn't talked about what he had said about their first kiss yesterday. They hadn't been alone for more than five seconds since that moment, unless sleeping counted, so he wasn't sure how Sasha felt about it. She hadn't pushed him away, but she also hadn't reached out since she was discharged from the hospital.

After everything that happened, Blake hadn't wanted to leave her side. But he knew that was a bit overbearing, even as the thoughts spiraled in his head. He had to do what was best for her. She needed time to process her thoughts, time to heal. So he'd watched as Margo's boyfriend and his mom picked them up from the hospital and took them home.

"Okay. But we'll be back soon, so make sure that truck is nice and cool for us when we get back." She winked at him.

Once Sasha and Margo stepped away, Blake clicked Porter's name and called him back.

"Blake. They're letting him go," Porter said. His voice was rushed and frantic.

"They're letting who go?"

CHAPTER FORTY-ONE

Sasha

The room was small and rectangular. Smaller than the one at county where her dad was being held. A long table sat in the center. Sasha folded her arms as she and Margo waited for Pamela to join them.

"Can I get you ladies anything to drink while you wait?" a deputy asked, peeking his head into the room from the open doorway.

Sasha glanced at Margo, who shook her head.

"No, thanks," she said.

Looking at the clock on the wall, Sasha exhaled loudly and tapped her foot on the tile floor as she grew increasingly impatient. They'd been waiting fifteen minutes already. Pamela had seemed eager to meet when she'd called, so she assumed she wouldn't be too late.

Five more minutes passed, and still nothing. Sasha pushed out of her chair when another deputy walked by. She was just about to say something when Pamela rushed in with Detective Spencer on her heels.

"Good news, ladies." She grinned. Tossing her briefcase onto the table, she tore it open and pulled out a folder. "They dropped the charges."

"They what?" she and Margo said at the same time. They locked eyes, confusion plaguing them both.

"Does the name Joanne Steele ring a bell?" Pamela continued, rifling through her papers. "Aha. Here it is." She pulled out a piece of paper and laid it flat on the table.

Margo leaned in first, then Sasha. It was a mug shot of a woman. Blond hair with streaks of gray that framed a thin face. Dark eyes, cold as stone, stared back. Deep wrinkles etched her skin, and sunspots dotted her forehead and cheekbones.

When neither Margo nor Sasha responded, Pamela went on. "This woman is your mom's sister. Well, not your mom," she corrected herself as she looked at Sasha. "But I suppose she would be *your* mom." Her words were slow as she focused her attention on Margo. As if it'd just dawned on her that Margo had a connection to the woman in the picture.

"So, she's my aunt?" Margo asked, raising an eyebrow. She placed a finger on the picture and pulled it closer. "Mom never mentioned a sister."

"Yes," Pamela responded unapologetically. "Your mom's maiden name wasn't Cohen. It was her married name. From her first marriage. Her maiden name was Steele. Sharon Steele."

"What does this woman have to do with anything though? Why was she arrested?" Sasha asked, pointing at the mug shot.

Pamela's eyes widened and a smile crept across her face. "It just so happened that Joanne was with Mitch when he was arrested.

Joanne's been on the run for years. Longer than you've been alive. She's part of a human trafficking ring. And we just took down one of their legs." There was a hint of giddiness in her voice.

"Let's not get ahead of ourselves here," Detective Spencer finally interrupted. He took Joanne's mug shot back and lifted it between his fingers. Without looking at it, he shoved it back into Pamela's folder. "This is still an ongoing case, so—"

"And I'm their lawyer. I am providing my clients with the information my private investigator found," she huffed.

The tension between the two of them grew by the second.

Pamela pulled a chair out and sat across from them, but Detective Spencer stood firmly at her side. She placed five more documents on the table. "After some digging, my PI found out that *your* mom," she eyed Margo, "was Sharon Steele. She was married to Henry Cohen in 1997." She pushed a marriage license in front of them. A picture of an unrecognizable man was stapled in the upper left-hand corner. It was labeled February 25th, 1997, Fairfax, Virginia.

"Sharon gave birth to Sasha Cohen in March 1997." She pushed a second document in front of them. It was an original birth certificate, with Sasha Cohen written on it. Not Sasha Patterson like the one she'd seen at her dad's house, though her last name wasn't what confused her. Her dad had confessed that he and her mom had legally changed it. What did confuse her was why Henry's name wasn't listed as the father. Not even on the original. Why was it left blank?

Pamela glanced up, as if reading her mind. "Henry wasn't Sasha's father. The PI found Henry's parents still living in Virginia. They confirmed that he didn't meet Sharon until she was six months pregnant. We're still digging around Sharon's past to see if we can come up with any leads."

After a few seconds, Pamela placed the third document in front of them. "In 2001, both Sasha and Henry were killed in an automobile accident. Sharon was listed as the only surviving passenger. It destroyed Henry's parents. And Sharon.

"Sharon admitted herself to a psychiatric hospital three days later. After she was discharged, she disappeared. Just up and vanished. That is, until she showed up in Cocoa Beach." A fourth paper was moved toward them. Sharon's discharge papers from the hospital.

"In August 2002, she began working as a first-grade teacher, where she befriended Olive Knight. Then, in July 2003, Paige Knight was kidnapped. You're Paige Knight." Pamela nodded in Sasha's direction.

"Your father," she glanced at Margo, "Dan Patterson, was still in the Marine Corps and was on duty the night of Paige's disappearance. Here is his duty log from that day." She placed the fifth and final paper in front of them.

"Does that mean they're letting Dad go?" Margo pushed her chair out, excitement rising in her voice.

Pamela nodded, a smile pressed to her lips. "There's not enough evidence anymore."

"What about the pictures? With Mitch and him. The ones at the café?" Sasha's voice trembled. She believed her dad was innocent, but the pictures didn't make any sense.

"He and Mitch did know one another, by his own admission. Just like Mitch also knew the Knight family. Joanne likely planned it all out. She knew her sister was ill. Between the depression and the loss of her family, Sharon was likely trying to replace the baby she had lost. You looked just like her. And if Joanne was going to help kidnap a little girl for her sister, they needed someone steady enough for the job. Someone who'd be able to deflect if things got out of hand. That's where Dan comes into play. He was the perfect man for the job."

"All right. That's all circumstantial. You can't go around telling people that story without any evidence," Detective Spencer growled.

"You know as well as I do that finding Joanne was like finding a needle in a haystack. Her last known whereabouts were deep inside Los Angeles, and that was ten years ago." Pamela collected her papers and placed them back in her folder, ensuring they were in the correct order.

Detective Spencer let out an annoyed exhale. "I'll need you both to come with me. Your dad is being transferred here as we speak. You'll get to take him home, but he can't leave Florida. Not until we finish the investigation."

Sasha scratched at her face, unable to wrap her brain around any of it. She stayed in her seat, thoughts circulating in her head as Pamela and Detective Spencer stood. "What about the others?" she asked before they reached the door, her voice full of dread.

Pamela looked toward Detective Spencer. He looked back at her. Lifting his arm, the detective rubbed at the back of his neck. Worry dripped from his face as he clenched his jaw.

"Honestly, I don't know. Sorting through this kind of evidence can take years. And I don't know how much luck we'll have reuniting anyone with their families. Joanne didn't typically take people, like you, from affluent neighborhoods. She abducted kids, babies, teenagers, and even women, from places they wouldn't be missed. She took advantage of their situations. We'd even heard some willingly gave up their children for money, drugs, a better life."

"But the pictures." A knot formed in Sasha's stomach. Grief washed over her, his words making her sick. "There were so many kids."

"We'll do everything we can to sort through the evidence. But it'll take time. Who knows? Joanne or Mitch may take a plea and offer up some useful information. It's too soon to tell."

Their reunion with their dad wasn't what Sasha expected. For as much excitement as Margo had shown earlier, she'd held back once their dad appeared in the hallway. The three of them shared glances and gave half smiles.

"You both came." Her dad was the first to speak. He clasped his hands together and rubbed them nervously.

"Of course we did," Margo said, oblivious to his surprise at seeing Sasha, and leaned in, giving him a hug. "Ready to get out of here?"

"I'd like nothing better to get out of here, but—"

"I took care of everything," Sasha interrupted, knowing he was probably worried about his house. "I called my friend Claire. She has a house on the bayside, not too far from here. She's in North Carolina and asked me to keep an eye on it. She knows what's been going on, so I asked if you and Margo could stay there until we can get back into your house and get the insurance involved to assess the damage from the fire."

"You didn't have to do that, sweetie. I can stay at a hotel or something." His eyes dropped to the floor, and a look of defeat etched across his face.

"Don't be silly." They lingered awkwardly, the three of them, before Sasha finally turned and led the way out the front doors. She heard his sigh, followed by his footsteps behind her. Her words had been short and cold, and she knew she'd hurt him, but what did he expect from her? She was still angry that he'd lied to her about so much. Even if he wasn't involved in the kidnapping, he was still at fault for so much. Right?

When the sun hit Sasha's face, tears pricked at the corners of her eyes. She lifted her hands to shield them from the blinding light. A sudden wave of dread and anxiety washed over her. She didn't want to sit in the car with her dad or watch Margo pack up her stuff. She didn't want to sit next to Blake as he drove them across town. Her heartbeat accelerated at the sudden heaviness.

In the not so far distance, she watched as Blake exited his truck. He didn't look surprised to see them walking with their dad. Instead, he extended his hand as they neared. "It's nice to officially meet you, Mr. Patterson."

"You're the fireman from the hospital. The one who saved…"

And there it was. The conversation stopper. Her name. Who was she? Because in that moment, she no longer felt like Sasha. Sasha had died in a car accident.

"Sasha," Blake finished for him.

Until then, that was exactly what she had wanted to be called. Blake knew this. Now though? She wasn't so sure.

"I heard you had a heart attack while you were at the hospital. How are you feeling now?" he continued as he opened the door. "I hope you don't mind climbing in the back with Margo. There's more room up front for Sasha's leg."

Sasha watched in amazement at how easily Blake handled the situation. How at ease he looked when talking to her dad. It settled her nerves ever so slightly, though it felt as if an elephant was sitting on her chest.

"You okay?" Margo asked, meeting her on the other side of the truck. She slipped her hand into hers. "You don't look so good."

Sasha looked at Margo. Her long strawberry-blond hair blowing in the wind. Worry radiated from her sad eyes. She wanted to say yes, that this was exactly what they'd wanted in the first place. Their dad was innocent. And yet, she didn't want to lie to her either. Telling her the truth, however, might cause Margo pain. It could put distance between them and cause more grief than she deserved.

"Look at me," Margo demanded. "You're my sister. No matter what. I know you think I'm still this fragile little girl who can't handle more bad news. But I'm not. You can talk to me."

Margo. Sweet Margo. Sasha pulled her sister close and wrapped her arms around her shoulders. Wasn't that what she'd told Blake? That she wasn't fragile. And yet she'd been treating her sister the way she'd found insulting. How had she not seen Margo blossoming into such a beautiful soul? In that moment, she knew honesty was her only choice.

"I'm not okay. Not yet. I don't know how to feel. I love Dad. He'll always be my dad. But then there's the Knight family. And I feel guilty that they lost their daughter. But I'm their daughter. Even if I don't feel like I am. And then there's this guilt sitting in my stomach. Like I'm the one who could cause so much pain for everyone. I'm afraid I'll let everyone down if I'm not ready to talk." As the words poured from her mouth, she knew she'd made the right decision. Keeping that bottled up would have caused more harm than good.

She realized, suddenly, that it wasn't just Margo listening. She turned and was met with the sight of her dad's sad, tear-stained face.

"I wish I could make all this pain go away for you. I wish I would have known. I can't even imagine what your family went through. All those years without ever knowing where you were. If you were dead or alive. All the while, I got to love you. Hold you. Call you mine. I loved your mother. But I hate her in this moment. For what she has done to you and your family." He made no effort to wipe his eyes as tears trickled down his cheeks.

CHAPTER FORTY-TWO

Two Years Later

Sasha

"Sash, you ready?" Blake called from the front door.

"Be there in a minute." Sasha quickly applied another coat of clear gloss to her lips. Closing the lid, she stole one last glance at herself in the mirror. "Good enough," she muttered. She smoothed her black knit pencil skirt and tucked in her cream-colored silk blouse. Then, grabbing a pair of nude heels and a black blazer, she ran down the hall.

Blake's attention dropped to her legs and then dragged up the length of her body until it landed on her face. "You are gorgeous." His eyes swirled with liquid fire.

"Put those sex eyes away. We don't have time," Sasha laughed, though it made her feel good to be looked at that way. Blake's attention always made her feel good. "It's not too much?" She scrunched her nose. She never dressed up professionally. Her wardrobe consisted of beach attire and sundresses. Even when she'd gone to the bank to sign for the loan on her new business venture, she'd walked in wearing an oversized sundress and sandals.

Blake wrapped his arms around her waist and pulled her to his chest. "You look like a million dollars." He kissed the side of her neck. "But you'll look even better once those clothes are on the floor," he whispered in her ear.

She flushed at his words. His touch, combined with the sound of his voice, always sent shivers up her body. But they didn't have time for that, not now. Instead, she ran her hand up his neck and placed a soft kiss to his lips. It had to be soft. Anything more, and she'd never make it to the courtroom on time.

A while later, Sasha and Blake squeezed onto the bench next to her dad, Olive, and Ned. Behind them sat Porter, Tina, Penny, Margo, and Drew. In the row behind that, Blake's parents sat with some of their close friends.

"You guys made it," Sasha said, glancing over her shoulder. She was happy to see them all, though the words were more for Margo and Drew. Their flight had been delayed two times, and hopping in a car to drive here hadn't been an option. Margo and Drew were students at Harvard and could only steal a few days from their studies to be here.

"Wouldn't miss it for the world," Margo said.

Turning back to face the front, Sasha caught sight of a reporter staring at her. Her body tensed until she felt Porter's firm hand fall to her shoulder.

"Don't worry about them. They don't matter. They'll get their story and then forget about us all over again," he whispered. His voice was calm and reassuring. In the last two years, Porter had transformed, and their relationship had grown by leaps and bounds as a result. No longer angry at what he couldn't change, he had given up all notions of control.

She suspected she'd changed too, but it was more noticeable with Porter. While she'd struggled with guilt and wanting to make her dad and Margo blend into their family with her, Porter had been angry and resentful about what he'd missed out on and the loss he and his parents felt over the two decades she'd been gone. He was a gentle soul at his core, but that had almost been ruined by how he'd had to grow up much too soon. Therapy helped. With Tina's encouragement, he began seeing a therapist, just as Sasha had. Looking back at even last year, Sasha could see how different he was. He smiled more, laughed more. Now Sasha didn't go a day without texting her brother.

She raised her left arm across her chest and laid her hand on top of Porter's. She nodded. "I'm good." Until now, Sasha had been a bundle of nerves. She'd written and rewritten her statement a hundred times in a hundred different ways. She tore them up. She cried. She started over, only to throw everything in the trash. Nothing she wrote ever felt good enough. No words could describe what she'd been through. And while Blake had helped soothe her nerves over the last several days, it was Porter who'd said, "Fuck it. Don't give them the time of day."

The room filled quickly as people took their seats. When the main doors closed behind them, a door next to the bailiff opened. Joanne and Mitch walked out, escorted by two police officers. When they stopped in front of their seats and sat down, Blake squeezed her hand. "You got this."

"All rise for the Honorable Judge Crawford," the bailiff announced as the judge entered the room.

For the next hour, Sasha listened to the prosecutor and defense attorney speak, each one trying to sway the judge into longer or shorter prison sentences. When the judge asked if there were any victim impact statements, the room fell silent. But Sasha didn't rise. She'd made the decision late last night that she wouldn't give the reporters another story that they could twist and turn for their own gains. She refused to let Mitch or Joanne be a part of her life any longer. Porter was right. Fuck them. Sometimes silence was louder than words.

When it was over and everyone stood to leave, Sasha turned and looked at her family. She smiled. Happiness filled her heart.

"Do you think twenty-two years was long enough?" She overheard Penny ask Margo.

"No, but I'm pretty sure they'll have more time tacked on with the Laurel case," Margo replied as Drew wrapped his arm around her waist. Laurel was the name of another girl the police had recently found. She was the first person Detective Spencer had been able to identify since they'd taken Mitch and Joanne into custody. It'd taken two years, but it left some hope in Sasha's heart that more people would, one day, be reunited with their families.

"Everyone ready?" Sasha's dad asked, already a step ahead. It was more of a statement than a question. He knew they were ready to shift gears and put the past behind them.

"I'm right behind you," Ned replied but paused to give Sasha a quick kiss on the cheek. "You did good. I'm proud of you. We'll see you over at the house." He and Olive hurried to catch up with her dad.

The three of them had grown close too. Once Sasha started her own therapy, she'd quickly realized how much both her families had in common. Rather than allow her guilt over wanting to keep her dad in her life as well as wanting to know the

Knight family more, her therapist suggested blending everyone together. Allowing them to equally love her. While difficult at first, it proved to be the second best decision she'd ever made. She still called Dan "Dad" and her biological parents by their first names, but that was a work in progress.

"Don't take too long, you hear me? Carter can't wait to see y'all," Porter said as he took Tina's hand in his. "You three coming or what?"

"We were waiting on you," Penny said, rolling her eyes. Penny, Margo, and Drew followed them out of the courtroom, leaving Sasha and Blake alone.

"Are *you* ready?" Blake threaded his fingers between hers.

Sasha took a deep inhale and then released it slowly, trying to calm the nerves that were building back up. "Promise me you won't let go of my hand. No matter how hard I squeeze."

Blake laughed. "I promise. Now let's get out of here."

CHAPTER FORTY-THREE

Blake

"Oh my God." Sasha gritted her teeth. "I need a break. I can't take it any longer."

The tattoo artist pulled back her tattoo pen, annoyance clear in the purse of her lips and huff of her breath. "Sweetheart, I'll be done in five minutes."

"I don't understand how people do this more than once. And you both have them all over," she said, nodding her head in their direction.

"The inside of the wrist is tender, but it'll be over soon. Unless you want me to stop." The woman's voice was soft but firm. She pushed back in her chair, testing Sasha.

"No. I want to finish." She closed her eyes and squeezed Blake's hand even tighter. "Go ahead," she said, giving her permission to continue.

When it was over, Blake wiggled his fingers free. "Open your eyes." He watched as Sasha's eyelids lifted and she tilted her palm to get a better view.

"It's perfect." She looked up to meet his gaze, a smile pressed to her lips.

Two small red maple leaves donned the inside of her wrist. One slightly larger than the other, just the way she'd wanted.

"You ready for a sleeve now?" the woman laughed.

Blake couldn't remember the last time he'd been so happy. Watching Sasha navigate life was something he couldn't get enough of. She was strong and vibrant. Full of life. She wasn't afraid to be herself, even when she didn't always know who that was.

Most people would balk at the idea of a tattoo that represented the object behind their trauma, but Sasha wasn't like most people. She embraced the chaos.

"You have a whole damn tree on your arm. The least I could do was get a few leaves," she'd said a few months ago.

The next day, Blake asked Olive to take a picture of the tree in their yard. Then he brought it into the tattoo shop and asked the owner if she'd be able to draw up a sample for Sasha. After his shift, he drove home to the condo they now shared and showed her. "I want that. Right here," she'd said, pointing at her wrist.

After shutting off his engine down the street from Dan's house, Blake walked around and helped Sasha out of his truck. Even if she weren't wearing a skin-tight skirt, he'd have helped her out. Maybe it was because he was keenly aware of how quickly someone could be snatched up by a stranger. Maybe it was because he'd been raised to be a gentleman. He preferred to think of the latter.

Taking her hand in his, Blake led Sasha down the sidewalk toward the newly remodeled house.

"I can't believe so many people are here," Sasha said.

"Your dad loves to celebrate." He squeezed her hand, suddenly nervous.

"Don't you think it's kind of weird to be celebrating like this though? He probably should have been a bit more discreet."

Sasha reached the door first and opened it. Inside, more than a dozen people milled around the living room, and Blake could see more people in the kitchen and out back.

"Sasha!" Carter yelled, running up to her. She lifted him into the air and swung him around. "Carter! You've gotten so tall in the last month. And what's this? A mohawk?"

"Yeah. Mom took me to get it cut like this yesterday."

Sasha put him back on the floor and touched the top of his hair. "I love it. Where's your little sister? I need to snuggle that girl."

"She's over there with Mom and your friends." He pointed toward the living room where Tina sat with Claire and Rebecca.

"Claire's here?" Sasha grinned and ran in her direction.

"Hey, Dad is outside." Margo sidestepped her way toward Blake and then nodded toward the back when he looked in her direction.

"Thanks. Keep her busy for me," Blake said.

She nodded and turned her attention back to Sasha, who was already deep in conversation with Claire.

Slipping away, Blake made his way outside. Dan and Ned stood at the grill, which was now on the opposite end of the patio from where it sat two years ago. His own dad stood next to them, and the three of them laughed together.

Dan noticed him first, and a grin spread across his face. "Hey. You're back." He placed a hand on Blake's shoulder. "She still inside?"

After a quick nod from Blake, Dan peeked around him, making sure Sasha was out of earshot. "Everything's set up. You ready?"

He was. He'd been waiting for this moment for the last several months. Earlier this year, Sasha had come home with a signed lease in her hands and jumped up and down before launching herself into his arms. He'd never seen her smile the way she did that day—eyes bright and pure joy radiating from her.

She'd worked tirelessly, drafting a business plan and looking for the perfect location to house her new coffee shop. Night Café. A play on words for her birth name. She'd decided to keep Sasha as her name—legally changing it from Paige—because that's who she'd been for the last two decades. Though she knew at the center of it all, there was still Paige, daughter of Ned and Olive Knight, and that deserved something.

Blake had already fallen in love with her by then. He'd told her within weeks of Mitch and Joanne's arrest. Both he and Sasha had been sitting in the grass, under the maple tree in the Knights' front yard. A gentle rain had danced across the sky as Blake told Sasha stories, memories he could recall of the two of them, three if you included Porter.

Everyone else had been in the house, sheltered from the rain. Even Dan and Margo. It was the first time they had joined. The first time they'd met the Knights. But in that moment, it was just the two of them.

"I love you, Sasha. I'm madly in love with you," he'd said, letting the words slip from his tongue and his hand tangle in her damp hair.

His mouth swept across her lips when she breathed the words back. "I love you too."

Everything else had been about timing. Blake hadn't wanted to move too quickly, yet if he'd had his way, they'd already be married. No. He'd known he had to wait. They needed to put Mitch and Joanne behind them.

Now that everything was over, they could start the next chapter of their lives. Tonight. Tonight was going to be perfect.

CHAPTER FORTY-FOUR

Sasha

The sun was setting, and Sasha was growing tired. It'd been a long day. She didn't want to be the first to leave since most of the people here had come to see her. She stifled a yawn before getting to her feet. She needed some fresh air. That might wake her up.

"Heading outside?" Tina asked, standing at the entrance to the kitchen. "I'll join you. It's gorgeous outside."

"Yeah. I want to find Blake. I kind of want to head home. I'm exhausted."

Tina stood, unmoving, a smile pressed to her lips. It felt a bit awkward. Sasha loved Tina, but she wouldn't move. And right now, all she wanted to do was get some fresh air. From the corner of her eye, Sasha watched as Margo and Drew pulled back the sliding glass door and walked out, followed by a few of the neighbors.

Lifting her arm in the direction of the door, Sasha arched her eyebrows. "Ready?"

"Oh. Yes. Of course." Moving slowly, Tina finally inched her way closer to the back door.

Sasha wasn't sure what was going on with Tina, but once the door opened and the lights flickered off, she suddenly didn't care anymore. Somehow, without her noticing, everyone had made their way outside. Strings of fairy lights dangled from overhead, stretching across in a zigzag pattern. Candles lit a path that led from the patio to the corner of the property line, where, against the fence, Blake stood.

Carter and his baby sister, Lila, suddenly appeared before her. Carter cleared his throat and touched her hand.

She looked down and caught his eye.

"This is for you," he said matter-of-factly. "Lila, give her the paper," he whispered.

Lila grinned and reached out her chubby little hand. In it was a small white piece of paper. The words "Don't just stand there" were written across the top in Blake's handwriting. Instinctively, she smiled and placed a hand over her mouth. That was just like Blake. To anticipate her thoughts ahead of time.

She was barefoot, but that didn't matter. She stepped off the patio and followed the candles that sat inside tall glass vases, creating a pathway of light. With the sun almost completely out of sight now, Sasha was unable to make out Blake's expression until she was a few feet away from him. It was his eyes she noticed first. The way they danced when he looked at her. Then it was the curve of his lips. His signature smile as he watched her sashay in his direction. Time froze as he bent down on one knee.

Then Blake's words broke the silence, his voice soft. "Marry me, Sasha. Tonight. Tomorrow. Next week."

Sasha inhaled deeply. She should have seen it coming. The setup alone was obvious. But his words still took her by surprise.

"I want to fall asleep with you in my arms every night. I want to wake up and kiss your lips every morning. I want to share the rest of my life with you and grow old with you. I can't imagine living another day without you being my wife."

Her heart thundered and her breath caught in her throat.

Someone in the distance yelled out, "Say yes!"

She turned, and in that moment, she saw everyone. Her family. His family. Friends and neighbors. They held up seven square signs, each with a letter on them that read "Say yes!" She was already nodding, wanting to say yes, but unable to force her lips to move.

Blake reached into his pocket and pulled out a small black box. He opened it and held out a brilliant round diamond solitaire ring. Taking her hand in his, he slid the ring onto her finger, gently pushing it over her knuckle. It fit perfectly. She looked at it and then at him as tears slid down her cheeks.

Once Blake was back on his feet, Sasha took his face in her hands and kissed him fervently. When their lips parted, she grinned. "So, Tina finally kept a secret."

Blake returned the smile, his green eyes gleaming. "She did good, didn't she? You ready to go home?" His voice was rough with need.

She nodded. She wanted nothing more than to go home. To get in bed. And to show him just how much she loved him back.

ACKNOWLEDGMENTS

If you read my dedication page, you'll see three names. Ang, Sue, and Sabrina. Collectively, these women represent the fictional character Blake in a weird hodgepodge sort of dynamic. I can always count on them to wipe away my tears with a metaphorical hand (because they live too far away to do it in a literal sense) and pull me up by my bra straps any time the going gets tough. No judgment passed. They are my people. And I'm genuinely grateful and honored to call them my friends.

Immense gratitude goes out to my editor, Beth at VB Edits. Thank you for lending me your expertise once again and bringing life to my manuscript. You are a rock star!

To my cover designer, Amanda Walker, PA and Design Services. Thank you for working tirelessly on creating another perfect cover. I cannot thank you enough.

To Sarah Burr at Reed Editorial Services. I'm so incredibly fortunate to have you jump on board so quickly and proofread my manuscript.

A special thank you to my husband, Pat, for telling me to keep writing, because maybe one day we'll be able to retire. And an even bigger thank you to my children, who keep me inspired. For reminding me that dreams don't have expiration dates and that anything is possible with some hard work.

I also have to thank my mom, because, well, she's my mom. She gave me life. But more importantly, because she encouraged me to write, without ever pushing me.

Finally, I can't end without acknowledging the elephant in the room. Sasha and her mom, Sharon. Like Blake, both of these characters are fictional, but represent the millions of people who grapple with addiction and mental health disorders. Sasha represents the strength that so many of us hope and want for our loved ones who struggle with trauma and dependency, while Sharon, unfortunately, depicts the opposite. It is here that I need to thank some very important people. For helping me understand the difference between supporting and enabling and how to stop trying to control things I have no business controlling. To Corey and Julie, thank you. To the members of FA and NA, thank you. And to Parkview Christian Church for reminding me that I'm not alone and to be patient because I can't always see the other side of the mountain. Thank you.

AUTHOR'S NOTE

If you or a loved one suffers from addiction, depression, anxiety, or any other mental health disorder, please know you are not alone. Reach out to someone, make a connection, or call one of the numbers below.

- Families Anonymous: (800) 736-9805

- SAMHSA: (800) 662-4357

- Suicide Prevention Lifeline: (800) 273-8255

- Veterans Crisis Hotline: (800) 272-8255

ABOUT THE AUTHOR

Manda Mazanec is a United States Marine Corps veteran and educator, committed to shaping a better and brighter future. While being an avid reader, writer, and runner, Manda is also an advocate for breaking the stigma associated with mental health illness, bringing to light how trauma can affect our everyday lives. Manda lives in Illinois with her husband, three daughters, and her two dogs and two cats.

 instagram.com/mandamazanec

 goodreads.com/mandamazanec

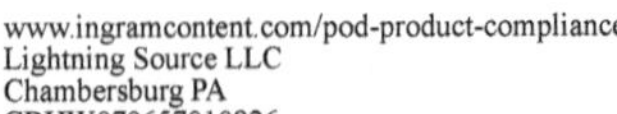